THE HESSIAN
LINK

BY

HENRIETTA F. FORD

Henrietta F. Ford

PublishAmerica
Baltimore

ISBN: 1-60474-058-2
PUBLISHED BY PUBLISHAMERICA, LLLP
www.publishamerica.com
Baltimore

Printed in the United States of America

DEDICATED TO

My sons, Scott and Brian, who spent many childhood
vacations probing dusty museums and exploring old battlefields.

Acknowledgments

I would like to express my gratitude to:

My husband, Jim. Thank you for your support and encouragement without which I could not have written this story.

Linda Ecceleston, my friend and neighbor. I give my deep appreciation for providing another pair of editing eyes.

PART I

PROLOGUE

1777 CHARACTERS

Captain John Ford—Revolutionary Patriot and Master of Oldfields Point.
Millicent Ford—wife of Captain Ford and Mistress of Oldfields Point
Caroline—sister of Millicent Ford
Anna—Millicent Ford's nurse
James—the carpenter

CHAPTER 1

AUGUST 25, 1777

The sunset over the Elk River turned the water into a lake of liquid fire. Gulls circled and screeched announcing the day's end, and ospreys circled their nests in the high branches of the great trees along the shoreline. A favorable westerly wind blew across the Bay on this August morning.

A young barefoot black boy walked cautiously along the rocky shoreline. He wore a faded tan smock and tattered leather breeches that were much too small. He picked his path carefully along the rough beach stopping often to stare into the woods and call for the lost goat that was his charge. Beyond the mouth of the river lay the restless Chesapeake Bay that stretched persistently until it reached the western shores. Once the boy had gone with his master aboard his schooner to help load supplies at Baltimoretowne and found the vastness of the Bay and the pitching of the boat so daunting that he had become sick. Since then, he tended the cows, goats, sheep, and chickens. The job of tending the horses remained in the hands of an older more experienced slave.

The boy knelt on the beach to examine a stone bruise on his heel. Suddenly, he realized that the gulls' shrieks took on a heightened frenzy.

He arose, dusted off his knee, and held his hand to shield his eyes from the setting sun. He looked out on the water and watched as a fleet of tall ships sailed slowly, silently toward the mouth of the river. Following a series of maneuvers, they began to drop their anchors.

The boy looked back toward the settlement where little pillars of grey smoke rose above the roofs of the cabins. He began to run in that direction leaving puffs of dust in his wake. Chickens squawked and scattered, startled horses reared, and cows with heavy udders mooed impatiently as he ran by. He ran pass bleating sheep, and pass women slaves with long skirts and swathed heads gathering vegetables for the evening meal. He ignored their questions and comments and continued running until he reached the cottage of the carpenter.

The English carpenter, James, had arrived at Oldfields Point as an indentured servant. He was an educated man; however, his choices in life had been limited by his affliction. James had a club foot. In return for his passage, he was to have worked seven years in construction and repairs at Oldfields Point, home of John Ford. However, after carving a magnificent grand staircase for the manor house he gained such favor with John Ford that he was forgiven three years of his servitude. So grateful was he that he stayed on as a paid hand at Oldfields Point. The carpenter had been patient and kind to the nervous boy and taught him to read and write his letters, skills often forbidden by other slave owners. A bond of trust was created between boy and carpenter so it was he whom the boy chose to report the event unfolding on the river. After only a few words of explanation the carpenter threw down his chisel and hobbled after the boy in the direction of the river.

The carpenter and the boy dropped to their knees on the knoll above the beach and stared in amazement at the scene below. At the mouth of the Elk River and extending around the bend into the Chesapeake Bay, a fleet of ships tugged restlessly at their anchors. A warship escorting the flotilla tossed menacingly like a great white swan hovering protectively over its cygnets. Most of the vessels were ship rigged with three masts. Guns peered forebodingly through the gun ports. The warship must have easily carried fifty guns, and several carronades were mounted on the highest deck.

The watchers gawked silently at the activity onboard the ships. Then a launch was lowered over the side of one of the troop transports, and soldiers wearing British uniforms dropped one by one into the boat. The carpenter nudged the boy and jerked a thumb in the direction of the estate. They crept over the crest of the hill and rushed frantically in the direction from which they'd come. They did not stop until they clamored breathlessly onto the front porch of the manor house. Simultaneously an old black woman wearing a long print dress, a spotless white apron, and carrying a broom positioned herself at the front door. She raised the broom in a threatening gesture instantly stopping the interlopers.

"What ya doin' a comin' here to da front door?" asked the slave as she eyed the carpenter with indignation.

"I must see Madam Ford immediately," he said breathlessly. "This is a matter of great urgency."

"Well, ya' jest take your matter of great urgency round to de back door where ya belongs," she said.

"This can't wait," the carpenter continued. "At this very moment…"

The terrified boy blurted, "Dar's soldiers and guns…"

Suddenly the old slave stepped out onto the porch and began whacking the boy on the head with her broom. "And ya' don't b'long to be here at de house at tall. Get ya'self back to ya' chickens and goats. Get outta here," she screamed punctuating her commands with blows to the boys head.

"Sara, Sara," said a firm but gentle voice. "What are you doing? What is the meaning of this outburst?"

The carpenter looked up at a lovely young woman with fair complexion, dark hair, and blue eyes. When she stepped onto the porch he could not help but notice her swollen belly. Embarrassed, he immediately diverted his attention to the woman who followed closely behind. Their resemblance was striking, and he knew her to be Caroline, sister of Millicent Ford, Mistress of Oldfields Point. The carpenter also recognized the tall black woman who closely shadowed Millicent Ford. Her name was Anna, and she had not left Millicent Ford's side since Captain John Ford went to fight in the war on the side of the Patriots. Anna was a free black woman. She had been nurse to young Millicent and

Caroline, and was given her freedom by their father. When Millicent married, Anna came to Oldfields Point with the young bride. She was present at the birth of her first child. Now that Captain Ford was away and Millicent was expecting their second child, Anna sheltered her even more closely.

"You must never leave Mistress alone," Captain Ford had charged Anna. "I am placing her under your care and protection." Anna took his order seriously and one never saw Millicent Ford unless Anna was nearby. It was even rumored that Anna hid a sheathed hunting knife beneath her apron during the day and under her pillow when she slept.

James spoke fearfully, "Mistress Ford, I have a most alarming report for you. At this very moment, British ships are anchored at the mouth of the river and on the Bay."

Millicent turned pale, gasped, and began to crumble. Anna stepped forward instantly and steadied her. Millicent regained her composure, swallowed hard, and said, "James, please how many ships are there?"

"I counted about twenty, but I'm sure that many more are anchored around the bend outside of eyeshot," James said.

"Why are they here?" asked Caroline. "There are no soldiers here save a few old patriot watchers."

James did not attempt to answer Caroline's question but continued his report. "But the most pressing circumstance," said James "is that as we speak, British soldiers have boarded launches and are rowing toward the beach of Oldfields Point."

"How many soldiers?" asked Caroline.

"I shall venture to guess about fifty in the first boats," said James.

Suddenly the broom swinging woman dropped her broom, clasped her hand to her heart, and pointed toward a cloud of dust yet some distance away. "Dare, dare dey be comin'," she yelled and fled into the house.

"Quick, James," said Millicent. "Go quickly through the house and out of the back door. Go and hide in the woods lest they conscript you. And take the male slaves with you also. Go, Go, quickly."

"No, Mistress," said James. "I cannot leave you to the mercy of British devils."

"James," Millicent said confidently, "I have not heard that the British affront women. We shall be safe, but they would surely conscript you and the male slaves. Go and seek the patriot sympathizers and tell them what transpires. Go! Go!"

James reluctantly stepped forward, looked soulfully into Caroline's eyes, and hastened down the dark hallway to the back of the house.

The women and the boy stood on the porch and watched as clouds of dust made red by the setting sun moved closer and closer to the house. Soon a young British Captain dressed in full uniform appeared leading a company of thirty British soldiers. He abruptly halted in front of the porch, gaped at the women, and touched his hand to his hat.

"Madam," he said with authority, "this property is hereby commandeered by General William Howe in the service of His Majesty King George III. Any attempt to prevent this occupation shall be considered an act of treason."

The Captain looked around at the startled faces of the black women and children huddled in the yard. Then he turned his attention back to the women on the porch. "Who is the Master of this house?" he barked.

Millicent stepped forward making no attempt to conceal her swollen body. "I am the Mistress, Sir," she said proudly. "You may speak to me."

"Where are the men slaves?" he roared.

"They have fled into the woods lest they be conscripted and forced to fight against their masters," she said.

"Madam," said the Captain, "should it be discovered that any adult males, slaves or free, are being hidden you could be arrested and tried for treason."

"Is it not enough, Sir," said Millicent defiantly, "that our men are forced to fight for our independence thus leaving their loved ones without their protection? Now you would register our male slaves who were left behind to watch over us? I was not aware that British soldiers were so indifferent to the welfare of ladies."

The Captain's face turned red and he bellowed, "Madam, you are also notified that this manor house is requisitioned to be used as headquarters for General Wilhelm Knyphausen, Commander of the Hessian Division. You are hereby commanded to vacate the premises forthwith."

Millicent turned pale and slumped forward. Anna was immediately by her side again comforting her. Caroline stepped forward, hate emanating from her eyes. "Have you no compassion? My sister is with child and her day of delivery is imminent yet you would force her from her own home?"

Millicent straightened, glared at the Captain, and shook her small fist, "I shall not leave my home. Never! All of my children will be born here at Oldfields Point as John and I planned, and no one, not even the devil himself shall make me leave." Then suddenly Millicent shrieked, tossed forward, and collapsed.

Now the Captain was shaken. Sweat appeared above his lip. He blinked uncontrollably, and shuffled from one foot to the other. As Anna and Caroline rushed to attend Millicent, the Captain regained his composure, cleared his throat, and said, "The decision is yours. However, let it be known that this evening General Knyphausen will establish his quarters here."

The Captain turned hurriedly and barked orders to his company. Then in exact precision they marched back toward the beach. As they left, other slaves rushed to the porch to help carry Millicent inside.

* * *

Night fell quickly on Oldfields Point bringing strange shadows and distance voices. The children hid themselves in the women's skirts as the slaves wondered aloud at what fate would befall them at the hands of the heathen Hessians. What tortures would be inflicted upon them? They had heard that Hessians spoke the language of the devil. How could they protect themselves if they could not understand what was said? An eerie stillness settled over the forest and swamps, and the moon slipped in and out from behind threatening gray clouds that hung heavily in the sky.

Suddenly an explosion of sound shattered the stillness. Shouts in an unfamiliar language reverberated from the camp by the river along with the clamor of metal on metal. Then a burst of light streamed up the hill as hundreds of torches charged towards Oldfields Point. The Hessians knew that fear was their most effective weapon in an initial assault. They were surprised when they met no resistance and found only black women, children, and very old slaves cowering in their cabins. They made teasing jabs at them with their bayonets and laughed at their fear. They cursed them in their native German tongue, and when they tired of this horseplay they turned their attention to the manor house. They had heard of the proud young women who refused to leave the house. They would have fun with these ladies.

Inside the manor house, Millicent felt helpless as she lay on her birthing bed hearing screams, cries, and crashing sounds as the soldiers poured through the house searching every room. Suddenly heavy footsteps raced up the stairs and soldiers speaking in a foreign tongue burst into her room. Caroline fixed a proud brave eye on the intruders and the Hessians halted abruptly and gaped at the scene before them. The black wet nurse sat nearby holding Millicent's other child who was pale and trembling with fear and a large black woman stood at the foot of the bed. Beneath her blood stained apron she clutched a large hunting knife. Millicent was begging for her mother declaring she would not have the baby until she arrived. The soldiers exchanged words, slowly backed out of the room, and disappeared down the stairs.

The women were not disturbed for hours. Millicent became weak and appeared to be giving up. Suddenly Caroline declared that she would fetch their mother.

"No, Caroline," cried Millicent, "you mustn't go. Unlike the British, the Hessians are fiends. Have you not heard of their wicked deeds? They do not even know how to speak English. Please, please don't go." And she began to sob.

Caroline knelt beside her sister's bed. "Millicent, dear," she whispered, "this birth has taken a bad turn. Your baby is coming into the world backwards. It is surely a curse brought on by the heathens. But you need Mama. Anna and I have not the skill to help you. So shhh. I shall be back soon, and Mama will be with me. She will know what to do."

Millicent swooned and closed her eyes exhausted. "Then if you must go," she said, "take it with you."

"What?" asked Caroline.

"Take it with you," said Millicent. "Take the necklace baring the Ford crest medallion that I wore the day John and I were married. I could not bear to think of it falling into the hands of the Hessians. Hide it. Hide it in the hem of your skirt lest they find it on you."

Anna was already opening the chest drawer. She unfolded a handkerchief, took out the gold necklace, and reached down to lift Caroline's skirt. Soon the necklace was secreted in the hem of her dress.

In spite of Millicent's tearful pleas, Caroline threw on her cape, rushed from the room, dashed to the end of the hall, and crept down the back stairs. The women could hear the callous voices of the soldiers who had found the ale stored in the cellar. Anna rushed to the window and looked down upon the confusion in the yard. Soon Caroline appeared. She carried a lantern, and its flickering light cast eerie shadows as she walked toward the backyard path that led to the home of Millicent's mother. As she disappeared around the back of the house, a shadowy figure crept after her.

PART II

JOURNEY TO THE ANCESTRAL HOME

Present Day Characters

Jeremiah Ford—(Jere) Richmond City Homicide Detective and amateur archeologist

Ingrid Fairchild—Jere's partner and also an amateur archeologist

Charles Ford—Owner of Oldfields Point and distant relative of Jere Ford

Martha Stevens—Housekeeper and companion to Charles Ford

Isodora Ford—Charles' aunt

Julia Caswell—Charles' stepsister

Bernie Caswell—Charles' stepbrother

Jefferson T. Wainwright—Isodora's alcoholic son

Alice Wainwright—Jefferson T.'s wife

Carrie Goldsmith—Isodora's party pal

Sheriff Regan—Sheriff of Cecil County, Maryland

Chapter 2

Present Day

Jere stopped his SUV at the junction of US Highways 60 and 13. The red traffic light shined like a crimson aura through the heavy morning mist. He squinted at the road sign across the intersection and read Chesapeake Bay Bridge-Tunnel. Underneath an arrow pointed left.

Jere glanced at the passenger sleeping fitfully beside him. Twitching hands and flitting eyelids revealed that his partner was sleeping soundly. Jeremiah Ford and his traveling companion were homicide detectives with the Richmond, Virginia Police Department. They graduated from the Police Academy at the same time and went on to become partners as street cops. Later they worked in homicide together, and when they took the test to become detectives, they studied together. After passing the test, they were assigned to work together as homicide detectives. It was unusual that they would end up as partners so often, but Jeremiah had no problem working with the same person for so many years. More specifically he had no problem working with a woman.

The bond between the two detectives was very tight. Ingrid Fairchild, often referred to as the Scandinavian Amazon, was quite a bit older than Jeremiah and had a son in college. She was five feet eleven and weighed one hundred and sixty pounds of solid muscle and worked out thirty minutes every day. In spite of her size, she was a very striking woman with thick blonde hair, large expressive blue eyes, and light golden skin. She was married and had one child, Shawn, who was her pride and joy. She put her career on the back burner until Shawn was well into school, and when she entered the academy she received a lot of ribbing from the younger guys. At the academy she was given the moniker, Mom. But soon her marksmanship and martial arts skills earned her the respect of not only the other candidates, but instructors too. She passed up an offer to teach at the academy and opted to work in the field.

Besides working together, Jere and Ingrid shared a common interest in archeology. The two detectives just completed a week of digging at historic Jamestowne, Virginia. They volunteered to help scientists and archaeologists dig at the site of the first permanent English settlement in the New World. In spite of the sophisticated equipment used to map the dig there was still much back-breaking work. The tedious job involved creating a record of where every object or bone was discovered. It was a daunting task because in a three year span in early 1600's, between four and five hundred people died. The detective skills that Jere and Ingrid brought to the dig were valuable because in a sense they were working a four hundred year old crime scene.

The traffic light turned green. Jere signaled, and turned left. Soon a sign warned that they were approaching a toll bridge.

"Hey Ingrid, wake up," Jerre said. Receiving no response, he nudged her and spoke louder, "Ingrid. Wake up Ingrid. We're approaching the bridge, and it's a toll. Got a five?"

Receiving no response from Ingrid, Jere began to fumble for his wallet. Suddenly he lost control of the SUV. It swerved and jolted onto the shoulder of the road and bounced over several enormous potholes in the process. Jere quickly recovered and with wallet in hand brought the SUV back safely onto the highway.

Ingrid bolted upright. "Hey Jer, what's going on?" She glared at Jere.

"Nothing, Ingrid. Everything's just fine. Go on back to sleep," said Jere.

Ingrid sat up and looked around confused. "You can't expect me to sleep with all that bouncing going on, now can you? How about keeping it on the road?"

Jere shook his head, rolled his eyes, and grinned. "Sorry about that, Ingrid. I'll try not to disturb you next time I almost have a wreck."

"Well, see that you don't," said Ingrid as she stretched her neck and began to survey the surroundings. "Where are we anyhow?"

Jere took on the tone of a tour guy speaking loudly and with great authority. "We are now approaching the Chesapeake Bay Bridge/Tunnel, one of seven engineering wonders of the modern world. Soon we'll be crossing twenty three miles of outstanding civil engineering achievement. We'll be dipping over and under anywhere from 25 to 100 feet of water." Ingrid shot him an impatient look.

As they approached the Toll Plaza, they gazed out upon an amazing scene. A heavy mist hovered above the Bay and swirled around the bridge and piers creating the illusion of a gigantic structure pushing its way through a great cumulous cloud. It was an eerie sight to see the road they were going to travel disappear into the bay.

"Whoa," said Ingrid, "Are you sure you'll be able to see well enough to drive out there?"

"Sure," said, Jere. "Just trust me." He stopped the SUV and handed the toll keeper a five.

Ingrid said, "Trust you? What…like when I took a little nap and you ran off the road back there?"

"A *little* nap? You were unconscious."

"Unconscious? You say…"

"Yes, unconscious. And I wouldn't have run off the road if I hadn't had to fumble around for my wallet?"

"Why didn't you just wake me up? I could have given you the money and you wouldn't have run off the road."

"Because you were *unconscious.*"

"You don't even know…"

The SUV drove off into the mist leaving a barrage of bickering in its wake and two toll gate keepers shaking their heads and laughing.

Once on the bridge, they discovered that the mist was more translucent than it appeared from a distance. Puffs of mist, like white balloons, blew up from the bridge as vehicles sped pass, yet nothing could be seen beyond the guard rails as the fog formed an opaque shield over the bay.

"We'll have to come back sometime when we can actually see the Bay," said Ingrid.

"If we want to see the Bay, we'll *have* to come back. Looks like this fog is going to be with us all the way across," said Jere.

Through the mist a sign appeared indicating that they were about to enter a tunnel and headlights should be turned on.

"I hate tunnels," said Ingrid. "Every time I go through one, I think this is it. This is the time that this thing isn't going to hold. How long is this one anyway?"

"Only a mile," said Jere. Then he added wickedly, "Why don't you just retreat back into your narcoleptic state and sleep through it?"

"Narcoleptic state you say," Ingrid shot back. "I was just catching a nap. There's no way I'll sleep through this. You might need me to fish out *my* wallet again."

Ingrid sat up straight, her eyes glued on the approaching dark hole. Then the SUV disappeared into the tunnel.

CHAPTER 3

The fog slowly dissipated, and a bright orange autumn sun pierced the mist to the east. The morning began to clear quickly as they left the bridge behind and drove farther onto the Delmarva Peninsula that runs along the eastern United States separating the Chesapeake Bay on the west from the Delaware Bay and the Atlantic Ocean on the east. The name given the Peninsula, Delmarva, is a portmanteau comprising letters of the three states that occupy it, Delaware, Maryland, and Virginia. Although there are several bridges that connect the Peninsula to the mainland, none are as amazing as the Chesapeake Bay Bridge/Tunnel.

While researching his Ford family line, Jere discovered that his ancestors first settled on what is now the Maryland segment of the Delmarva Peninsula commonly referred to now as Eastern Shore Maryland. In 1632, King Charles of England granted Peninsula land to Englishmen to insure a stronghold for English colonization. The promise of these charters was most appealing to the English Colonists. British subjects not only obtained good land, but were also free from the religious and political strife that was taking place in Europe at the time. It was under a grant from King Charles, that the ancestors of Jeremiah Ford emigrated from England.

When Jere sought genealogical documentation, he was pleased to learn that the Ford family name was still prevalent on Eastern Shore, Maryland. He soon established communication with several Ford family members living there. The most forthcoming and responsive of them was Charles Ford. Jere was excited to learn that Charles Ford lived at Oldfields Point, the home of Captain John Ford. Both Charles and Jere were direct line descendants of this Revolutionary War Patriot.

Charles had shown great interest in meeting Jere, and he was particularly curious about Jere's job as a homicide detective. So when Charles learned that Jere would have four weeks off in September for 'R and R' following an especially difficult and brutal murder case, he invited Jere and his wife to come to Oldfields Point for a visit. It would, after all, be much like a pilgrimage for Jere. Jere explained to Charles that his wife, Lily, died the previous year having lost a three year battle with cancer. So Jere asked if his partner, Ingrid, might accompany him. He wasn't sure how Charles would react to a relative bringing another woman on the trip, so Jere explained that Ingrid was an older woman and had been his partner for many years. Charles extended an invitation to Ingrid without hesitation. Jere received an email in which Charles expressed great excitement in having *two* detectives visit. It read:

"…I was saddened by the news of Lily's death. Please accept my sincerest sympathy. I am, however, pleased that you will be paying us a visit. Perhaps a trip to Oldsfields Point may be an appropriate diversion for you at this time. We are also delighted to learn that your partner, Ingrid Fairchild, is interested in visiting too. I can't believe I'm fortunate enough to have a PAIR of detectives visit. How lucky! We have many 'unsolved mysteries' here at Oldfields Point. There is one in particular I feel would interest you. Perhaps I can impose upon the two of you to provide a modern detective's insight into this puzzle. At any rate, welcome Jere and Ingrid!

* * *

Jere drove slowly enjoying the Peninsula scenery for the first time. Ingrid yammered on about anything that caught her eye. Soon they crossed the Maryland State line. They drove by farmers' stands of fresh vegetables…tomatoes, green beans, fresh greens, and corn. They passed poultry farms with low out buildings where large transport trucks labeled Perdue Farms stood ready to be loaded.

The towns were small and each one boasted at least one Mom and Pop restaurant with the best food on the Peninsula. The restaurants' advertisement boards reminded them that they hadn't eaten since six o'clock that morning. Early breakfast, plus what Ingrid described as a nerve-racking drive across the Bay, made them especially hungry.

"What about lunch?" asked Ingrid.

"How hungry are you?" said Jere.

"So hungry that my stomach's shaking hands with my backbone," said Ingrid.

Jere smiled. "Well, if you can hold off for a while longer, we can cut off up here and drive over to St. Michaels. In the letter I got giving me directions to Oldfields Point, Cousin Charles recommended a restaurant in St. Michaels, the Sailor's Choice. Said the seafood was the best on this route. What do you think?"

"I think," said Ingrid, "that I can hold off that long, but as far as his glowing recommendation is concerned, you don't even know *Cousin Charles*. You know how picky I am about my crab cakes. I don't settle for just any crab cakes. Crab cakes have to be done *just* right. Otherwise, you end up with a glob of fillers and no crab. Do you think we can trust Cousin Charles' opinion simply on the basis that you two are from the same gene pool?"

Jere laughed. "First of all, Cousin Charles and I are just barely from the same gene pool. He's like a sixth cousin or something X number of times removed. Second of all, I know nothing about his taste in crab cakes. So take your chances or not. What do you say?"

"Let's live dangerously," said Ingrid, "St. Michaels it is."

Jere accelerated and after leaving Highway 13, made a series of left turns until they reached a board that read St. Michaels 5 miles. Soon they drove into a quaint waterfront village. The streets were lined with delightful inns, charming bed and breakfasts, saloons, gourmet restaurants, and all kinds of specialty shops. Women with large purses and hefty shopping bags scurried from one shop to another. They drove past a magnificent church as its bell peeled a reminder to shoppers that it was lunchtime. They reached a sign that pointed the way to the Chesapeake Bay Maritime Museum, and they realized that they would soon be leaving the village. Just in time they spotted a small sign that told them a right turn would take them to the Sailor's Choice Restaurant, the Best Seafood on the Eastern Shore.

Jere parked in front of a wooden structure that was built on pilings with piers extending into the Miles River that empties into the Eastern Bay. Sailors were attempting to get in one more good sail before the fall weather turned cold. The river was so full of boats that it appeared one could walk across the river simply by stepping from one boat to the other. All the slips were taken. Anchored sailboats, catamarans, and sleek power boats dotted the water. An enormous yacht anchored at the mouth of the river appeared to be out of place beside the smaller sporting vessels. A uniformed steward could be seen serving drinks to a gray-haired man wearing a captain's hat. Lounging beside the older man was a young, long-legged, suntanned, bikini-clad, bottle blonde.

Jere and Ingrid climbed the steps to the Sailor's Choice Restaurant. The place was large and packed with diners. The view was breathtaking. The room overlooked the boat-filled river. They were told they would have at least a twenty minute wait.

"Why do they always say a *twenty* minute wait? Have you ever noticed that? Why not fifteen minutes or thirty minutes? Why always twenty minutes?" Ingrid was getting hungry, and it was no picnic being around Ingrid at feeding time.

Somehow the wait did not seem that long. They settled back to enjoy the view and talk with other waiting customers.

Finally Jere and Ingrid were seated at an enviable spot. From their table, they had a perfect view of the river and all the activity. They watched a 42 ft. Hunter sailboat motor into the mariner and attempt to squeeze into a narrow slip. A waitress with a Russian accent brought them water, and they learned she was an exchange student scheduled to return to St. Petersburg the following week. Jere ordered a combination platter, and Ingrid ordered two crab cakes, both served with slaw, corn on the cob, and hush puppies. They ate leisurely and watched intently as the Hunter was finally maneuvered into the slip. Jeremiah's interest peeked as a tan woman with short dark hair and a voluptuous figured bounced around on the deck securing the lines.

"Well," said Ingrid, "what do you think?"

"Well, I, I, I," stammered Jeremiah trying not to stare at the woman who was attempting to tie a hitch.

Ingrid laughed. "I mean what do you think of the crab cakes? How do they stack up?"

"Stack up? Why do you say stack up?" spluttered Jeremiah.

Ingrid laughed so hard tears rolled down her cheeks.

Jere stood, shook his head, and tossed a bill on the table. The waitress appeared instantly. Jere waved her off and said keep the change. Ingrid scrambled to her feet and scurried after him.

As Jere and Ingrid reached the SUV, Jere said, "How about you driving now?" asked Jere. "I'll read Cousin Charles' directions and navigate."

"Sure," said Ingrid as she opened the door on the driver's side. "At least I can keep it on the road."

CHAPTER 4

"Okay, Jere," said Ingrid, "what does Cousin Charles recommend as our first point of interest on this Ford family pilgrimage?"

"Let me see," said Jere. "He writes:

'May I suggest that you include a short detour to Turkey Point? This was the home site of your earliest immigrant ancestor, Richard Ford. The records of Richard's estate establish the Ford family as among the oldest in the area. The view at the site is breathtaking, and I am sure you will not regret the diversion. It is only a short distance from Oldfields Point. Richard and wife Elinor settled there on land they called Beaufort Farm. They built an imposing home on the hill overlooking the Elk River. As you will see, the house would have commanded a magnificent view of the Chesapeake Bay.'

"That's it. There are really no directions other than a mention of Turkey Point, Elk River, and Chesapeake Bay." Jere reached for the map.

"Sounds like a scenic view opt. We've got the time. Might as well take it," said Ingrid.

"Wait," said Jere snapping a map, "I've found it. Turkey Point. Looks like we cross the Elk River and drive to the very end of a small peninsula. Road goes through Elk Neck State Forest."

"Sounds simple enough," said Ingrid.

On the map the distance to Turkey Point appeared to be much farther than it actually was. The ride through the State Forest was peaceful, and after the heavy lunch at Sailor's Choice they began to feel lethargic.

"Want me to drive?" offered Jere.

"No, you did quite enough this morning," said Ingrid with a grin, "Besides this is an easy drive."

They drove in silence soaking in the peaceful scenery. They only passed a few cars as they rolled through stands of sweet gum trees and through swamps where 60 feet tall cypress trees were covered with resurrection ferns. They passed ruins of old churches and buildings hidden by willows and vines. In places the forest was so thick and dark that one could only imagine the many haunting legends that grew out of such a setting.

Finally the road narrowed, and a sign told them they had arrived at Turkey Point. Ingrid parked in the crushed shell parking lot. Then they stepped out and viewed a scene so spectacular as to be sacred. Boaters had been forced ashore as twenty mile an hour winds caused the Bay to toss and roll in a dramatic display of its energy and command. Four and five feet waves churned up white caps and tossed foam upon the shore.

"Wow! This place just blows me away. I'd say this was really worth the drive, Jer," said Ingrid. "Can you imagine living here?"

"I cannot," said Jere.

Then they stared mesmerized and watched the as Bay continued its compelling performance.

Jere said, "You know, I read once that if you ever live near the sea salt water gets in your very soul, and you won't be content until you return there. Do you suppose this urge could be passed from one generation to the next?"

"I don't know, Jere," said Ingrid. "I don't think a person would have to have a genetic predisposition to want to live here. Why I could move here in a heart beat…if I had the money."

"Same here," said Jere, "I suppose we better move on. I wrote Cousin Charles that we'd be there for dinner tonight, and I still don't have a handle on how to get to his place."

"You're right," Ingrid joshed. "Let's continue the search for your ancestral home."

* * *

It was a large, well equipped, kitchen with devices that would be the envy of any gourmet chef. At one end of the room everything was modern, shining, and stainless steel with an assortment of pots, pans, and utensils that hung within easy reach over a gas ten-burner stove. In contrast, at the other end of the room was an eight foot long brick fireplace with stone benches at each end. In the jamb of the chimney and near the fireplace was an oyster oven about three feet deep and over two feet wide. The brick appeared to be very old, yet the oven showed signs of continued use. The floors in the entire room were made of brick.

A man was seated on a tall stool watching a woman slowly stir the contents of a bubbling pot. He looked to be about sixty years old. He wore tan corduroy pants and a matching tweed jacket over a brown turtle neck sweater. He had a ruddy complexion, a mop of unruly auburn hair dappled with gray, and a ready smile.

"Martha," the man said, "I can hardly contain my excitement."

"I know, Charles," said Martha, "I'm so excited I'm afraid I'll leave something out of one of the recipes."

Martha was about fifty years old. She stood tall, straight, and confident yet unpretentious. Her brown hair was flecked with gray, and she wore it pinned back in a severe bun. She wore very little makeup, and she hid a slim attractive figure beneath a cotton print house dress. At first glance one would view her as quite plain, yet, there was a softness about her. Her skin was clear and virtually unwrinkled, and her smile was warm and genuine. It was almost as if Martha went to great lengths to appear homely and unassuming.

Charles smiled indulgently, "What do mean 'leave something out'? One thing is sure, Martha, when you are in charge of dinner, no mistakes are made. That's why I appreciate your offering to take on tonight's dinner single handedly."

Martha paused and her voice took on a serious edge, "Oh Charles," she said, "I only hope they can help us."

Charles spoke reassuringly, "I feel confident that they can. After all, Jeremiah Ford and his partner are homicide detectives. Why they solve these kinds of crimes all the time. I'd venture to say that this will hardly be a challenge to them."

"Charles," said Martha, "I just don't want you to be disappointed. After all, Caroline disappeared over two hundred years ago."

"Not just disappeared, Martha," Charles said emphatically, "...murdered. Caroline was murdered."

"Yes, dear," Martha said, "murdered."

CHAPTER 5

As luck would have it, finding Oldfields Point wasn't as difficult as Jere and Ingrid feared. After leaving Elk Neck State Forest they actually spotted several markers giving directions to Oldfields Point, Home of Captain John Ford, Revolutionary War Hero. They simply followed the markers, and soon they turned onto an unpaved drive lined so thickly with cedar trees that the road seemed to disappear into a dark tunnel. Just before claustrophobia gripped them the drive ended, and they found themselves in front of an impressive, well tended manor house.

Oldfields Point resembled photos of houses Jere had seen in Virginia Historical Preservation magazines. The two-story house stood in a stand of very old, tall trees. Large English boxwoods hugged its walls. The manor was built of brick probably brought from England and used as ballast in the ships. The bonds in the walls of the house presented amazing patterns. There were several chimneys, and dormer windows projected through the slate roof providing light to the third floor attic. Extending across the front of the house was a long porch with a brick floor. Deacon benches were pushed against the walls and rocking chairs positioned to create several conversation spaces. Stretching above the entire length of the porch was a balcony with doors opening into second floor rooms. White wicker furniture with plush cushions was sited to provide a stunning view of a green that sloped to the river. The sun was beginning to set, and a soft peaceful glow radiated from the water.

Jere and Ingrid walked towards the house. The crunch of their footsteps on the shell covered walkway announced their arrival. Simultaneously with the noise, the front door opened and a man stepped onto the porch. As he approached, Jere and Ingrid noticed that he walked in a stiff manner, and his arms swung loosely at his sides. He extended a trembling hand. Jere approached him, shook his hand, and said, "You must be Charles Ford. I'm Jeremiah Ford. Just call me Jere. This is my partner and friend Ingrid Fairchild. Thank you so much for inviting us. I wouldn't have missed this for anything." Jere looked admiringly at the house and grounds.

Charles continued to smile and shook hands first with Jere and then Ingrid. "Welcome, welcome to both of you. This is such a special occasion for me. I couldn't believe that you were actually coming. Thank you, thank you. We seldom have visitors here at Oldfields Point. Welcome"

Jere felt slightly embarrassed by Charles' effusiveness.

"So what do you think about the old place? Your ancestral home so to speak, Jere." Charles had used Jeremiah's moniker and Jere was pleased that he seemed to find it comfortable.

"Charles, this is amazing," said Jere waving his hand about. "I never expected…well, I don't know what I expected. But this is far more impressive than I'd ever dreamed," said Jere.

"And, thank you for including me in your invitation," said Ingrid looking toward the river. "What a marvelous setting."

Charles rubbed his hands together and grinned even wider. "Really? Then you aren't disappointed?"

"No!" Jere and Ingrid said in unison.

"Then please come inside. I can hardly wait for you to see the inside," Charles turned and shuffled toward the porch. "We have prepared several rooms for you. You may take your pick. Whichever ones you think will be most comfortable. Oh, this is so exciting."

As Charles opened the door he called, "Martha, Martha, they're here. They finally made it."

Jere and Ingrid gawked at the amazing entrance hall. The floors were of heart pine probably shipped up from Carolina. A fine woolen rug made more beautiful by the many years of weathering covered the area under a tiger oak hall table of 18th century design. Fresh flowers were displayed in a large pewter bowl. Straight-back waiting chairs rested against the wall. The spectacular mahogany molding and balusters were intricately carved. They would learn later that the work had been done by an indentured craftsman who earned his freedom when he completed the work. A large ornate hall clock stood like a sentinel beside the staircase. Its mellow sound reverberated throughout the hall. The face of the clock was adorned with Masonic symbols, and there was a mechanism that indicated the cycles of the moon, a function frequently consulted by early farmers. On the wall along the stairwell portraits of men and women dressed in colonial attire stared with authority at the visitors.

"Oh, Martha," said Charles, "there you are. May I introduce Martha Stevens. Martha this is my distant cousin Jeremiah Ford, and his partner, Ingrid Fairchild. Martha is my most valued housekeeper, friend, and companion."

Martha was smiling as she looked from Ingrid to Jere. "You can't imagine how delighted we are to have you as our guests. Charles and I have looked forward to your visit for days. Please let me know if there is anything I can do to make your stay more enjoyable."

She paused and looked at Jere. Then she continued, "You'll be hungry after your long drive. I am preparing a typical Eastern Shore dinner for your first meal. I hope it will be to your liking."

"I'm sure it will," said Jere.

"I look forward to it, too," said Ingrid. "It's been some time since we ate at St. Michaels."

"Then I shall get about it right now," smiled Martha. "Excuse me." And with a nod and a smile, she quickly disappeared down the hall.

Charles ambled toward a door off the entrance hall gesturing for the guests to follow him. "St. Michaels, aye?" said Charles. "I hope I steered you well. How did you find the food at Sailor's Choice?"

"Superb," said Ingrid.

Jere laughed. "Ingrid considers herself a connoisseur of

seafood…crab cakes in particular. She gave the crab cakes at Sailor's Choice five stars."

"Sure did," said Ingrid. "I'd like to try them again on our trip back."

"Ah, a return visit," said Charles, "the ultimate endorsement."

They entered the parlor. A fire was burning in the fireplace, and the lights were dimmed enhancing the golden glow of the late afternoon sun. Oil paintings of landscapes, seascapes, and horses adorned the walls of the room. Shudders were still open, and a window seat provided a breathtaking view of the river. Stationed against the wall was a tall secretary with tiny drawers and nooks. It was cluttered with envelopes, papers, and unopened correspondence confirming it as a legitimate work station. A loveseat and two stuffed chairs were positioned in front of the fireplace. A small table was placed in front of the loveseat and on it set a decanter and three crystal snifters.

Two portraits gazed down from the wall over the mantle. One painting was of a beautiful young woman dressed in a blue satin dress with ruffles and lace. She had dark hair, blue eyes, and fair skin. She smiled coyly at her admirers. In her hand she held a fan, and she wore a small peacock feather in her hair. A gold necklace graced her long white neck, and hanging from the necklace was an engraved medallion. The other portrait was of a commanding young man wearing a Revolutionary War uniform. His arm rested on a table beside a military hat. The yellow cockade on his hat identified his rank as captain.

"Won't you have a seat," invited Charles gesturing toward the chairs in front of the fireplace.

Jere and Ingrid sat in the side chairs and using the arm of the loveseat for balance, Charles slowly lowered himself.

"You must excuse my awkwardness," said Charles. "I was recently diagnosed with Parkinson's disease. My medication is not yet adjusted, and when I go off, as they say, I become quite stiff and sometimes tremble. I hope you will not find those times disconcerting."

"Don't give it a second thought, Charles," said Ingrid. "My mother has Parkinson's disease, and I recognized the symptoms immediately."

Charles seemed relieved.

Jere said quickly. "Seems to me like you manage very well. I'm sure keeping up this place is a lot of work."

"It does require effort, but it is a labor of love for me. Now let's toast to your visit." He reached for the decanter then suddenly paused. "That is if you like brandy. If you prefer something else, I'm sure I can accommodate most any preference...or if you don't care for spirits, something softer is available. I never thought about..." Charles looked mortified at a possible breach of etiquette.

"No, no," said Jere sensing Charles' embarrassment, "brandy is fine. Believe me, brandy is just fine."

"For me too," said Ingrid. "That's exactly what I'd order if I were dining out. Nothing says celebration like brandy."

Charles seemed relieved. "I suppose I try too hard," he said reaching for the decanter. "It's important to me that your visit be as pleasant as possible. As I said, we don't have many visitors at Oldfields Point."

Charles handed snifters to Ingrid and Jere. Then he struggled to his feet, lifted his glass, and said, "To a pleasant and successful visit to Oldfields Point."

They said, 'Here, here' and sipped. As Jere and Ingrid were preparing to sit again, Charles added, "And Jere, here's to your joining the family circle."

"Thank you," said Jere. "I'm honored." And a little confused he thought...*successful visit?*

They sipped their brandy in silence as Jere and Ingrid studied the room and its furnishings. Eventually all eyes were drawn to the two portraits above the mantle.

"Jere, these are your ancestors, Captain John and Millicent Ford. Remarkable couple aren't they?" asked Charles.

"They certainly are," said Ingrid.

"But Charles," said Jere, "they look so young."

Charles took a sip of brandy. "Well they were, Jere," he said. "Captain John was eighteen and Millicent was sixteen. That would be unheard of today."

"Unheard of and in some instances not allowed," agreed Jere.

"Sixteen...seems awfully young for a girl to be leaving home," added Ingrid.

"She didn't go far from home," said Charles. "She was born and raised just across the river. Her Mother was always nearby. Millicent and John married, built Oldfields Point, moved in, and began having babies immediately. They had ten children, you know."

"Yes, I recall reading that," said Jere.

"He cuts a fine military figure," said Ingrid.

"He does, doesn't he?" Charles said proudly. "He started his military career with the Maryland Militia when he was quite young. He was eventually commissioned Captain of Militia, 13th Battalion of Cecil County. Then when the Revolutionary War began, he served quite widely. Archives indicate that Captain John Ford fought in the Battles of Long Island, Germantown, and Monmouth."

"He really got around didn't he?" said Ingrid. Charles nodded.

"Charles, it seems like I read somewhere that John Ford was captured at Camden, South Carolina," said Jere.

"Yes, that's correct," confirmed Charles. "When the British undertook their Southern campaign sometime in the 1780's, Captain John fought in South Carolina at Camden. He was briefly imprisoned there but was freed in a prisoner exchange. He then went on to fight at the Battle of Guilford Courthouse in North Carolina."

"That's quite an impressive military record," said Ingrid.

"Indeed," agreed Charles. "As you may know the Continental Army was stretched quite thin. Young men were sent to fight wherever needed."

"Amazing," said Jere.

"Makes one quite proud doesn't it?" asked Charles. Jere nodded.

The men sipped their brandy in silence and stared at the portraits of the brave young soldier and his beautiful wife. Then a soft voice interrupted their concentration.

"Pardon me," said Martha beaming proudly, "your dinner is served."

CHAPTER 6

Martha did not join them for dinner. Charles explained that they usually dined together, but Martha was so determined that everything be perfect for the guests' first dinner, that she chose to supervise the kitchen. She also served each course.

Candles glowed from a chandelier hanging above the table, and the rich smell of wax filled the room. Their brilliance provided a gracious ambiance as the glow was reflected in the English bone china and sparkling pewter. Fine linens and fresh flowers adorned the table and pitchers filled with cool ale set at both ends of the table.

"This ale is so refreshing," said Ingrid dabbing foam from her lips.

"This is English ale," said Charles. "Traditionally we serve English ale just as Captain John and Millicent would like."

Jeremiah thought it fascinating that Charles spoke of Captain John and Millcent Ford as if they were still alive or only recently deceased.

The meal was exquisite. Smiling, Martha entered the dining room with bowls of mouth-watering crab bisque so smooth and thick that Ingrid declared she'd 'died and gone to heaven'. Then Martha removed the empty bowls and soon returned with a salad of mixed greens topped with a thick creamy dressing unlike any dressing the guests had ever enjoyed. A bread basket filled with Maryland biscuits traveled about the table continuously. But the entree was by far the most scrumptious course. Martha ceremoniously tied oyster napkins around each one's neck and laid an oyster knife at their places. Then with aplomb she set a large platter of roasted oysters in front of each guest.

"Now there's plenty oysters in the kitchen," she said proudly.

"So this must be the delicious aroma I've been trying to identify," said Ingrid eyeing the oysters eagerly.

"Yes," said Charles, "roasted oysters have been a favorite at Oldfields Point for generations. As a matter of fact, our oyster oven was well documented by Bishop Asbury in his 1781 journal following one of his many visits here. He described our kitchen in detail and mentioned that in the jamb of the chimney was an oyster oven."

Jere who was tackling his first oyster said, "You've seen this journal?"

"Oh, yes, and I have copies of it," said Charles. "The Bishop most specifically described the oyster oven as being about three feet deep and over two feet wide with a long gridiron that could hold as much as a half bushel of oysters at a time. It could be slid in and out to load or unload. And, Ingrid, you will be interested to know that he too spoke of the delicious smell of roasting oysters that permeated the house."

Ingrid whose mouth was full acknowledged Charles's account with a nod, swallowed, and went in for another oyster.

"Are there remnants of that fireplace or oven?" asked Jere.

"Remnants? How about the *entire* fireplace and oven?" Charles beamed.

"What," Jere exclaimed. "How could it be?"

"Well, knowing that the old kitchen fireplace and oven are an important element of our family history, residents over the years have been very diligent in its care and maintenance. Granted, some brick have been replaced and structural problems had to be addressed, but the original fireplace and oven are here, patches and all," Charles said. "As a matter of fact, this very meal was prepared in the old oyster oven."

Ingrid swallowed, took a sip of ale, and said, "That's amazing. I'd like to see it. You're not going to tell me that Martha still cooks over an open fire are you?'

Charles laughed. "No," he said. "Not that it couldn't be done. The fireplace and oven are quite functional. We have, however, done quite a bit of modernization to the rest of the kitchen over the years, but certain things just need to be left as they were. The fireplace and oyster oven are examples."

They ate in silence savoring the succulent oysters and replenishing their mugs. Soon the ale made them feel relaxed and glib. Conversation flowed freely and soon took on a more personal nature.

Charles said, "Jere how did you become involved in the archeological digging at Jamestowne?"

Jere quickly finished chewing a mouthful of oysters and swallowed hard. "It's just a hobby. Something I started doing during my college summer vacations. Places that have a wealth of finds, such as Jamestowne, rely heavily on volunteer diggers. Of course, all volunteers receive instructions before going into a field, and when important finds are unearthed more experienced archeologists take over."

"And you Ingrid. How were you drawn into archeological digging?" asked Charles.

"Jere." said Ingrid again wiping foam from her lips. "It was one summer like this when both of us had R and R coming. He invited me to give it a try, and I got hooked."

"Jamestowne's not the only historical site that relies heavily on volunteers," Jere added. "Volunteers are used at such places as Colonial Williamsburg, sites of old native American villages, battlegrounds, places where prehistoric fossils have been found. It's an exciting activity."

"It's *really* exciting to find a bone or some other artifact for the first time," added Ingrid. "When I first started digging, I imagined all kind of explanations for the objects I found. Example: Suppose you found a four hundred year old skull of a young boy with a bullet hole in the back of his head. Just imagine what kind of story you could come up with."

Charles looked shocked. "Did you?" he said. "Did you find such a skull of a child?"

Ingrid winked at him. "Sure did," said Ingrid. Then she qualified her response, "Well not *me*...but one of the diggers did."

Jere smiled, "Yes, working Jamestowne is sorta like working a four hundred year old crime scene."

Suddenly, Charles' face lit up. "How exciting! After so many years you can establish the circumstances that led to a death."

"Not always," said Jere, "but we try."

The diners fell silent, and Charles seemed to slip deeply into his own thoughts. The oyster platter never emptied, the pitchers were bottomless, and smiling Martha floated continuously between the kitchen and dining room.

Charles suddenly stirred into awareness. "Ah Ingrid…Jere tells me you have a son," he said attempting to rekindle the dinner conversation.

Ingrid never missed an opportunity to talk about Shawn. She set her mug on the table and said, "Yes, Shawn is a sophomore at the University of Virginia in Charlottesville," she said.

"A sophomore?" said Charles. "You must be very proud. What is he studying?"

"Criminology," said Ingrid. "He wants to go into law enforcement when he graduates."

"How do you feel about that? With your knowledge of the dangers involved in law enforcement, aren't you anxious?" Charles asked his voiced etched with concern.

"Of course, I am," said Ingrid reaching for her mug, "but law enforcement is an obvious choice for Shawn since both his parents are in the business."

"Your husband is a policeman, too?" asked Charles.

"No, Art is with the FBI," said Ingrid.

"The FBI?" Charles asked with interest.

"Yes he is out on the west coast right now. He'll probably be there about six weeks. It's a homeland security assignment. I don't know anything about the specifics, but then I never do."

"Amazing," Charles said. "Of course, your son will follow in the footsteps of his parents. He must be so proud."

"Thank you," said Ingrid. "We are proud of Shawn."

As if realizing that tongues were loosened and lightheartedness had begun, Martha appeared with two more pitchers of ale. She smiled and accepted the compliments graciously. As she removed platters and walked in and out of the dining room she glanced at Charles. Her face beamed with happiness. Silence again descended on the diners as they enjoyed their dessert, a Brule topped with fresh raspberries.

Finally Charles folded his napkin and placed it beside his plate.

"I hope you enjoyed your first meal with us. Martha came up with several ideas for a menu, but then we decided that a traditional Eastern Shore meal would be the most authentic fare for Oldfields Point guests," said Charles.

Charles paused as if reflecting. Then he said, "What exciting lives you live. Homicide detectives, FBI…"

"And don't forget mother of a college sophomore," Ingrid interjected.

"Oh, yes, of course," Charles laughed. "Ah, how exciting! How fortunate to have such knowledgeable guests. How fortunate indeed."

"Fortunate?" thought Jere. "What a strange choice of words."

Charles stood. "Shall we have a liqueur in the parlor?"

Jere stood to join him. Ingrid steadied herself by holding onto the arms of the chair. Jere smiled. He was always amused that such a hefty woman had so much trouble holding her liquor.

"I'll join you," said Ingrid, "but I'll pass on the liqueur. The ale gave me quite enough cheer for tonight."

When they settled into the parlor, the momentum of the evening slowed. They were satisfied, comfortable, and tired. When Martha appeared with a tray carrying a carafe of brown liquid, Jere noticed that the tray held four glasses instead of three. Martha set the tray on the table and then joined Charles on the loveseat.

Jere noticed that Martha fit quite comfortably beside Charles.

"Shall I pour?" asked Martha.

"Please," said Charles. Martha lifted the carafe.

"None for me, thank you, Martha," said Ingrid.

"Very well," said Martha and she filled three small glasses.

The three glasses were raised in a silent toast.

"Martha, my dear, a lovely evening made more enjoyable by your delicious dinner," said Charles.

"Thank you, Charles," she said demurely.

"I'm anxious to see the kitchen, Martha," said Ingrid, "especially the fireplace and oven."

"Oh, it will be a pleasure to give the grand tour so to speak," said Martha.

Jere noticed that both Martha and Charles appeared to be quiet comfortable as they sat side by side like a married couple on a loveseat. Jere was glad. He had immediately liked Charles, and was glad that Cousin Charles was not shut up in this two hundred and fifty year old mansion with only family ghosts to keep him company.

"Charles, have you told Ingrid and Jere about the celebration party?" asked Martha.

"Oh no, I haven't. Thank you, dear, for reminding me," Charles leaned forward in his seat and beamed at his guests. "Jere, Ingrid, we have planned a little get-together in your honor. We are so excited because we seldom host such festivities at Oldfields Point."

Jere who wasn't big on parties of any kind struggled to hide his consternation. "Oh, Charles, I hope you haven't gone to a lot of trouble for us," he said. "Just visiting with you here at Oldfields Point is as much as we'd hoped for. Right Ingrid?"

Ingrid who knew of Jere's aversion to such social gatherings jumped in to support her partner. "Right," said Ingrid. "We certainly don't want to be an imposition…"

"Imposition? Why Charles and I have had so much fun with the preparations…the guest list and caterers. We've even hired three workers to help out in the kitchen. Then there was the menu and the floral arrangements. Why we've never had so much fun. Have we Charles?" Martha did not give Charles a chance to respond. She continued. "We haven't had so much fun since…since…"

"Since never," Charles completed Martha's answer.

Martha reached over and patted Charles' trembling arm. Jere and Ingrid exchanged defeated glances.

"Why, of course, if you have already planned…," Jere stammered.

"It sounds like a lot of fun. Doesn't it Jere?" Ingrid interposed quickly. "Just think a party here at Oldfield Point."

"Yeah," said Jere.

Charles said excitedly, "Mostly we have invited family and a few close neighbors. They are all looking forward to meeting another cousin."

"Isn't it exciting?" said Martha beaming.

"Yes," said Jere hopelessly, "exciting."

Conversation slowed. A log dropped in the fireplace shooting sparks up the chimney like fireworks reaching into the night sky. The long drive, sightseeing, and delicious meals along with the excitement of meeting a new cousin, left Jere exhausted. He stifled a yawn, and recognized that Ingrid was having trouble staying awake, too. Jere felt that Charles and Martha could easily pull an all-nighter, but he knew he wouldn't last.

Finally Jere slipped forward in his chair and said, "Martha, Charles, thank you for a wonderful evening. I wish it could continue through the night, but I'm completely exhausted. And Martha, your dinner served as perfect comfort food. I know I'll sleep like a log."

"Me, too," said Ingrid. "Thanks for inviting me to be a part of your family reunion."

Charles and Martha stood. "Of course, we understand," said Charles graciously.

"Of course," chimed Martha.

The two hosts began to walk toward the door. "Your luggage has been taken upstairs. Now, as Charles may have explained," said Martha, "we prepared several rooms for you. We wanted to give you a choice. Chose the ones you think will be most comfortable."

Martha stopped at the foot of the stairs. "Charles will show you the rooms. Although this was a magnificent day, I am a bit tired myself," Martha said, "So, if you will excuse, I think I'll say goodnight also." She smiled, turned, and walked down the hall.

Ingrid and Jere followed Charles up the long stairway. They quickly realized that Charles climbed much slower than they. He lifted one foot to the next step first, and then he'd pull his other up to rest beside it. This way he managed his balance. He used this progression and slowly moved up the steps. In order to avoid rushing Charles, Ingrid and Jere would occasionally pause and examine the portraits hanging along the stairway.

"Charles you have a family gallery here," said Jere.

"Yes, this is quite a collection," said Ingrid. "How did you come about all these portraits? The frames look like originals."

Charles paused and looked proudly into the faces of his ancestors. "Most of them have always hung here at Oldfields Point. Others, I had done in oil from existing photographs. Let me introduce you to some of them."

So as they slowly ascended the stairs, Charles paused and rattled off the names of ancestors long passed as if they were in residence today at Oldfields Point…men with stern faces in military uniforms; tired white haired old ladies; bearded gentlemen with jewel-handled canes; and lovely young girls with coy smiles stared back at the strangers.

When they finally reached the second floor, they stood face to face with the portrait of a breathtakingly beautiful young woman. Dark curls softly framed her oval face, and piercing violet eyes stared confidently back at them. Her lace gown was cut bolder than might have been approved of at that time revealing creamery white shoulders and firm youthful breasts. A sapphire attached to a gold chain complimented her eyes…eyes that seemed to conceal some secret or memory that she chose not to share.

"What branch of the Ford tree did that peach fall from?" asked Jere. Remembering that Charles held the family in great respect, he immediately regretted the flirtatious remark. "Sorry, Charles. I shouldn't have…"

Charles immediately interrupted. "No, no, Jere," he said with a little laugh. "She's beautiful isn't she? A real goddess."

"So who is she?" asked Ingrid.

"Well, she isn't a Ford," said Charles. "This lovely creature is Caroline, Millicent's sister."

"So what is she doing here on the Ford Family Wall of Fame?" asked Jere. His first attempt at humor passed so he thought he'd try it again.

Charles rewarded his efforts by smiling. "Millicent and Caroline were very close. There was almost an uncanny bond between the sisters. Caroline spent as much time at Oldfields Point as she did at her home." Charles stared at the portrait for a brief second, turned, and said, "I hadn't intended to get into the story of Millicent and Caroline tonight. This should best wait until morning."

Charles turned and started down the hall. "After all, we must save some mystery for tomorrow."

He looked back at Jere and grinned. "He's trying to make a joke too," thought Jere.

Jere looked down the long cavernous hall. It reminded him of a hotel. "Charles this is such a big place. Other than Martha, do you live here alone?"

Charles paused and turned to face Jere. Another sly grin spread across his face. "Oh no, Jere," he said. "I also live with them." He made a sweeping gesture toward the portraits on the stairwell.

Jere was confused. "But...they are dead."

"Oh no, they aren't dead." Ingrid and Jere looked startled.

Charles continued, "They live as long as they are remembered, and it is my mission to see that they are remembered."

Charles turned and continued down the hall. He showed them five bedrooms. All were neat and set with vases of fresh flowers. In every room the beds were turned down and the white crisp linens looked inviting.

"The only thing missing is a mint on the pillow," whispered Ingrid.

Three of the rooms had doors opening onto the balcony. The view was dramatic. An autumn moon illuminated the green where a deer grazed on the grass. An owl hooted mournfully, and a fox barked in the distance. Shadows created by leafless branches danced across the lawn as a gentle breeze blew up from the river, and moonlight on the water created a peaceful, serene ambiance.

"I think I'd like a room that overlooks the green," said Ingrid. "This view is so peaceful. I'll fall asleep before my head hits the pillow."

"I feel the same as Ingrid," said Jere. "I'd like one of the rooms that open onto the balcony."

Charles seemed pleased. "Excellent choices!" said Charles. "Now...these two have their own bath, and there's a bath at the end of the hall there." He pointed in the designated direction. "My room, on the other hand, is at the other end of the hall." He pointed in the opposite direction.

Charles began to totter toward his room. Then he turned and said, "This is going to be so exciting. I can't wait for tomorrow to come. I feel like a child waiting for Christmas." And he quickly hobbled away.

Ingrid and Jere picked up their luggage that had been placed in the hall.

"I'll take this room," said Ingrid nodding toward one of the opened doors. She picked up her bags.

"And I'm right beside you," said Jere heading toward the adjoining room bag in hand.

Suddenly Ingrid stopped, moved close to Jere, and whispered, "Hey Jer, meet you on the balcony in fifteen minutes."

"You bet," whispered Jere.

CHAPTER 7

Jere stepped onto the balcony and was awestruck by a magnificent celestial canopy. A million silver stars were pasted against a black satin sky, and a sliver of moon slipped behind a dark cloud. Somewhere in the distance a boat chugged down the river. Lines from a childhood poem kept running through his mind:

"By the shores of Gitche Gumee,
By the shining Big-Sea-Water,
Stood the wigwam of Nokomis,
Daughter of the Moon, Nokomis."

He could almost envision a young brave beaching his canoe and walking through the woods toward the house.

Jere stretched his arms upward, and breathed deeply of the cool night air. Suddenly he coughed and sputtered. He turned and followed the rank smell of cigarette smoke. Ingrid was engulfed in a cloud of smoke. She sat in a high back wicker chair, her legs curled underneath her. She wore plaid drawstring pajamas pants with a matching tank top and held a long filter tipped cigarette.

Jere looked down at Ingrid with a disgusted look on his face. "Isn't there any place you don't smoke?" he asked irritably.

Ingrid blew a heavy cloud of smoke upward. "You want to discuss my nicotine addiction or you want to talk about what's going on here?"

Jere pulled a chair closer and sat down. Then he said in a whisper, "I want to talk."

"You're not going to brood over this family celebration thing Charles and Martha are planning in your honor are you?"

"No, that's not it. I don't have the heart to deprive them of their celebration. I want to talk about Charles. Some of the words coming out of Charles' mouth make no sense."

Ingrid said, "You mean how they both talk kinda...well, kinda funny. Like from another era."

Jere said, "No, I couldn't care less about their speech patterns. He's talking but not telling us anything."

Ingrid nodded, "Go on. I'm curious if you have the same questions as I."

"I can understand Charles being excited about meeting a distant relative who until now was unknown, but I'm puzzled by his degree of exuberance," said Jere.

"And Martha's conduct," said Ingrid, "is peculiar, too."

"Right," said Jere, "it's one thing to be ecstatic over filling in a blank on your family chart, but why should it mean so much to Martha."

"It could be a love thing," said Ingrid.

"*Love thing?*" exclaimed Jere.

"Shhh," cautioned Ingrid. They both looked towards the door. She continued in a low voice. "Surely you realize that Martha is in love with Charles. Why she dotes on him constantly. It's like this is his world and she's fortunate enough to live in it."

"Well," said Jere, "I never thought love, but she certainly indulges him. You would notice love quicker than I. Give me evidence."

Ingrid nodded. "Evidence? Take for example when we first got here. He was way too anxious to let Martha know that we arrived. It was like they had been waiting anxiously *together* for us to get here."

"And from that you think they are in love?" asked Jere skeptically.

"I haven't finished," said Ingrid irritably. "Martha in turn welcomed us by saying *We* are delighted to have you as *our* guests. "

"You're overstating the significance of that," said Jere. "I think she was just reflecting Charles' enthusiasm. I thought Charles was right up front when he introduced her as his friend, companion, and housekeeper. He clearly defined her role right then."

"Huh," grunted Ingrid. "Her *role* is too compliant if you ask me. I can't imagine preparing five rooms so *his* guests can take their pick. And that dinner…she apparently prepared it single handedly. Then she didn't even eat with us."

"Now what you just described doesn't sound like love to me," said Jere. "You make her sound like a doormat."

"Not quite. After she jumped through all those hoops for him," said Ingrid, "she joined us in the parlor and without hesitation sat beside Charles on the loveseat? It's obvious to me that this was an evening ritual she was accustomed to."

"Well, if it will put your suspicious mind to rest," said Jere, "just remember that his room is on the second floor and hers is on the first."

"And you never heard of a back stairs?" she said. Ingrid was hanging on like a bulldog with a bone. She was like that. She liked nothing better than to spar with her partner.

"What difference does it make?" said Jere. "You're just too suspicious."

"Well, that's what I get paid for…to be suspicious," said Ingrid with a big grin.

As always, Jere relented. He shrugged, "I couldn't care less about the love life of Cousin Charles. There are other things that make me uncomfortable. Maybe you're right. It is our job to be suspicious, and it is hard to turn it off even when we're on vacation."

Ingrid took a pull on her cigarette and tapped the ashes into her hand. "Tell me about the 'other things' that make you suspicious."

"Well, as I said before Charles' exuberance is unsettling. He went to such extreme for our visit," said Jere.

"Yes, like preparing five rooms so we would have a choice," said Ingrid. "I've already conceded that's strange."

Jere continued. He was also used to her interruptions. "Another thing, did you notice his curiosity about our jobs?"

Ingrid nodded.

Jere continued, "At first I thought he was just making polite conversation, but then I began to feel there was a reason for his questions about our work."

"Like what?," Ingrid asked as she looked around for a place to snuff out her cigarette.

"When we were telling him about the dig in Jamestowne, he got real excited because I said it was like working a four hundred year old crime scene," said Jere.

"Yes, I remember that," said Ingrid as she held the cigarette up and prepared to flip it onto the green.

"Don't," snapped Jere.

Ingrid lowered her arm, dropped the cigarette butt on the floor, and crushed it out with her foot. She blew the ashes she'd held in her hand into the air.

"That's disgusting," said Jere.

Ingrid ignored Jere's disapproval and simply continued, "I remember something he said that made me raise an eyebrow."

"Go on," said Jere.

"After we spent a lot of time at dinner talking about our jobs as homicide detectives, Charles commented about how fortunate he was to have such knowledgeable guests. I remember thinking that 'fortunate' to what end? It just seemed like a strange choice of words."

"I caught that, and I thought it was strange too. One of the last things he said tonight was that he was going to save some of the mystery for tomorrow," said Jere.

"So you're thinking that there's an ulterior motive for his inviting us here?" asked Ingrid.

"Oh, I think Charles is sincere in his hospitality, but yes, I think he has something else up his sleeve," said Jere.

"You've got a gracious cousin, Jere, but he is a little peculiar," said Ingrid. "When he welcomed you to the 'family circle' I expected to see hooded people in long black gowns appear and form a circle."

"Family circle!" Jere laughed. "The term is so outdated isn't it? How about that creepy comment he made about the people in the portraits? That made the hair on my neck stand up."

"You mean what he said about 'keeping the dead alive if you just remember them'?" said Ingrid.

"Yeah," said Jere, "and that he considered keeping their memory alive to be his mission."

"Now that's sad, Jere," Ingrid said sympathetically.

"Yes, sad and weird," said Jere.

"Can you imagine what it would be like if the only thing you had to live for was dead people?" said Ingrid. She unfolded her legs, bent over, and picked up the crushed cigarette butt. "But I find this whole experience quite enlightening."

"What do you mean?"

"I mean that it's interesting to see how other immigrants lived. Take my family for example—my grandparents hitched a ride on a freighter. They didn't have two kronors to rub together and couldn't speak a word of English. That lets you know what kind of family stories I grew up hearing," said Ingrid as she stood. "So as Cousin Charles said, 'I can't wait till tomorrow. It's like waiting for Christmas'."

CHAPTER 8

Jere slept fitfully. He heard creaks and groans from far-off reaches of the ancient house, and he lay awake for hours trying to identify them. The enormous clock by the stairwell struck loudly taunting Jere that another sleepless hour had passed. He finally sat up and looked down on the green. An early morning wind stirred the naked branches of some trees forcing them to writhe and bend like dancing skeletons against the dark gray sky, and the ground fog drifted slowly upward until it dissipated. A rabbit hopped undeterred across the lawn after a night of foraging, and somewhere in the distance a bird chirped its early morning song.

Then Jere heard a door slam. Soon the delicious scent of brewing coffee wafted through rooms, up the stairwell, and down hallways until it found its way to Jere's room. Jere reached for his watch and saw that it was five forty five. He stumbled to the bathroom, brushed his teeth, and waited for the hot shower spray to fill the room with steam. When he emerged twenty minutes later his hair was dripping wet and his skin beet red. He reached into his canvas bag and drew out a pair of khakis and a tee shirt that had Jamestowne's 400th printed on it. He picked up his boat shoes and stole barefoot from the room. He knew that it would take an earthquake to awaken Ingrid, and he was glad because he desperately needed to have his first cup of coffee alone.

Following the aroma of delicious coffee Jere made his way to the dining room. There he found the buffet set with a huge pot of coffee, a plate of tempting pastries, and ice cold juice. He poured himself a large glass of juice and drank it on the spot. Then he poured a mug of coffee, snatched a pastry, and turned to walk toward the porch.

Then a much too cheerful voice stopped him. "Good morning, Jere."

Jere turned to see a smiling Martha entered the room from what he supposed was the kitchen. She looked so chipper, crisp, and fresh that he was temped to splash her with orange juice. Instead he said as cheerfully as his pre-coffee condition would allow, "Good morning, Martha. Thought I'd steal a cup of coffee if it's okay."

"Oh please help yourself. And if you'd like to have your coffee in privacy while you wake up, feel free to slip into the parlor or out on the porch. Charles always wants time alone while he has his first cup. Could be a family thing." Martha smiled, turned, and went back into the kitchen.

Martha had won a reprieve. Jere took his coffee and pastry and headed to the porch. He sat and watched as life began to stir along the Elk Riverbank. There was the sulfur smell of rain in the air. Cedar trees along the bank swelled with the wind, and dappled sunlight filtered through the remaining sweet gum leaves turned bridle from the hot autumn sun. A smoky mist swirled above the marsh grass and wafted upward taking on the appearance of phantoms rising from the river. He imagined the mist as spirits of his ancestors whose images were immortalized in portraits on the stairwell. He thought of Charles' mission to keep them alive through their descendants' memories and wondered if the river phantoms reached out to enable Charles in his undertaking.

"Good morning. May I join you?" Jere's fantasy was interrupted by a dry sleepy voice. He turned to see Charles standing in the doorway holding a cup of steaming coffee. His hand trembled slightly.

"Yes, by all means," said Jere. "Morning is my favorite time of day, and what a marvelous scene to wake up to."

Charles pulled up a chair and joined Jere. "You would think that after all my years at Oldfields Point I would not be so deeply affected by this river, but that's not the case. Looking at its beauty every morning is like breathing new life into my very soul. It's just in my blood."

Jere was silent for a few minutes, then he said, " I understand what you mean. I think if I lived here I'd feel the same way."

They sat without speaking for a long time and relished the serenity. Jere's thoughts turned to his discussion with Ingrid the night before. He replayed events that had aroused their curiosity…Charles' unbridled exuberance at their visit; his intense interest in their jobs as homicide detectives; Martha's unusual role at Oldfields Point; the gallery of family portraits that Charles honored. Jere also thought of the one portrait at the top of the stairs that was not a Ford family member and yet Charles paid it such special homage.

Jere broke the silence. "Charles, may I ask you a question?"

"Of course, Jere," said Charles.

"I'm very curious about the lady in the portrait at the top of the stairs," said Jere. "Granted she's very beautiful but since she's not a Ford how does she rate being there at the top of the wall of fame? When I asked you about her last night, you said you would tell me this morning."

"Wall of fame," repeated Charles with a chuckle. "You have such a sense of humor Jere. As I said, the beautiful lady is Caroline, sister of Millicent Ford. The two sisters had an unusual bond, and Caroline spent many days and nights at Oldfields Point."

"I remember your telling us that. So just spending time here with her sister earned her a prominent spot on the wall?" asked Jere skeptically.

Charles paused and took a sip of his coffee. "Cold," he said and set the cup on a table. Then he continued, "You see Jere, there was much more to it than that…"

Charles was interrupted when Martha appeared at the door. "Breakfast, gentlemen," she announced happily.

Charles pushed himself up and said, "I promise to continue telling you about Caroline at breakfast. Shall we go in now? Martha thinks breakfast is the most important meal of the day as you will soon see."

And Charles was right. The sideboard was set with several kinds of breakfast meats, eggs, grits, gravy, hash brown potatoes, hot Maryland biscuits, and a fresh platter of homemade pastries. "This spread could feed a crew of field hands," said Jere.

Ingrid was already in the dining room and filling a plate. "Morning guys," she said. Charles grinned at being called a 'guy'. He appeared to enjoy the informality of his guests.

Ingrid quickly returned her attention to her full plate. "This looks delicious, Martha. You're some cook."

Martha smiled delightedly as she picked up a plate. This morning she joined them for breakfast. At first they sat in silence and ate hungrily as if they had not eaten at all the night before. Then after each dish had been sampled, the conversation turned to the Ford family and Oldfields Point.

Charles said, "Ingrid, earlier I began telling Jere about Caroline, Millicent's sister. While Captain John was off fighting in the war, Millicent was expecting her second child. Caroline was already at Oldfields Point, so she, and two black women were to attend Millicent. The British and Hessians seized Oldfields Point, and the chaos caused Millicent to go into labor."

Ingrid said, "So Caroline helped deliver Millicent's baby and therefore earned herself a place on the Ford Wall of fame."

Jere shot Ingrid a look of disdain. "Ingrid likes to cut to the chase."

Charles laughed, "Cut to the chase...I really enjoy your way of putting things. But, Jere, there's much more to the story," he said. "I have documents that explain it better than I."

"I would certainly like to read them," Jere said enthusiastically.

Charles beamed, "I was hoping you'd say that. Perhaps after breakfast"

"I'd like that," said Jere.

"So Charles, the entire house is the original?" asked Ingrid.

"Well, not exactly," said Charles. "We have done a few updates such as a part of the kitchen, but we have kept that sort of thing to a minimum. Then, of course, there was the fire in 1777 which required some restoration. Other than that, we can say that Oldfields Point as you see it today is authentic."

"Fire?" said Jere. "I didn't know that Oldfields Point burned down."

"Oh no," said Charles. "It wasn't completely destroyed just one wing badly damaged."

Jere still looked at Charles questioningly.

Martha spoke up and said, "Perhaps you should explain more fully, dear."

"Of course, I didn't mean to be vague." Charles smiled and continued more specifically, "You see," he said, "At the same time Captain John was off fighting for American independence, General Howe and an army of British and Hessian troops left New York with the intention of capturing Philadelphia which was the capital at the time and where the Continental Congress was meeting. He was going to slip in the back door so to speak. So he took a rather unusual route. He sailed down the coast, up the Bay, and disembarked at Oldfields Point on August 25, 1777. When the property was seized many slaves and other workers fled into the woods and swamps to escape conscription.

"It was not surprising that General Howe chose to disembark at Oldfields Point. Oldfields Point was a very large and prosperous estate. To give you an idea of its enormity, there was this house, houses for tenants, slaves, free blacks, and indentured servants. There were many barns and other out buildings, and an abundance of livestock and poultry. The shoreline was cleared creating a wide and easily accessible beach. There were docks and a boathouse for the smaller boats. The family even owned a schooner that sailed once a month to Baltimoretowne for goods, groceries, and supplies. Howe confiscated the entire property, and this house was used as headquarters for Hessians, under the command of General Wilhelm Knyphausen. Hessians, as you probably know, were German soldiers fighting with the British."

"Hessians? All I know about Hessians is that they were German mercenaries and wore those funny tall brass hats," said Jere

Charles smiled. "Well, there are a couple of misconceptions there," said Charles. "There is a popular belief that all Hessians wore tall brass hats, when in fact the mitre hat, as it is called, was worn only by Hessian Grenadiers. Most of the Hessians in America and the ones who occupied this house were Musketeers and wore tricorn hats and carried muskets like the other soldiers in the war."

"And the other misconception?" asked Jere.

"That Hessians were mercenaries," answered Charles. "Technically they shouldn't be called that. They weren't personally paid by the British themselves. The term is misleading. The Hessian soldier did not receive *extra* pay for fighting in the American Revolution. While serving here, the

Hessian soldier was paid only his usual salary by the German state of his origin. The term mercenary came about because the British paid the German princely *government* for hiring out its soldiers."

"And the family lived here while the place was occupied?" asked Ingrid.

Charles said, "Yes, they were here."

"Just imagine the horror of having foreign soldiers burst into your home and take over. It must have been terrifiying," said Ingrid.

"It was horrible," Martha exclaimed as if she'd been there. Her outburst startled Ingrid and Jere.

Charles said calmly, "Yes, that was a dark time for our family, Jere. You see the men were away fighting, leaving the women, children, and slaves to fend for and defend themselves. An inventory of property stolen by the Hessians and British listed 3 horses, 4 cows, 38 sheep, 13 large hogs, 36 geese, 100 bushels of corn, 8 bushels of herring, 1 dozen shad, and a pound of salt. And then there was the fire." Charles was breathless following this recitation.

Jere was astonished that Charles had committed the entire inventory of stolen property to memory as if the theft occurred only yesterday.

Jere said, "Charles what about the fire?"

Charles continued, "From here, General Howe simply continued his campaign to capture Philadelphia. It was dastardly enough that they stole our winter supplies, but as they left they torched the house intending to burn it to the ground. Fortunately, when the Hessians rode off the men hiding in the woods and swamps came back. These men, women, children, and slaves were able to extinguish the fire. They were also able to make substantial repairs before the harsh winter set in."

Ingrid exhaled loudly. Even though she had heard the story many times Martha's face was flushed with excitement. Jere was surprised that he felt anger after being told of an assault that happened so long ago.

Ingrid said, "Seeing your home burn has got to be one of the most traumatic experiences I can think of," Ingrid said with empathy.

"It was for Captain John," said Charles. "Although Captain John wasn't here when the fire was set, he never forgave the insult. Some time later he acquired a Hessian sword and displayed it proudly in his study. I think it served as a reminder that ultimately he'd won."

"What happened to the sword?" asked Jere.

"Oh, it's right here at Oldfields Point hanging in Captain John's study. I wouldn't allow it to be anyplace else. Would you like to see it?"

"Most certainly," Jere said excitedly.

Charles seemed pleased. "And while we're at it, I'll share some more family history with you."

"Oh, this is so exciting," said Martha. She looked at Ingrid. "Don't you think this is exciting?"

CHAPTER 9

Ingrid excused herself for an early morning jog along the riverbank explaining that this was part of her exercise routine. Now Jere knew better. He knew this was only a pretext to sneak a smoke. After breakfast and at bedtime were two times Ingrid had to have a cigarette or there was hell to pay for those around her. Incredibly, Jere had sat with her for hours on stake-out when she never smoked, and she was none the worse from it. But he knew better than to stand between Ingrid and her after-breakfast smoke. Jere was one of the few people who even knew Ingrid smoked.

"Either give it up or come out the closet," Jere would chide her.

Charles pushed open the doors to the library. Jere followed him inside and surveyed the room with its leather chairs, two library tables, and gigantic desk. A library ladder leaned against bookshelves that reached to the ceiling. They were crammed with books and worn leather bound journals that appeared to have seen much use. Jere was also interested to see that Charles was not just a pencil pusher who rejected technology. There was a work station complete with the latest computer, fax, copier/printer and other electronic equipment necessary for Charles' research. Several books and journals lay on the library tables and slips of white paper peeped out from between pages that might contain important information. Jere eyed the books curiously. He thought of how he'd love to spend hours lost in these volumes. Oriental rugs lay on the floor with stuffed chairs strategically placed on them. A hearth rug positioned in front of a large fireplace was flanked by two comfortable leather chairs.

Charles said, "Come in Jere. Please come on in." Then he hobbled proudly into the room, stood before the fireplace, and gestured. "There it is Jere. There it is…the symbol of Captain John Ford's eventual victory over the Hessians."

Jere moved to the fireplace and looked where Charles pointed. Above the mantle were two portraits…one of Captain John Ford and the other of Millicent. These portraits were of a somewhat older couple. However, the Captain still proudly wore full military regalia. Millicent looked solemn, and she was not dressed as gaily as in the younger portrait. A sword hung beneath the two portraits, and it was unlike any sword Jere ever saw.

It was a large sword, about forty inches long. The blade was smooth with sharp edges and a silver finish. Engraved on the blade was a hunting scene in which a hound fought furiously with a wild boar. The cross guard was sturdy bronze, and the grip was made of ivory engraved with a vine of roses. The pommel was shaped like a small finely carved crown.

"Charles, it's magnificent," said Jere.

"I know," Charles said delightedly. "I also know how proud Captain John is that it is still in the possession of his family and hanging in his own study at Oldfields Point over two hundred years later."

Jere noticed that Charles spoke of Captain John in the present tense. "Has it ever been out of the family?" Jere asked.

"Not really. For a short time a descendant not in direct line had it. I invited him to spend some time here at Oldfields Point. He was quite elderly and so impressed with the care we have given the ancestral home that he willed the sword to me. And there it will stay," said Charles proudly.

After inspecting the sword, Jere walked around the room reading titles of the books on the shelves. "May I?" asked Jere as he reached for a book.

"Of course," said Charles rubbing his hands together gleefully. "I am so delighted that you are interested. Examine any one you'd like. And I took the liberty of pulling a few volumes I thought you might find particularly interesting."

Jere worked the bookshelves pulling out book after book for closer examination. There were books on the Revolutionary War and Cecil County Maryland. There were old books; new books; maps of the area from different eras; charts of the Chesapeake Bay; ledgers. Spiral bindings held copies encased in sheet covers of land grants; church records; birth and death records; wills; inventories of property; sales of property; and probate records. Most of the documents related to the Ford family.

"Charles, this is incredible," said Jere. "You've done a remarkable job! What you've done is build a Ford Family library."

Charles smiled broadly. "I know."

"Is all this information cataloged?" asked Jere.

"Not all of it Jere," said Charles. "I have been so busy over the years collecting the materials that I'm a little behind in the cataloging. Don't get me wrong, I have notes and records on everything here I just don't have it recorded and organized as well as I'd like. Mostly Martha and I work on that in the evening."

"Charles, this represents a lot of work," said Jere. "I know you're glad to have Martha's help."

"Oh, I couldn't get along without Martha," said Charles.

They looked up as Ingrid hurried breathlessly into the room. "That wind has really picked up out there, and it's a cold wind, too." She hugged herself and rubbed her bare arms. "Hope I didn't miss anything," she continued while taking in the packed bookshelves. "Charles, what an impressive collection of books! These must have taken years to collect."

"That's not all, Ingrid," said Jere. "Take a look at this sword."

Ingrid crossed the room and stared up at the ornate sword. "Whew! That's some piece of weaponry, Charles. I've never seen the likes of it."

Charles was bursting with pride. "You know I love my work here," said Charles. "And I would be happy to spend the rest of my life just collecting and preserving documents and artifacts belonging to my family, but I must admit that it brings me great pleasure to share all this with others...especially with other Ford descendants. Your visit has brought me much happiness."

"How sad," Jere thought, "that Charles chose to shut himself up in this house day after day and year after year with no other apparent interest than family history."

Ingrid studied the portraits of Captain John and Millicent. "They look older in these portraits," said Ingrid. "Captain John still fits into that uniform though."

"Oh yes," said Charles. "He had a fine physique even at that age, and he took every opportunity he could to wear that uniform."

Ingrid walked slowly around the room absorbing the complete scene with the trained eye of a detective. She walked toward the large desk set in the back of the room. Hanging above it was a portrait…another portrait of Caroline, the young woman at the top of the stairs.

"Jere," said Ingrid, "look here. It's the girl at the top of the stairs. You know Millicent's sister."

Charles and Jere joined her in front of the portrait. Charles said, "As I said earlier she was Millicent's only sister, and under the very dangerous circumstances I described she was present when Millicent labored with her second child."

Charles turned and walked back to one of the library tables that held several volumes with certain pages tagged by pieces of paper.

"I took the liberty of selecting some readings you might find interesting. These are accounts of colonial life in Cecil County during the Revolutionary War period," said Charles, "but more importantly for our purposes it tells how isolation fostered the dependency that family members had on each other for survival and companionship. In referring to Millicent and Caroline's relationship, one young writer called their attachment to each other a 'bond that extended beyond the grave'."

Jere sat with Ingrid reading silently the selections Charles had flagged and wondered what all this had to do with them. Charles said it was important to "our purposes"…just what purposes was he talking about. If Charles needs their help, then why doesn't he just come out with it instead of feeding them endless family stories that seem to go nowhere?

Suddenly Jere said, "Charles, I have a feeling there's something you want us to do. If so, just ask us."

CHAPTER 10

As if on cue, the library door opened and a pleasant voice said, "Am I interrupting anything?" They looked up as Martha walked quickly through the door.

"That is too much of a coincidence," thought Jere. "She had to be listening outside the door and doesn't want to miss anything."

"Of course not Martha," said Charles, "please come in and join us. I've just been briefing Jere and Ingrid on life at Oldfields Point during the days of John and Millicent. "

"And Charles was about to answer my question," Jere was determined not to be to be put off again. "So Charles what would you like us to do?"

"Jere, I want you to solve a murder," Charles blurted.

"A murder?" repeated Ingrid and Jere.

Suddenly the room grew silent and a surge of energy shot through Jere much like the feeling he experiences when he first begins a case.

"Charles," Jere said eagerly, "what murder? Here? When did it happen? Who was murdered? What did the police say? Fill me in."

Charles appeared so excited that he could hardly contain himself. He slipped to the front of his chair, leaned forward, and blurted out, "You don't know what a relief it is to finally find someone willing to listen to me. Others think it ridiculous and a waste of time and resources to pursue. Yet

I feel compelled to investigate…to get to the bottom of a mystery that haunts me. Thank you, Jere, for showing an interest."

"Wait a minute, Charles," Jere said taken aback, "Are you telling me there was a murder here and someone doesn't want it investigated? Who? Were the police notified?"

"Charles," Martha interrupted gently, "you have digressed again. Remember we must first determine if it were murder or some other crime."

Ingrid looked confused. Jere was confused too and shot Ingrid a wary glance. Had a crime actually occurred in this remote place? Had these two reclusive gentle people witnessed some horrible act? Had Charles been warned not to talk about it? Now it made sense. So this was Charles' ulterior motive for inviting them to visit, and this is why Charles was interested in their job as homicide detectives.

Ingrid said, "Some other crime? Charles, start from the beginning. Tell us about the murder…or whatever?"

"Yes, yes. I'm so sorry. I have a habit of getting ahead of myself. In a sense I have dreaded asking you for help. I was so afraid that you would consider me an eccentric recluse with a grand imagination."

"Charles…" Martha said gently.

"Charles, we don't consider you eccentric. I think you're a well focused, intuitive researcher," said Jere reassuringly. "And if you feel you've stumbled on a crime, I respect your opinion."

"Now tell us the problem," Ingrid said sharply.

"Thank you, Jere, Ingrid. I'll cut to the chase," he said and smiled at Ingrid. "I hardly know where to begin. For our purposes, I felt it most important that you fully appreciate the bond between Caroline and Millicent and have a feel for life at Oldfields Point during the time of the Revolutionary War."

"Charles is most methodical," said Martha. Ingrid shot her an intimidating look that said 'back off, he's finally getting to the point'.

Charles continued, "As I told you, in August 1777 the War came to Oldfields Point, and Millicent was expecting her second child. The chaos from the Hessian occupation caused Millicent to go into labor. When the delivery took a difficult turn, Millicent called for her mother. Caroline feared her sister might die. So in the darkness of night amidst the turmoil of the Hessian occupation and the treachery of the Loyalists that roamed the woods hoping to hookup with the British, Caroline prepared to fetch their mother. Millicent could hear the Hessians plundering downstairs and asked Caroline to take a valuable family artifact with her. The relic was a gold necklace baring a medallion with the Ford family crest engraved on it. The medallion is the one you see in the portrait of young Millicent. But what I have not told you is that neither Caroline nor the artifact was ever seen again. In fact, the last person to see Caroline was Millicent's nurse, Anna. She peered out the window just as Caroline carrying a lantern disappeared into the shadows around the house. There was a backyard path that led by the kitchen door, pass the cellar, and through the woods to her mother's house. Suddenly Anna saw something most alarming. A figure stepped out of the shadows and crept closely behind her.

"When the Hessians left to continue the campaign, those who had fled into the woods came out of hiding. First they turned their attention to putting out the fire. Then they realized that Caroline was no where to be found. A search ensued…this house, Caroline's home, the woods, the riverbank, the river itself…all were diligently searched for days. They even used scent hounds. Not a trace of Caroline was ever found. They found no clues…footprints, necklace, clothing, lantern, or disturbed earth that might indicate a grave. It was as if Caroline had simply vanished from the face of the earth.

"Millicent was never the same after that. Oh, she and Captain John went on to live a long life here at Oldfields Point, but it was as if Millicent's very soul had been ripped from her. You noticed the change reflected in the two portraits of Millicent. It wasn't just age that made that difference. Millicent grieved for Caroline until she joined her in death."

Jere and Ingrid were astonished. They now realized that the murder Charles wanted them to investigate happened over two hundred years ago.

"So Charles, explain to me exactly what it is you want us to do," Jere stammered.

"Find her, Jere. Please find her," Charles pled. "I just know Caroline was murdered."

"How do you know that, Charles," asked Jere.

"Because of this incredible bond I spoke of. She would never leave Millicent. And another thing, she's here. I know she's here at Oldfields Point. I sense it. I sense her presence here. If you find Caroline, Jere, you'll also find the crest medallion. The crest will identify her."

Jere's first reaction was to say something cynical like 'you've got to be kidding', but he felt sorry for Charles who was so wrapped up in family lore that his ancestors were as real to him as any relative living today. Jere took a deep breath and thought about the best way to respond.

Finally Jere said calmly, "Charles, I want you to look at this through our eyes as modern homicide detectives. You see, you don't have any evidence; you don't have a body; therefore, you don't have a case."

Charles looked stunned. "But you told me when you were digging at Jamestown it was like working a four hundred year old crime scene."

"Yes," said Jere, "but we uncovered results. We knew where to dig. We knew the location of the village site. Not a day went by that we didn't find artifacts and sometimes a whole skeleton. We examined and tested the artifacts and from the results we could piece together a scenario."

Ingrid looked at Charles who appeared to be on the verge of tears. She said, "Charles, Jere's right. We have nothing to go on here. Not one shred of evidence to help us. If the searchers didn't find anything over two hundred years ago, what are our chances today?"

Charles covered his face with his hands. The silence was deafening. Martha reached over and touched Charles.

Suddenly in the distance they heard the sound of a car engine, and Martha hurried to the window. Ingrid and Jere continued to explain why it would be impossible to use today's investigative methods to solve a crime committed over two hundred years ago.

Then Martha cried out, "Charles, Charles, it's Isodora. Oh dear, what a wretched way to start the day!" She patted her hair, straightened her dress, and hurried from the room. "I must go and open the door," she mumbled to herself.

Charles looked distraught. "Jere I had hoped to spare you this unpleasantness until our family gathering, but Aunt Isodora is most determined. She is eighty years old and nothing deters her. I feared when

I told her about your visit, that she would make a visit of her own. I had only hoped that we would have an opportunity to discuss our case, before she appeared." Charles obviously had not accepted that Jere and Ingrid didn't think there was a case.

A loud knock reverberated through the entrance hall followed by the patter of hurried footsteps. The front door opened and indistinguishable voices floated down the hall toward the library. Suddenly the library door burst open, and Jere and Ingrid gaped in amazement at the woman in the doorway.

●

CHAPTER 11

The woman who stormed into the room was unlike anything Jere expected. To him, eighty years old meant a little old gray haired lady, bent and gnarled, wearing comfort shoes, and dowdy attire. Instead the intruder caused Jere and Ingrid to gawk in amazement.

Even in three inch heels, Aunt Isodora was barely five feet tall and could not have weighed over ninety five if she weighed a pound. She had bright red hair compliments of Miss Clairol teased and fluffed in an effort to make her look taller. She had penciled-on eyebrows and false eyelashes. Her face was lifted so tautly that tiny blood vessels could be seen through the pale thin skin that stretched severely over her fine cheekbones. Her white face was excessively powdered and blushed making her bright red cupid-bow shaped lips look surreal. She wore black silky slacks and a flowing floral blouse over a knit chartreuse green sweater. She wore several gold bracelets and dangling gold earrings that almost touched her shoulders. Around her neck were several long gold chains.

Charles struggled to stand up. "Jere, Ingrid, I'd like..." he began.

Aunt Isodora ignored his attempt at an introduction, marched straight to Jere, and looked up at him confrontationally. Several moments of silence went by as she stared him up and down. Then she said, "Charles told me he had found a long-lost cousin and invited him to come and stay here in the house. So since I wasn't invited to this soiree, I thought I'd better come over here and find out about this missing relative for myself."

Jere was speechless, but it made no difference. Isodora apparently did not require another person to have a conversation. Her eye twitched involuntarily as she continued, "So who are you?"

Jere introduced himself. "I'm Jeremiah Ford…"

Aunt Isodora interrupted, "That's not what I mean. Who's you daddy? And your grandfather?"

Jeremiah underwent a lengthy interrogation about his lineage, and answered every question that Aunt Isodora spit out. She listened intently to his answers, and Jere quickly realized that Aunt Isodora was also quite knowledgeable about Ford family genealogy.

"So where did you get all this genealogical information that led you to us?" Aunt Isodora asked suspiciously.

"Research," said Jere.

"Where'd you find your documents?" she asked.

"Different places. Libraries, courthouse, internet…" said Jere growing tired of being cross examined.

"I don't trust the internet," Aunt Isodora said dismissively.

Aunt Isodora suddenly seemed to realize that Ingrid was in the room. She turned, walked to her, and took her stand. "And who the hell are you?"

Ingrid who had been watching the whole horrible scene would have none of it. She stepped forward, hands on hips, towered over the little woman, and in her most commanding voice said, "I'm Ingrid…who are you?"

Aunt Isodora was taken aback only briefly. She resumed her stand, looked Ingrid straight in the eye and asked sternly, "Are you a Ford?"

"No," Ingrid said yielding no new information.

"Then what is your *relationship* to our newly found cousin?" Aunt Isodora said sarcastically as she jerked her head in Jere's direction.

"Our *relationship* is that we're partners," Ingrid said not giving an inch.

"Partners in what?" Aunt Isodora prodded suspiciously.

"Homicide detectives in the Richmond City Police Department," said Ingrid.

Isodora froze for a moment, a look of shock on her face. Then a light came on in the old woman's eye. With hands on hips she walked to Charles, took a firm stand in front of him, and said accusingly, "Oh, I see, Charles. I see the method in your madness…and I do mean madness…you've pulled a distant relative out of nowhere, brought him here with his partner, and fed him the story of Caroline and the missing Ford family crest. Now you'll probably expect these detectives to help you play out your fantasy of finding Caroline's remains and the necklace."

Aunt Isodora suddenly realized that Martha was still in the room. "You're dismissed," she barked. As Martha hastened out of the room she anxiously looked back at Charles who slumped back onto the loveseat.

"We've had enough complications from family members getting involved with the help," Isodora snapped.

Jere looked at Charles who had begun to shake.

"Chasing the wind," Aunt Isodora continued cruelly pointing a boney finger at Charles. "That's what he's been doing for years. Chasing the wind. He's shut himself up in this house, collected all this stuff, and for what? What do your efforts amount to?" She waved her hand about the shelves. "Who'll care about all this when you are gone? Nobody. Nobody, Charles…the house, the books, all this stuff. Nobody else cares about it, so when you're gone what's going to happen to your stuff? All your efforts down the toilet. You're chasing the wind, Charles."

Now it was Jere and Ingrid's turn again. Aunt Isodora turned on them and said, "It's been worse since he's been sick. He's become a driven man. He and that housekeeper (or whatever she is) immerse themselves in family research, and obsess over the disappearance of Caroline and the damned necklace with the family crest. If you ask me Caroline shouldn't have been allowed to take it anyway. She wasn't a Ford."

Isodora's eyes suddenly went to the fireplace and the sword hanging there. She walked authoritatively across the room, stood with her hands on her hips, and glared maliciously at the sword.

"And this," she screeched waving a hand at the sword, "hanging on to this symbol of hate and revenge for over two hundred years…brooding over it day in and day out. No wonder you're sick."

She went back to Charles. "Let go Charles. Let the whole damned thing go…Caroline, the necklace, your obsession with the Hessian occupation," she screeched. Then she turned to Ingrid and Jere and added, "And if you have any conscience, you won't encourage him. It's futile."

Then Aunt Isodora turned and stomped out of the room. Jere and Ingrid had never seen so much fury and passion come out of such a diminutive woman. It wasn't until they heard the front door slam and the car engine start that Martha dashed back into the room. She rushed to Charles and began to comfort him.

CHAPTER 12

Jere and Ingrid were stunned by Aunt Isodora's chilling performance. They looked at each other in disbelief. How could she be so rude? How could she be so cruel? Jere watched as Martha attempted to console Charles.

Then the front door clicked open causing everyone to turn back in dread toward the library door. Was this to be a hysterical encore by Aunt Isodora? The footsteps in the hall were urgent, yet not heavy and challenging. The door sprang open and the blur of a young woman raced across the room and knelt beside Charles.

She was tall and thin and wore a white medical uniform, white comfort shoes, white trouser stockings, and carried a small black leather bag. Her soft brown hair was cut short to frame her oval face, and her large brown eyes were wide with alarm.

"Charles, are you all right?" she asked grabbing his wrist to measure his pulse. Charles did not respond. He sat rigidly and drool appeared on his lower lip.

The lovely intruder turned toward Martha. "Martha, what happened? I just saw Aunt Isodora tear out of here like a bat out of hell. She almost ran me down."

"Bat isn't strong enough, Julia," said Martha fighting back tears. "She came in uninvited, humiliated Charles, and was rude to our guests. She was awful, awful."

Julia's face reflected anger as she reached into the medical case and took out a syringe and a vial filled with liquid. She held up the vial, inserted the needle, extracted a measured amount of fluid, and injected Charles. In a few minutes Charles relaxed and everyone breathed a sigh of relief.

The lovely heroine stood and for the first time seemed to notice Jere and Ingrid. She stepped forward, extended her hand, and said, "I'm Julia Caswell, Charles' sister. Sorry we had to meet under such atrocious circumstances." She shook hands with Ingrid then Jere.

"Who was that crazy woman?" asked Ingrid.

Martha looked up with tears streaming down her cheeks. "Oh, she's horrible, Ingrid. Just horrible. She treats Charles awful, and I think she's jealous…just plain jealous. She thinks of herself as the Ford family materfamilias who knows everything. But deep down inside she knows that Charles has far more knowledge of family history and everything than she. She's just plain jealous."

"Well, she acted like a lunatic. What right does she have to come into Oldfields Point and attack Charles that way?" Jere asked angrily.

"None," Martha said flatly. "None at all! This is Charles' place plain and clear. She's always acted high and mighty, and the family just placates her because she's old. I believe that age is no excuse for rudeness and cruelty. Since Charles got sick, she takes advantage of the situation suggesting that he's not capable of making decisions for himself. She's getting more and more intrusive, and she knows Charles shouldn't be upset like this." She dropped to her knees again and began gently stroking Charles' arm.

Julia began to place things back into her bag. Charles struggled to the front of his seat. "Thank you, Julia," he said. "I feel so much better now. I'll walk you to your car."

"NO!" they all blurted out at once.

Jere hurried toward Julia and took the bag from her hand. "I'll see Julia to her car, Charles. That'll give me a chance to get to know yet another cousin."

Julia bent over and kissed Charles affectionately on the cheek.

"Thanks, Jere," she said. "You sit still Charles. Now I have to pay Aunt Isodora a little visit."

Jere and Julia walked to the car in silence. Jere was still stunned by Isodora's dramatic performance. When they reached Julia's car Jere opened the driver's door and handed Julia her bag. He noticed that her nails were clipped short. Jere assumed this was to prevent the puncture of rubber gloves.

Jere stammered, "I…I didn't know Cousin Charles had a sister. And such a good looking one at that. Seems I've found myself another cousin. Well, that's my luck…as usual."

Julia smiled, slid into the driver's seat, and started the motor. She looked out the window and said, "Charles is my stepbrother."

Jere looked confused. It took a few minutes to realize the significance of her remark. Finally she said, "Then you and I aren't cousins. We aren't blood relatives at all."

The car began to slowly roll away. Jere shouted after her, "Hey, does that mean we can be 'kissing kin'?"

Julia stuck her arm out the window and waved good-bye.

Jere smiled, broke into a trot, and jogged toward the house. He reached the porch and grasped the doorknob. Suddenly he stood motionless. His mind clicked back to Charles and the awful scene with Aunt Isodora. He struggled to think of some way to comfort his cousin. This lonely, sick man who cloistered himself with his books and maps…a man who had put his hopes in a distant cousin he'd never met and now saw his hopes dashed. Jere couldn't bear the thoughts of Charles being disappointed any more. He knew Ingrid would feel the same way.

When Jere entered the library he immediately walked over to Charles. Charles looked up at him. He was pale and still trembled. He said, "Jere, I apologize for Aunt Isodora's rude behavior. I'd hoped to spare you her madness…at least until the family gathering."

Jere said, "Don't worry about it. You're not responsible for her lunacy."

"Yeah, she's just a toxic old biddy," said Ingrid.

"Meeting Julia cancels out Isodora's hysterics. Julia's certainly devoted to you. Is she your neurologist?" Jere asked.

"Oh, no," said Charles. "I see a neurologist at Johns Hopkins Hospital. He's an old friend of Julia's, and she assists him in whatever way he feels she can…such as giving injections when necessary. Actually Julia is our county medical examiner."

"And she just adores Charles. Why they couldn't be closer if they were blood kin," said Martha. "Not like that evil Isodora…"

Jere interrupted her, "Look Charles, forget about Aunt Isodora. Forget what she said about your research. What does she know? Don't give up trying to solve your family mystery if this is what you want to do. Now I'm going to stay honest with you. Since we have no evidence, I think it will be impossible to determine exactly what happened to Caroline by investigating the way we do in Richmond today. But suppose we take another approach. Suppose we use your research and your intricate knowledge to look into this mystery. We might be able to come up with some possible scenarios. It may not answer *all* your questions but, hey, you could end up with more than you have today."

Charles lifted his head. "You would help do this?"

Sensing what Jere was doing Ingrid said lightheartedly, "Sure, why look at all this stuff…books, maps, journals, letters, all kinds of documents. Seems a shame to just leave it setting there. Let's take a trip back in time and solve a crime."

"Oh, thank you," Charles said relieved. His eyes welled up with tears. "We've felt so alone with this conundrum. Haven't we Martha?"

Martha nodded fighting back tears.

"First of all," said Jere "Ingrid and I need to familiarize ourselves with your setup here. We need to know how things are organized and take some time to peruse the volumes, maps, etc.. Charles, will you give us a guided tour?"

"By all means," said Charles. He pushed himself upright. It was as if new life were breathed into him.

Then with flair, Ingrid bounced up and announced, "Then let the games begin."

Martha jumped up and trotted toward the door. "And I'll make a tray of sandwiches and light the tea kettle. We'll just snack while we *peruse*. Isn't this exciting? Oh it's so exciting!"

Charles proudly walked Ingrid and Jere through the shelves of volumes, maps, and other documents. He also explained his computer file system and apologized that the work wasn't complete.

Martha returned quickly with a tray of sandwiches, cups, and a large pot of tea. Ingrid whispered to Jere, "She certainly got back fast. I bet she'd already made the sandwiches and put the kettle on."

Jere grinned and said, "Martha, you're certainly on top of things."

Martha set the tray on the library table. "Here's our lunch. We can accomplish more if we snack while we talk.

"Ingrid," Martha continued, "you know that cool wind you spoke of this morning? It's bringing quite a weather change. Earlier I heard on the radio that radar is tracking a nor'easter headed in our direction." Then to Charles she added, "We can expect some pretty heavy rain later on. I had so hoped that the cellar could be repaired before another big storm. It leaks like a sieve."

"And I hope the rain will hold off until after the family gathering tomorrow night," Charles said a look of concern on his face.

They placed the most comfortable leather chairs beside the large library table. Martha poured tea and passed around the tray of sandwiches...cucumber, chicken salad, and soft shell crab. As usual, Martha's fare was scrumptious.

Jere took a bite of a soft shell crab sandwich, leaned back, closed his eyes, and savored the taste. After he'd tried all three choices, he brushed his hands together and said, "Now, let's talk about this. You know the first thing we need to do is come up with a strategy."

Charles' face lit up, "You mean like a war room."

"Yes, like a war room," said Jere with a smile. Ingrid smiled, too.

Charles seemed no worse for wear. He seemed to have forgotten all about Aunt Isodora. Jere really liked Cousin Charles. His simple, almost childlike persona made him quite an endearing character.

They spent the entire afternoon discussing possible strategies, perusing materials, and generally shooting the breeze. Jere and Ingrid occasionally related an account of one of their Richmond homicide cases, and Martha and Charles sat wide-eyed devouring every word.

Soon Martha excused herself to prepare dinner. It was her usual gourmet delight featuring two seafood pastas, a salad, and Peach Melba for dessert. They chatted about the afternoon's accomplishment and about the family gathering to be held the following evening.

"I'm so sorry I can't spend tomorrow morning with you in the library," said Martha. "Things will start hopping in the morning. The florist, the caterer, the gardener, and the kitchen helpers will show up bright and early so I shall be very busy."

"Your presence will be greatly missed," said Charles, "but the family reunion is most certainly our priority tomorrow." Then he smiled at Martha and added, "I am so fortunate to have you, my dear."

Martha returned his smile. It was as if for the moment Jere and Ingrid were not in the room. "Thank you, Charles," Martha said softly.

They retired early, and when Charles and the two detectives finally reached the top of the stairs, Charles turned and said, "Today I am a happy man. If I were to die tonight I would die happy." And he turned and walked down the yawning dark hall.

CHAPTER 13

Early the next morning Jere and Ingrid awoke to the sound of groaning truck engines, slamming doors, and loud voices. They both rolled out of bed and appeared on the porch at the same time.

"What's going on?" asked Ingrid in a deep scratchy voice. Her hair was platted in a long blonde braid and sleep creases marked the side of her face. Her pajama top and pants were wrinkled and one trouser leg was twisted awkwardly around her leg.

"Damned if I know. What time is it anyway?" Jere had slept in a tee shirt and boxers. Suddenly he looked down, swore, and made a dash inside.

Ingrid's curiosity outweighed any embarrassment she felt, and she continued to hang over the railing her wide eyes glued on the hubbub below. When Jere reappeared, he wore jeans, boat shoes, and another Jamestown 400 tee-shirt—this one was orange and inscribed with bold black letters that read 'I Dig Jamestowne'.

"So what do you think?" asked Ingrid again.

"I think you better get some clothes on," Jere said tersely.

Ingrid looked down at her wrinkle pajamas, shrugged her shoulders, and pranced slowly inside.

As Jere and Ingrid started down the stairs, they were astonished by the excitement and commotion taking place in the hall below. Doors leading from the grand hall into the parlor, dining, and drawing rooms were slid into their pockets thus opening up the rooms and converting the first floor into one large gathering area. Sweaty workmen wore sleeveless gauze shirts that exposed their large biceps. With little effort they demonstrated their brawn as they lifted heavy furniture and carried it away to some unknown place in the house. The drawing room which had been quite over-furnished was no longer cluttered. Now it contained only several groups of comfortable chairs with small tables placed purposefully nearby. Extra chairs were also placed in the parlor and grand hall. In the dining room additional tables were pushed against the wall, and two women in blue and white uniforms covered them with thick cotton pads and then topped them with fine crisp linen cloths.

Jere and Ingrid reached the first landing of the stairway. They were so amazed by the bustle below, that Ingrid wasn't mindful of where she stepped and almost stumbled on a musical instrument case. "What the..." she started to say.

"Watch it, Ingrid," said Jere as he caught her arm.

They looked down at the landing floor in disbelief. There was an arrangement of three chairs and several musical instrument cases on which was printed, The C. C. Trio. They gawked at each other in disbelief.

"Is all of this for us? Ingrid, this is embarrassing!" said Jere.

Ingrid suppressed a giggle. "Not for us, Jer...for you."

Below an older gentleman with pinkish complexion, white hair, and a snow white beard flitted from one room to another. He was dressed in a green uniform with a logo that identified him as Josh of Josh's Horticultural Heaven. He was accompanied by three young assistants who stood transfixed by the splendid mansion and ogled all the elegant trappings. Josh struggled for their attention and snapped off instructions about floral arrangements and their placement about the house. Soon the entire first floor took on the scent of roses, lilies, and some plants unfamiliar to Ingrid and Jere.

And amidst all this pandemonium was Martha, cheeks aglow with excitement and enthusiasm. Her expertise and command of the task were beyond question. She stood in the hall and scrutinized every move made by the workforce…sometimes making corrections and then correcting her corrections. Martha was most certainly in her element. She turned in the direction of the stairs and spotted Jere and Ingrid. She darted across the hall and up the steps.

"Isn't this exciting? Oh, I've not had so much fun since…" Martha paused as if trying to resurrect some joyous memory. She couldn't. "Oh, well let's just say I've never had so much fun. Come." And she started down the steps.

Jere and Ingrid followed her dodging florists, movers, and caterers as they wove their way through the chaos. Martha led them into the dining room where a huge urn of coffee, cold juice, disposable cups, and an enormous platter covered with foil were laid out on one of the side boards. Closer examination revealed that underneath the foil was a large stash of hot Maryland biscuits and baked ham.

"Please forgive the informality," Martha said. "But I instructed the workers to come early, and they did just that. Please help yourself to the ham and biscuits and coffee. As you can see, the rooms have been opened up to accommodate our…I shouldn't say *our*…I should say *your* guests. I did, however, lock the door to the study and you are welcome to continue *perusing* if you'd like. I'll be glad to unlock it for you."

Martha looked hopeful. Jere knew that Martha would prefer that he and Ingrid hide out in the library and stay out from under foot.

Ingrid had sensed the same thing and said, "That would be great, Martha. Just let me grab a few of these." And she snatched three ham/biscuits.

"Martha," said Jere somewhat painfully. "I thought that the family gathering was going to be just a few family members and friends. I never dreamed you'd go to this…"

"Oh, shush," said Martha. "It's no trouble at all. You know how it is. You begin a guest list and before you know it…" She shrugged her shoulders, spread her hands in a questioning manner, and lifted her eyebrows. Not being a gregarious person, Jere had no idea what she meant. He was just flabbergasted. Ingrid was amused.

"We understand…don't we, Jere?" and without waiting for Jere's answer, Ingrid said, "Now if you'll unlock the study door…"

Jere and Ingrid balanced coffee, juice, and biscuits on small trays and followed Martha to the library. Jere felt self-conscious as all eyes seemed to follow the procession. He supposed that they were all thinking '*so that's the guy who rates all this*'.

Once inside the library, Martha helped them clear a place on the work table for their food. Then she said, "Charles asked me to explain that he decided not to come down this morning. He is unaccustomed to this much activity and excitement."

"I'm *unaccustomed* to this much excitement, too," Jere muttered. Ingrid elbowed him.

Martha did not appear to hear him. "Julia insisted it would be best if he stayed clear of the ruckus. So Charles is going to remain upstairs and try to relax although he is so excited that I doubt he'll do much relaxing."

Jere said, "When did Charles see Julia?"

"Oh, Julia was by bright and early this morning," said Martha as she turned and scurried away.

Jere was disappointed that Julia had been at Oldfields Point and he'd missed her. He reached for his coffee and took a big gulp. Suddenly he coughed, sputtered, and grabbed the cold juice. "Burned my damned tongue," he gasped.

Ingrid grinned, "Mad 'cause you missed her?"

"What? Who are you talking about?" said Jere.

"Julia. You mad 'cause you missed Julia?" She repeated.

Jere looked disgusted, took another swig of juice, and said, "We've been working together too long."

They ate in silence realizing once again that their appetites had become gargantuan. Perhaps they were just finally relaxing after a hectic year; or maybe it was the fresh air off the Bay; or maybe…just maybe…it was Martha's skilled cooking that could turn a simple cucumber sandwich into a culinary delight.

The morning passed quickly. The clamor in the hall served as background noise as they acquainted themselves with Charles' library. They discovered that the volumes were not confined solely to the Revolutionary War era but covered a much greater span of time. There were lists of Fords who fought in the Indian Wars, the War of 1812, World War I and II, up through the most recent Desert Storm. There were records on the earliest Ford immigrant who had arrived in America from England before 1700. There were letters and diaries relating the joyous birth of a baby and the sad passing of a cherished relative; announcements of weddings and celebrations of anniversaries; and invitations to christenings and holiday celebrations. The hours passed swiftly as Ingrid and Jere took a romantic journey back in time. They were startled when the library door opened and Martha walked in. She was carrying a picnic basket, a large beach blanket, and a flask of wine.

"Lunchtime," she announced cheerily. Jere looked at the mantle clock and was surprised to see that it was twelve o'clock. "I thought you might enjoy a picnic down on the beach. The weather is supposed to take a nasty turn so you might be wise to take advantage of this lovely day. There are sandwiches and wine and a surprise dessert. Now you two go along and have a nice outing."

Martha was herding them toward the door much like a kindergarten teacher might direct her class to the playground. Jere took the basket, and as they walked through the grand hall Jere felt the eyes of the workers follow them.

Once outside Jere muttered, "This is humiliating!"

"Oh, come on Jere," said Ingrid. "They're proud of you. They want to show you off."

"Well I wish they'd find some less ostentatious way to do it," Jere grumbled.

"Oh, get over it, Jere," Ingrid snapped angrily. "Give the poor couple a chance to shine. Stop thinking about yourself."

"Okay," he said startled by Ingrid's reproach.

Jere didn't speak for a few minutes. They reached the bottom of the hill and spread the beach blanket in the dappled shade of a large tree. It became apparent that the barometric pressure was dropping. The light wind that reached the river beach had a distinct chill about it. The air smelled wet and salty, and the mist above the water had not yet dissipated. Wildflowers were still beaded with dew, and enormous clouds moved swiftly across the sky from the northeast. Just above the marsh grass, which flapped noisily in the wind, a snake sunned itself by hanging from a tree branch. Little waves washed ashore reminding Jere of small wraithlike hands stretching out of the water.

"I hope this weather holds," said Ingrid reaching eagerly into the basket and removing a crust-free sandwich. "It would be sad if the festivities were disrupted by a storm."

Jere opened the wine bottle and filled two glasses. "Yeah, we wouldn't want that to happen," he said cynically.

Ingrid shot him a stern look and Jere continued wearily, "All right. I'm gonna brace myself and put on my best social face. I know it's not so much about me as them. After all they've done for us by providing us with a free vacation and the best meals I've had in a long time, the least I can do is be nice."

"There you go," Ingrid quipped cheerfully. "Just pretend you're working security at a political fund raiser and you have to mingle inconspicuously. Just mingle."

Ingrid was pleased that Jere acknowledged Charles and Martha's efforts, and she yammered on endlessly. Jere just smiled and half listened. Then he finished a sandwich in one bite, gulped some wine, and lay down on the blanket. He put his hands behind his head, stared up at the swiftly moving clouds, and detected the shape of a large three-masted ship. He even envisioned guns protruding from its ports. To the right of his fantasy ship another massive cloud took the shape of a white crane gliding aimlessly across the sky. He visualized other objects and creatures as he indulged in a game he hadn't enjoyed since he was a child. Finally his eyelids grew heavy, and he was lulled asleep by the sounds of the river.

"Jere, Jere! Are you listening to me?" Ingrid said irritably. Then as if to answer her own question she continued, "You don't ever hear a thing I say."

Jere stirred into wakefulness, raised himself on his elbow, blinked hard, and focused on his partner, "How can I not hear you?" Then he looked in the direction of the house and watched as workers loaded their trucks and began pulling away. "What's going on anyway?" he asked sleepily as he stood and began to fold the blanket.

Ingrid stuffed the last triangle of a sandwich into her mouth and began to load things into the picnic basket. "Looks like the stage is set for your debut. It's time to party!"

CHAPTER 14

Jere stared at himself in the full length mirror. He was dressed in a navy blue coat, a white mock turtle neck sweater, and taupe slacks. Martha had assured the two detectives that tonight's celebration was to be a casual affair.

"Casual!" scoffed Jere as he turned and walked from his room. He rapped on Ingrid's door, and she opened it immediately.

"What took you so long? I've been ready an hour," she said with a gleam in her eye. Ingrid wore a simple black thing. Her only accessories were gold earrings and a gold locket that Sean had given her one mother's day.

"An hour...I bet," Jere muttered.

They began to walk toward the stairway. "Now remember, Jere, you're going to be nice and you're going to mingle. Right?"

"Yeah, mingle," Jere scoffed.

They descended the stairs, passed the musical trio that was warming up, and gazed down into the grand hall with its polished floors and copious floral arrangements.

"Casual...huh. Looks like a funeral parlor," Jere complained.

Ingrid stopped abruptly, turned to Jere, and said in a stern voice, "Now listen here Jere, this is not about you. Get over it. It's about two lonely people who want to show a neglectful family that they have friends in their own right. You want to deprive them of that? You want to embarrass them like Isodora did the other morning? If so, you can just walk on down these steps by yourself."

Jere was instantly contrite. "I know, I know, you're right, Ingrid. Thanks for straightening me out again. I sure don't want to offend Charles. Let's go smile and mingle."

When Jere and Ingrid entered the parlor, Charles was seated on the loveseat. Martha sat beside him and held his hand. Their faces glowed with excitement and eagerness. Martha stood as the house guests entered, but Charles remained seated.

"Oh how nice you both look," said Martha.

"You most certainly do," Charles agreed. "It has been so long since we had such a celebration at Oldfields Point that I'd forgotten just how exhilarating it can be. Of course until now, we've had little to celebrate."

Martha added as if to prevent the conversation from taking a negative turn, "But tonight we shall make up for all those other times. This will be a celebration to end all celebrations at Oldfields Point."

"Martha the cheerleader," thought Ingrid.

Martha continued, "Now Charles and I were just discussing your introductions. Jere, Ingrid, since you do not know any of the guests, we thought a reception line in the front hall would be appropriate."

"A reception line?" Jere repeated horrified.

Martha continued undeterred, "You will stand beside me, and I shall introduce you to each guest. Charles, of course, is not up to standing that long. Therefore, after each introduction we shall direct the guest to the parlor to be welcomed by Charles."

"We could just wear name tags," suggested Jere. Ingrid delivered a hard jab with her elbow.

Martha twittered, "Name tags! Oh, Jere, you are so funny."

"He's a stitch all right," said Ingrid.

Suddenly car headlights swept the room. "Our first guest," chirped Martha, and she bent over and spontaneously kissed Charles on the cheek. Charles looked surprised, and Ingrid wondered if that were the first time Martha had shown such affection.

Martha quickly herded Ingrid and Jere into the hall and positioned them by the door. Martha assumed the first position then Jere and Ingrid. Martha gave the signal, and the trio began to play. As each curious guest arrived Martha introduced Jere as Charles' cousin and Ingrid as his detective partner. The guests carefully scrutinized Jere as they looked for family resemblance, quizzed him about his lineage, and welcomed him to the family. However, more than one eyebrow was raised as they considered Jere's very attractive *partner*. As the guests made their way to be greeted by Charles, laughter floated from the parlor. From the corner of his eye Jere saw tears of relief and joy well up in Martha's eyes.

Jere felt himself relax as he was embraced by guest after guest. Then she arrived…Julia in all her simplicity and loveliness. She wore something that was soft and flowing and light green that highlighted the tiny green flecks in her brown eyes. She was smiling and animated as she kissed Martha on the cheek. She moved on to Jere and reached for his hand. She held his hand briefly and looked warmly into his eyes. As she began to speak, Jere looked over her shoulder and saw a man…Julia's escort. His heart plummeted. He had never considered she would have a date. How could he have been so naïve? Of course, Julia would have suitors. He was foolish to have thought such a beautiful, intelligent woman would hide herself away and pine for someone like him to rescue her from her cold, sterile laboratory. As Julia moved on to greet Ingrid, her companion stepped forward, smiled, and extended his hand amiably. Jere was so crestfallen that he didn't even catch his name. He found himself mumbling something that sounded like 'glad to meet you' as he felt heat rush to his face.

Julia's presence did nothing to prepare him for the next arrivals. The racing sounds of car engines caused Jere to peer outside as a caravan of three or four vehicles in close procession trudged up the road to Oldfields Point.

"Oh, my," gasped Martha. "Isodora and her entourage have arrived." She instinctively patted her hair and straightened her dress…neither of which actually needed attention.

As if foretelling some catastrophic event there was a distant rumble of an approaching storm and lightening pulsated on the horizon. Car doors slammed consecutively in precision, and footsteps crunched their way along the walkway, up the steps, and across the porch. Then Isodora's pale shriveled face appeared at the door. Heavy eyeliner and thick shadow made her wide eyes appear even more sunken. Her chicken neck supported a face that was powdered so heavily as to look surreal, and her cheekbones looked like small pumpkins. Her lips were painted bright red, and long, heavy earrings threatened to rip the lobes from her ears. She wore the most garish garb. It was a long fluid caftan of a green, red, and purple floral design on black background. A purple silk shawl was wrapped tightly about her shoulders.

Isodora stepped inside, stopped in front of Martha, and scowled at her furiously. Satisfied that she had sufficiently intimidated Martha, she moved on to Jere. She tried her look of disdain on Jere but before she had the chance to snub him, Jere affected a country twang and said, "Howdy, Aunt Isodora. Glad ya' made it to our little soiree."

Isodora looked stunned. Speaking to neither Jere nor Ingrid she turned abruptly and stormed off toward the parlor to stake her territory.

Following closely behind Isodora was a tall boulder of a man who was already several sheets to the wind. His stance was a series of balances and counter balances. He thrust his bulbous head forward as if using his double chin to balance his protruding stomach, and he spread his feet far apart for the same purpose. He had a red veined nose and rummy eyes. He wore a three-piece suit, a gold watch chain, and a white shirt with gold engraved cuff links. He completely ignored Martha and stepped in front of Jere. He did not extend his hand instead he eyeballed Jere suspiciously, assumed a knowing contemptuous smile, and moved on. When he took his place before Ingrid a look of astonishment crossed his face. He recovered quickly and slowly looked her up and down lecherously. As he swaggered away he smiled and winked.

"That's Jefferson T. Wainwright, Isodora's ner-do-well son," whispered Martha. "Pass it on." Jere leaned toward Ingrid and *passed it on.*

Following closely behind Jefferson T. like a whipped pup was a tiny, mousey bit of a woman. Her taste in dress was quite different from Isodora. She wore a gray suit, much too tailored for the occasion, a straight short hair cut, comfortable shoes, and carried a large pocketbook.

Martha introduced her as Alice, Jefferson T's wife. The hand Alice extended to Jere was damp, cold, and limp. Her face was lined with fatigue. She squeaked some incoherent greeting and moved on to Ingrid. When she looked at Ingrid a look of sadness washed over her face. She mumbled a few words and slunk off behind her husband. She looked like the walking wounded. Ingrid felt sad for her and wondered how many times Alice had compared herself to other women that her womanizing husband winked at.

When the parade of guests dwindled, Martha turned to Jere and Ingrid and suggested, "I'll announce that the buffets are ready in just a bit. In the meantime why don't you two go in and mingle."

Jere and Ingrid grinned at each other. "Okay," said Jere. "We'll go mingle." Jere headed toward the parlor, and Ingrid went into the drawing room.

CHAPTER 15

Ingrid entered the drawing room and surveyed the scene. It appeared that the 'Grand Dames' had assembled here. The room was filled with gracious white-haired ladies wearing black lace and smelling of lavender. A dark skin young man walked toward her balancing a tray of crystal wine glasses.

"Champagne?" he offered.

Ingrid smiled and took a glass. She edged into the room and walked toward two ladies their heads together and speaking softly. Ingrid cautiously approached them and introduced herself. They seemed startled and acknowledged her greeting curtly. Ingrid stepped back, sipped her champagne, and continued to look about the room.

Her eyes fell on a tiny snip of a woman huddled into a large stuffed chair. The woman looked her straight in the eye, lifted a bony hand, and wiggled a gnarled finger at Ingrid. Ingrid smiled and crossed the room to join her. The lady patted the chair beside her and said, "Have a seat, my dear."

Ingrid sat. The lady leaned in close and said in a pleasant voice, "My name is Mrs. John Wesley White. Now, dear, tell me all about this *partnership* you have with Jeremiah Ford."

"Well, it's just that...we're partners. He and I are homicide detectives in the Richmond City Police Department, and we work together as partners. We're a team."

"Hmm. And for you, my dear, was your desire to *partner* with my relative derived for purposes of occupation or passion?" the lady said with a twinkle in her eye.

Ingrid smiled and laughed. "I can assure you Jere and I are only partners…and friends."

The old gentle lady lay back against the cushions. A wistful expression crossed her face. "Ah," she mused. "It wasn't that way in my day you know. To begin with a lady of my station should never have thought of an occupation other than wife, hostess, and mother. Why it was unheard of. It wasn't to be even considered."

Ingrid looked sympathetic. "But you thought of it didn't you? Thought of having an occupation other than homemaker?"

She smiled. "Yes," she said sadly. "Yes, I did."

Ingrid leaned back in her chair fascinated and said, "And what occupation would you have chosen?"

Mrs. White's dim eyes brightened and she answered unequivocally, "An architect. I should have been an architect. How exciting it would have been to draw something and then watch the drawing come to life! How exciting!"

The two women talked and laughed and Ingrid explained her work as detective. The woman was bright, quick, and interested. Ingrid felt an immediate bond with this woman of another generation who had struggled with the same aspirations as today's women but was unable to realize them.

Ingrid decided to dig for information about Isodora the Terrible as she had come to think of her. "Are you acquainted with Isodora Ford?" Ingrid asked simply.

Just as the question was out of her mouth, they were joined by yet another lady in black. The newcomer heard the question and jumped right in without invitation.

"Isodora Ford? Lordy honey, why I knew her when she was just plain Izzy Beck living in a fishing shack with her father down by the river," the interloper offered.

"Ingrid, dear, this is Mrs. Anthony Gray. She is a very close neighbor of your host, Charles Ford," Mrs. White said.

"Then you must know Isodora's son, Jefferson T. Ford," Ingrid said.

Mrs. Gray made a disgusted face. "To begin with his name is not Ford, he's Jefferson T. Wainwright. He's a miserable creature. Usually he's drunk as a lord, and he makes that poor wife of his miserable too. He's some kind of political feather weight who likes to throw names around. Most of them, I've never heard of, and I've lived here all my life." Then she leaned in close and whispered, "He's just a middle-aged sot waiting for his worthless mother to die." She nodded with conviction. "That's right. And he thinks he'll get some of this some day, too." She rolled her eyes about the room.

"She is referred to as *Aunt* Isodora," said Ingrid. "Just how is she related to Charles?"

Mrs. White answered, "Isodora married Charles' Uncle Dan Ford, now deceased. After Dan's death Isodora just assumed she'd earned the role of matriarch."

Mrs. Gray added, "Yes, poor Dan. He was a sweet man. Real tender-hearted. He died just three years after marrying Isodora. Probably died just to get away from her. She never loved Dan anyway she'd really set her cap for Charles' father, Richard. But he wouldn't have any part of the likes of her. Besides he'd already fallen like a ton of bricks for Julia's mother."

"I'm afraid that Isodora has not always been kind to our Charles," said Mrs. White sympathetically. "She seems to take his father's rejection out on him. And there's the German heritage factor, too."

"What do you mean the German heritage factor?" asked Ingrid.

"I'm sure you are aware of the Hessian occupation of Oldfields Point during the Revolutionary War," Mrs. White said.

"Yes," said Ingrid.

"Charles has spent a great deal of time documenting that event. Since Isodora Beck Ford is of German ancestry, she took his interest in the Hessian occupation of the Oldfields Point quite personally. She has grown increasingly critical of poor Charles," explained Mrs. White. "She has been especially vengeful since Charles fell ill. Her behavior has been quite taxing for him you know. We are all most concerned for his welfare."

"And," whispered Mrs. Gray, "she thinks she'll make that bastard son of hers heir to Charles's estate."

"Jefferson T. being the bastard son?" Ingrid asked.

"Mrs. Gray," Mrs. White said with distaste, "granted Jefferson T. is a person of courser sensitivities, however, we mustn't repeat sidewalk gossip to our guests. What must Ingrid think?"

"Oh, I am not easily shocked," said Ingrid. "I hear far greater lascivious remarks in my job."

"Really?" Mrs. Gray said expectantly and leaned in close. "Please tell us about it."

Mrs. White ignored her friend's curiosity and continued, "You see, my dear, Isodora was introduced to the family as a widow with one child, Jefferson T. Wainwright."

"I've never known of any Wainwrights around here, and I've lived here all my life," Mrs. Gray said.

Mr.s White ignored her friend and continued, "Dan raised Jefferson T. as his own child, but he never adopted him nor gave him the Ford name, much to Isodora's disappointment."

Mrs. Gray jumped in again, "That's why we think he's a bastard. Dan probably knew and didn't want to give a bastard his name."

"That's merely supposition, Mrs. Gray," Mrs. White said reproachfully.

"Then both Charles' father and uncle married widows with children," Ingrid said in summation. The ladies nodded.

Other ladies had noticed that two grand dames were involved in ear-bending conversation with Ingrid so gradually they moved closer to voice their corroboration or dissent of what was being reported.

"Oh, but we mustn't let her think that Julia is anything like Jefferson T.," a tiny voice said from the back of the crowd. Murmurs of affirmation drifted through the group.

"Oh, I've met Julia," said Ingrid. "She seems to have Charles's best interests at heart. But what can you tell me about Alice, Jefferson T's wife?" asked Ingrid.

"Oh, I'll tell. Let me tell," said another newcomer to the group. "We call her Alice in Wonderland. That's because she seems to be in some fantasy universe most of the time."

There were giggles followed by an admonishment from Mrs. White who said, "The poor woman must live a miserable life. I would suppose that from time to time she uses a prescription to make the abuse tolerable."

"Well, she's not the crème-puff you'd think," said a voice from yet another chatterbox. "I've seen her mistreat more than one person…a bag boy down at the grocery store for instance. Poor kid. She sounded just like Izzy on one of her tirades." There were murmurs and nods of agreement.

Mrs. White intervened. "Please, we must give the poor woman the benefit of the doubt. After all, a temper can sometimes serve as a safety valve."

Then their tête-à-tête was unexpectedly interrupted when a melodious chime announced that buffets were now set.

* * *

When Ingrid entered the dining room, she spotted Jere staring down at a silver platter lined with a bed of fresh parsley topped with a delicious array of appetizers.

"Just look at all this. Stuffed celery, stuffed mushrooms, stuffed shrimp, and stuffed crab. I've never seen so much stuff," Jere quipped. Ingrid grinned at her partner's attempt at humor.

"I've really been getting an earful from your elderly kinfolk," Ingrid said as she picked up a plate and took one of each kind of appetizers. "What a riveting family saga! I never knew my quiet unassuming partner had such hot blood pulsing through his veins."

Jere shot Ingrid a curious look. "What did you hear?"

"Later, partner, when the guests are gone and our hosts are asleep, I'll tell you about the seamy side of your family tree," Ingrid said as she turned and headed back toward the drawing room.

"Ingrid and her love of drama," muttered Jere.

"What dear?" Martha had walked up quietly behind him.

"Oh, hello Martha. I'm just muttering about Ingrid. She's certainly enjoying the party," Jere stammered.

"I'm so glad," Martha twittered. "And you Jere. Are you having a nice time?"

"Oh, nice doesn't even begin to describe it. Martha you shouldn't have gone to all this trouble," Jere said for about the hundredth time.

"Don't be foolish. As long as you and Ingrid are having fun, then that makes us happy." And she waved to someone across the room and scampered off.

Jere scouted the different buffets nodding and greeting guests as he piled his plate much too full. Then he turned and walked slowly back toward the parlor and resumed his post. As usual, the food was delicious, and Jere was tackling a mouthful of stuffed mushroom when a seductive voice behind him almost caused him to choke.

"Hello Jere," said Julia with a roguish smile. "You know if I didn't know better, I'd think you were trying to avoid me."

Jere coughed and swallowed hard. "Avoid? Oh no," Jere said. "I haven't been avoiding you, Julia. I just didn't want to butt in on you and your date."

Julia laughed, "My date? So that's what this is all about. Jere my *date* just happens to be my brother, Bernie. I appreciate your not wanting to intrude, but you could have simply introduced yourself and found out who he is."

Jere was mortified. "I'm sorry, Julia. I feel like I've wasted half the evening. I'm not so good at these social things…especially when I'm supposed to be the guest of honor. Forgive me?"

Julia gave Jere a warm smile and said, "There's nothing to forgive." Then she looked across the room and gestured to Bernie who was sitting on the couch beside Charles. Jere prided himself on being able to recognize the origins of different southern accents. And when Bernie moved through the reception line, Jere thought he recognized a North Carolina intonation. Bernie crossed the room and joined his sister.

"Bernie," said Julia. "This is Jeremiah Ford, guest of honor. Just call him Jere. Jere…Bernie."

The two men shook hands. Jere saw little resemblance between the siblings. Bernie had sandy hair, blue eyes, and a beach tan. He was no taller than Julia and of small build, but his handshake was firm and his smile genuine.

"I'm so glad to meet you Jere," Bernie said. "What a difference your visit has made to Charles. I haven't seen him so enthused in years. You may not realize it, but your visit is a God-send."

"Thank you," Jere said a little embarrassed. "Charles is quite the guy."

Bernie cast an anxious eye in the direction of the couch. "Better get back," he said. Then he added, "I'm running interference for Charles." He scowled in the direction of Isodora.

As Bernie hurried off, Jere said, "So you and Bernie are Charles' stepbrother and sister?"

"Yes," said Julia. "Our mother was a widow and Charles' father, Richard, a widower. Our mother and Richard were madly in love. It was like a storybook romance, and Richard made Bernie and me feel like we were his own. And Charles…he was the big brother every little girl and boy dream of having. Oldfields Point was thrown open to our explorations, and we spent many a rainy day rummaging through old trunks and clothes in the attic. Even back then Charles was engrossed in Ford family history. He told us exciting stories of the early days of his family on the Eastern Shore. It sounded so romantic, so adventurous. Charles never resented Bernie and me. He helped us with our studies, encouraged us, dried our tears, and protected us." Julia hesitated and looked toward the couch where her brother and Charles sat. They laughed as Bernie patted Charles' shoulder.

Julia continued, "You see, Bernie was thin and small as a child. Unfortunately he inherited my mother's petite stature. Consequently, he was teased and bullied unmercifully at school, but then Charles would intervene. Charles was a gentle giant. That's why it's so painful to see him like this. As a boy his mere intercession prevented playground fights. Bernie has never forgotten those times, and even though Bernie now lives in North Carolina the relationship between the two of them couldn't be tighter."

A troubled expression crossed Jere's face. "Julia, why is Isodora so opposed to Charles searching for Caroline and the family crest?"

"To begin with," said Julia, "Isodora has no understanding of Charles' work. Charles would like to find out what happened to Caroline simply because it's another aspect of the family history. He's dedicated his whole life's work to tying up such loose ends, so to speak."

"And the crest?" Jere said.

"Oh, the crest is another story. You see to Charles it is just another missing family artifact that can be used to identify Caroline. Isodora appears to think he's concealing it because it is a valuable heirloom. She'd give anything to get her hands on it," Julia explained.

"One of Charles' neighbors told me that Isodora actually snoops around Oldfields Point when Charles is away...sometimes even at night," Jere said.

"Sounds like Isodora," said Julia. "That woman knows no boundaries."

A young man in uniform appeared and took Jere's empty plate. Jere stood silently for a moment and observed the interactions of the guests much as he would if he were working security at a high-level event in Richmond. Isodora, her son, daughter-in-law, and several inebriated friends stood across the room glaring at Charles and Bernie. Isodora had a vinegary expression on her face, and Jere heard her say something like 'a reckless waste of time...' A smirk rippled across Jefferson T's face, and he lifted his glass and threw down the fine champagne without bothering to savor it. Then he staggered to the closed bar, stepped behind, cracked open a bottle of Jack Daniels, and poured himself two fingers. Alice Wainwright stood frozen and stared vacuously into space.

"Isodora is at it again. She won't be happy until she creates a ruckus. She thrives on controversy especially if it disturbs Charles," Julia said.

"Maybe I can..." Jere began and starting to walk in that direction.

Julia put out a hand to stop him. "She gets really mad if someone interferes."

Their voices grew louder and the tenor became angry, contemptuous. Jere had witnessed this kind of escalation before and knew that without intervention it was only a matter of time before there would be an ugly scene.

Jere whispered to Julia, "Do me a favor will you? Find Ingrid and tell her I need her right now."

Julia looked puzzled. "Please," said Jere and he moved toward Isodora and her cronies.

Julia was gone like a flash. She found Ingrid in the drawing room engaged in animated conversation with Mrs. White and her cohorts. Julia leaned close to Ingrid and whispered Jere's message. Ingrid stood, begged her leave, and rushed out of the drawing room leaving disappointed ladies to speculate on her abrupt departure.

Ingrid hurried to the drawing room and surveyed the room. She'd observed this scene many times and immediately recognized the gravity of the situation. Jere had edged into Isodora's clique and taken a menacing position close to Jefferson T. even allowing his arm to occasionally bump against him. Jefferson T. looked confused, daunted, and sweat popped out on his swollen brow. Isodora was oblivious to Jere's close proximity and continued her harangue. Ingrid moved slowly, deliberately into the room her eyes locked ominously on Isodora. Then Isodora spotted Ingrid and hushed mid sentence. Her mouth flew open. Ingrid continued her piercing stare and slow approach. Isodora stepped back and her mouth dropped open. She looked around for Jefferson T. and for the first time saw Jere. A glowering look spread across Jere's face, as he moved even closer to her son. Bernie and Charles appeared oblivious to the circumstances around them. They still sat on the couch laughing and deep in conversation.

Isodora slammed her glass on a nearby table, gathered her shawl tightly about her, tossed her head, and said, "Well, I can see that I'll not have an opportunity to converse with our host tonight so we might as well leave." She stomped toward Jefferson T., grasped his arm firmly, gave it a tug, and started toward the door. In the process, she almost ran Alice down. "Watch where you're going, you despicable weakling," Isodora said hatefully as she continued toward the door. Poor Alice would have been knocked down had it not been for Jere's quick thinking. He caught her arm, steadied her, and asked if she were all right, but Alice said nothing and trudged stiffly toward the door.

When Isodora and company exited en mass, Charles and Bernie realized that they must have missed something. "Is something wrong?" asked Charles with concern.

"Nothing wrong," Ingrid said cheerily. "Isodora just remembered she hadn't unplugged the coffee pot." Everyone laughed.

At first Charles looked confused. Then he too laughed and said to Bernie, "Bernie, Ingrid has the most delightful sense of humor. She keeps us laughing constantly."

Jere whispered to Julia, "That was some dramatic exit!"

"Oh, that's Aunt Isodora. She knows a good stage when she sees it. She's quite the Thespian."

The evening wore on and guests stayed late. Julia expressed concern for Charles several times, but one glance at his smiling face and animation soon led her to realize that her concerns were without merit.

The rain arrived just as the guests began to leave. Jere grabbed an umbrella from the hall stand and walked with Julia and Bernie to their car. Jere opened the door for Julia as Bernie scurried round to the driver's door. Jere looked down at Julia's pixy chin and impish eyes, and without thought bent down and kissed her wet cheek. At first Julia looked startled. Then she smiled.

"When will I see you again?" he whispered hoarsely.

"How about tomorrow?" she said breathlessly, and she slid into the car.

As they drove away, Julia lowered her window, stuck her arm out into the rain, and waved.

CHAPTER 16

When the last guest left, the house suddenly fell eerily silent. Charles, Ingrid and Jere wearily climbed the stairs. Jere's awkwardness at having been the center of attention completely vanished when Charles turned a smiling face toward them and said, "No words can express my happiness and appreciation to you for an unforgettable evening." Tears began to well up in his eyes.

Embarrassed, Jere said, "Thank you, Charles, for the opportunity to meet so many members of the family…and their friends." Then in order to elevate the mood of the conversation he added cheerfully, "Have a good night, Charles. Don't forget…tomorrow we begin our investigation."

Jere and Ingrid trudged to their rooms. It was raining steadily now and the sound of the raindrops on the porch roof had a soothing effect. Jere thought he would sleep soundly tonight. Just as he was preparing to undress, there was a rap on the porch door. He opened the door to find Ingrid standing there, cigarette in hand. She was in pajamas, but this time she wore a long fleece bathrobe over it.

"Why are you standing there in the rain?" he asked.

"Ah, come on out. I've pulled some chairs back against the wall and besides, the porch roof protects you. We can exchange stories," Ingrid said enticingly.

"Let me grab a sweater," said Jere.

When Jere came out on the porch, he found Ingrid sitting in a chair with her bathrobe pulled tightly about her. She was lighting her second cigarette. Jere was too tired to lecture her, so he sat down in the chair next to her.

Jere said with a twinkle in his eye, "I'll tell you mine if you'll tell me yours."

"Sounds like a pajama party," Ingrid laughed. "To begin with, you'll be interested to know that I had a hard time breaking the ice with some of your very honorable lady family members. They thought we were lovers." Jere looked shocked. Ingrid continued. "Don't worry, I set them straight."

Jere was relieved. "Thanks for that. I guess I hadn't seen that coming."

"Well, don't look so damned horrified. You could do worse than me you know," Ingrid teased. Then she continued, "I also learned that Aunt Isodora actually had the hots for Charles' father, but had to settle for Charles' Uncle Dan. Who, by the way lived only three years after the wedding."

Jere raised his eyebrows and said, "Three years? Go on."

"Into this brief union Aunt Isodora brought her son, Jefferson T. Rumor has it that Jefferson T. was illegitimate. He's a sot who hopes to someday live in Oldfields Point. It is said that Alice, his seemingly timid wife, can have quite a temper and has demonstrated it publicly on several occasions. Jere, this is a powder keg waiting to explode."

Jere looked concerned. "Anything else?" he asked.

"Isn't that enough?" said Ingrid. Then she added. "One school of thought concerning Isodora's hatred for Charles is that she is taking out his father's rejection on his son. Just a theory."

Jere exhaled loudly. "That's as good a theory as any."

"One other theory," said Ingrid, "it seems that Isodora has German ancestry so she takes it personally when Charles recounts the Hessian occupation of Oldfields Point," said Ingrid.

"You got as much as I did," said Jere.

"Tell," said Ingrid as she shivered and pulled her bathrobe tighter about her.

"To begin with, Julia's escort was her brother, Bernie," said Jere.

"Bet that was a relief for you," said Ingrid.

"Charles' father married Julia's mother and accepted Julia and Bernie as his own. Julia describes life at Oldfields Point like living at Disney World. The blended family bonded immediately. Julia described Charles as the big brother they'd always wanted. Apparently the feeling was mutual and Charles became their teacher, helper, protector."

"What's her take on why Isodora hates Charles?" Ingrid asked.

"She hinted at jealousy also," Jere replied.

They both sat silently processing the information they'd shared. Then Ingrid flipped her cigarette into the yard below.

"Don't," said Jere as he stood.

"What are you going to do...go out in the rain and pick it up?" Ingrid said. "It's biogradeable."

Jere shook his head disgustedly and walked to his room.

* * *

Next day the rain fell much harder and they commented on how fortunate it was that the weather had held until after the festivities. Breakfast conversation centered about the events of the night before. Martha and Charles were still elated over the success of the evening. The phone had not stopped ringing as family and friends called to express their congratulations on such a gala event. Workers worked diligently to put the furniture back in order and clean away the remnants of the happy occasion. No one mentioned Isodora's abrupt departure. They all enjoyed their second cup of coffee and planned their investigation.

Soon they were gathered in the study and seated around the large worktable. All eyes turned to Jere. "What we need is a big piece of poster board and some magic markers..."

Before he could finish Charles struggled up, hurried off, and returned with several markers and some poster board. "Will this do?" he asked waving several pieces of board. "I trace maps onto these."

"Perfect," said Jere. "First, Charles, we have to get to know the victim...in this case, Caroline."

Charles looked confused. "But Jere," he said, "I've already told you what I know about Caroline."

Ingrid said, "What Jere means is we need to know about Caroline's personality; what kind of friends she had; how did she act in a stressful or threatening situation...that type of thing."

"How did she dress," Jere picked it up, "what did she and Millcent do at Oldfields Point, etc. etc. etc. Get the picture?"

Charles nodded, "Oh, I see what you need. You want a personal profile."

Martha exclaimed, "Certainly, a profile!"

Jere smiled and repeated, "We need to know everything we can about the victim."

Charles appeared lost in thought. "There's so much to tell," he mused. "Why not ask me questions."

"Good idea," said Ingrid. "What can you tell us about Caroline's personality?"

"Oh Caroline was not sedate. She was full of life. There are many entries in journals and diaries that refer to her being gregarious and assertive. You see, that was not exactly how ladies of the gentry were expected to behave back then."

"It seems like that might have caused some family problems. How did she accept criticism?" asked Jere.

Martha and Charles exchanged knowing glances. Charles slipped forward in his chair and said, "Not very well according to a letter Caroline's mother wrote to Capt. John. She complained in great detail about Caroline's unruly behavior and strong will. You see, she felt that Caroline's only reason for spending so much time at Oldfields Point was because she had more freedom here. Freedom, I might add, was unacceptable for a young lady back then."

"Then would you say Caroline was defiant?" asked Ingrid.

"Most definitely," Charles said without hesitation. Then he added as if defending her, "But remember, in those days, social restrictions on beautiful young ladies was to a certain extent...well, harsh."

"Do you think that Caroline would stand up to anyone trying to force her to go or do something she didn't want to do?" Jere asked.

"Most certainly," said Charles. "Oh, from what I've read about Caroline, she was courageous to a fault."

"What about lady friends?" asked Ingrid.

"None but Millicent that I'm aware of," said Charles.

"What about suitors?" asked Jere.

"Now that's a different story. Caroline had many suitors. There's one of her journals over there," Charles said pointing to the book selves, "devoted entirely to her beaus."

"I'd like to see that journal," Jere said. Charles started to stand. "But not right now. Did her family approve of her choice of suitors?"

"There were a few that they liked, but for the most part, they didn't like her choices," Charles said sadly.

"Tell us," said Ingrid.

"In the eyes of her parents, Caroline always seemed to attract the most questionable men," said Charles. Then he leaned forward as if to share a secret and in a low voice said, "There was this Loyalist...yes Loyalist...who was quite smitten. Caroline showed him favor for a while and then she had the most horrible time rejecting him."

Martha added, "And Caroline's brothers drove him off several times. They threatened to tar and feather him. But he just snuck back."

Ingrid and Jere exchanged knowing glances. "Do you know of any other boyfriends her family didn't approve of?" asked Ingrid.

Martha and Charles appeared to be most uncomfortable. Finally Charles said, "There was one other that I am aware of..."

"Oh, he caused quite an uproar," Martha interjected.

"Yes, indeed," said Charles. "I mentioned him when you first arrived, and Aunt Isodora alluded to him. The carpenter who carved the balusters in the hall was quite taken with Caroline...and unfortunately she was with him."

"Why do you say unfortunately?" asked Jere.

"Because he was *most certainly* not of the gentry. He came to Oldfields Point as an indentured servant and earned his freedom by working for Captain John. Captain John rewarded him for the fine work he did on carving the baluster by giving him several years off his bond. Oh, he was a strange one."

"From what you've read about Caroline, would you say that it would be out of character for her to slip out to meet men?" Jere asked candidly.

"No," Charles replied bluntly.

Jere tapped his pen on the table, looked at Ingrid, and said, "What do you think? We got enough to get started?"

"We got a strong willed, assertive, beautiful, sought-after, young woman who spent most of her time here at Oldfield Point with her devoted sister so she could do what she damned well pleased," said Ingrid taking a deep breath. "Yes, I'd say we have a pretty good idea of who we're working with."

"Ah, Jere," Charles interrupted, "may I make a suggestion?"

"Sure, Charles, this is your ball game," said Jere.

Charles laughed, "*Your ball game*…you certainly know how to make one feel relaxed," he said and reached for a journal that lay on the table, a white slip of paper slipped between pages. "I thought since we are conducting this kind of investigation, it might be helpful if you have a thorough knowledge of the sisters' relationship. I don't want you to think that Caroline stayed at Oldfields Point just so she could have more freedom. There was a real bond between Caroline and Millicent. One that is often difficult for us to understand today. There's a short selection I think will help you understand their devotion to each other and Millicent's endless mourning at the loss of Caroline. It may also help you to understand why I feel Caroline would never abandon Millicent…and why I think Caroline is still here at Oldfields Point.

"I'd like to read it," said Ingrid. "You see, what I'm beginning to realize is that it's not just Millicent who couldn't get past Caroline's disappearance. Millicent's grief has been passed down to her descendants." She pointed a finger at Charles and saw Martha nod in agreement.

"Here, let me show you," Charles said eagerly and reached across the table.

He opened the journal to the designated place. "This journal belonged to the great granddaughter of John and Millicent Ford. She documented several family stories told to her by her father and grandfather." He opened the book to a certain place and tapped the page. "This particular entry gives a detailed account of Millicent and Caroline's childhood. It explains how their dependency upon each other fostered an incredible bond. It explains the importance of Caroline's role in the Ford family narrative and why Millicent looks sad and much older in that portrait." Charles nodded toward the portrait above the sword.

"Want to read it together?" asked Jere.

Ingrid nodded. They sat down at the library table, opened the journal to the selected entry, and began to read. It was a photo copy of the original journal and bound in a leather cover. The reading was dated November 18, 1868 and the author was identified as Martha Ford, great granddaughter of Captain John and Millicent Ford. The penmanship was beautiful and flowing. They began to read:

I am the great granddaughter of Captain John and Millicent Hyland Ford. This is an account of the undying devotion between two sisters, Millicent Hyland Ford and Caroline Hyland. I shall endeavor to explain how life in their home served to create a bond between Millicent and Caroline that survived beyond the grave.

Life in this past society was quite different from that of today. All phases of education for the six Hyland sons and two daughters were conducted at home by an elderly lady of genteel disposition know as Auntie Teenie. It is not known if Auntie Teenie was a true relative or if the forename was simply one of handiness. However, the education and school schedule for the Hyland children was left entirely to her discretion, and school days extended from seven in the morning until six at night yielding only half hour for breakfast and one hour for dinner. It was sometimes necessary, however, to dismiss school early in the winter days because of failing light. Millicent and Caroline often spent these long winter evenings in their room sharing their girlish hopes, dreams, and promises made to each other. One such promise was so sacred that they penned it and sealed it with a drop of blood from each young girl. That sacred promise was to never leave each other.

Aunt Teenie's school was well thought out and strictly managed. Letters were taught first by writing on a slate and then later with a pen. Reading and writing English, recitations, arithmetic, and French comprised their studies in their early years. Later Millicent and Caroline were trained in housewifery skills such as needlework, knitting and cooking. All of these skills Millicent and Caroline learned together while their brothers practiced more challenging arithmetic problems.

When the children reached adolescence, the boys were given tasks befitting young men, while Millicent and Caroline together were taught female accomplishments expected by a genteel society. Most common were dancing and music. However under Auntie Teenie's relentless tutorage the Hyland girls also spent hours of practice in deportment. They walked about with a book balanced upon their head. They practiced incessantly sinking into a chair graciously while being cautioned to keep their knees together and their hands in their laps. They were instructed to hold their heads up lest they acquire a double chin. They were cautioned to never use a sliding, shifty eye but look people straight in the eye when engaged in conversation. Since Millicent and Caroline were the only Hyland daughters, they heartened each other during this zealous training.

As the Hyland sisters became older, Auntie Teenie slowly relinquished her duties to their mother. Mother provided increased social encounters and introduced her daughters to household tasks. In addition to attending weddings, balls, and family gatherings, Millicent and Caroline assisted their mother during birthings, illnesses, and lying ins. And when Auntie Teenie lay on her death bed, Millicent and Caroline sat sadly beside her with their heads up, their knees together, and held her hands until her death rattle ceased.

When Millicent and Caroline came of marrying age, they were allowed to go together unaccompanied by adults on long visits to the homes of friends and relatives. Caroline was disarmingly beautiful, and she enjoyed the attention of many suitors. Millicent had a warm smile and a lilting laugh that shy young men found most alluring. It was on one such visit that Millicent met and fell in love with John Ford. Millicent married John at the age of sixteen. Caroline had not yet committed herself, and the two sisters remained inseparable with Caroline spending as much time at Oldfields Point as at her own home.

After the tragic matter that separated the two devoted sisters Millicent spoke despondently of times when she thought she heard the light-footed tap of Caroline's slippers in the hall and awaited her cheery greeting.

Jere and Ingrid leaned back. Ingrid exhaled loudly.

Jere looked up at Charles and said, "Charles this is an amazing account of the lives of young girls in the eighteenth century."

"I'd say this is the earliest form of home schooling," said Ingrid.

"Now don't you feel you know the sisters much better?" asked Charles. "Do you understand why I believe Caroline would never abandon Millicent?"

111

"*I* certainly do," said Ingrid.

"Me too," said Jere. Then he added, "With stories like this being passed from one generation to the next, it's understandable why the family hasn't affected closure in over two hundred years."

CHAPTER 17

Ingrid stood at the window looking out on the luscious green that reached to the river. Enormous raindrops peppered the river creating dimples that gave the appearance of someone throwing pebbles into the water. The wind increased steadily. Soon the rain in tandem with the intensifying wind caused Martha and Charles to scurry off to fasten shudders and check on the leaky basement.

Ingrid turned and said, "Can you imagine what it was like for those girls to live out here on a day like this? This kind of weather would make anyone feel isolated."

"Well, it would make me feel that way, but this was what they were used to," said Jere. "I doubt that they felt *isolated*. However, that way of life requires that you depend upon each other. And I'm not sure that dependency was all that bad. Families were closer back then because they looked to each other for companionship as well as survival. I don't think it was a bad way of life. It was just different…and in some ways better."

"You're right," said Ingrid. "We can't measure yesterday's way of life using today's yardstick. And Charles is right, too. The journal entry we read gave me a better perspective of Caroline and Millicent's relationship. Now I understand why Charles insists that Caroline didn't just abandon Millicent."

"Whoa…," said Jere. "What is this? Are you actually conceding that I'm right and Charles is too? No argument? No fight? Get the calendar. Circle today in red. Miracle of miracles!"

Ingrid laughed. "I'm not that argumentative. It's just my job that makes me skeptical…my job and my partner."

Jere laughed and walked away. He stopped and stood before the portrait of Caroline. She was enchanting. He understood how easy it would be to become obsessed with such a beauty. Her eyes were piercing, and her powdered shoulders and arms were smooth and white. The slight curve of her mouth made Jere feel that she was hiding some mischievous, closely guarded secret. He felt that at anytime she would reach down, gently take his hand, and whisper to him why she summoned him here.

"She getting to you too?" asked Ingrid interrupting his fantasy.

"I suppose," said Jere, "but I can't think of any safer way to be seduced than by someone over two hundred years old."

"I suppose, but don't become obsessed like Charles," Ingrid cautioned.

"I won't," said Jere. "You know what? I'd like to give this our best shot for Charles' sake. I don't mean to be duplicitous, but what if we work this *case* like he thinks detectives would. Then when we can't find out what happened to Caroline maybe he'll move on."

"And give Martha a chance," added Ingrid.

"That too I suppose," said Jere.

"Okay, I'm with you. Let's show them an investigation like they expect detectives to conduct," Ingrid said. Then she looked at Jere quizzically. "Say Jere, your sudden interest wouldn't have anything to do with spiting old Aunt Isodora would it?"

Jere grinned and said, "Well, maybe a little bit."

They heard excited voices in the hall and turned as Martha scampered into the library. She seemed befuddled and concerned.

"Charles asked me to explain the interruption. We have the most awful mess in the cellar. It's real bad. It's been giving us problems for quite some time, and last spring it started leaking. Now it seems like every time we have a big rain, the flooding is worse. Right now we have about three inches of water down there," Martha said in frustration.

Jere and Ingrid started toward the door. "Maybe there's something we can do to help," said Jere.

"Oh no," said Martha lifting her hands. "Charles is speaking with the plumber right now. He promises to come just as soon as the nor'easter passes. He knows our cellar quite well and sees nothing to be gained by coming before the rain stops."

Ingrid said, "Well, if you're sure there's nothing we can do…"

Ingrid stopped as Charles came into the library. "How inconvenient," he said. "Martha and I have waited so long for you to come and help us with our conundrum, and now this has interfered. I deeply apologize."

"No need," said Jere. "Any time you're ready."

They walked back to the library table, sat down, and folded their hands on the table. All eyes turned expectantly to Jere.

Jere cleared his throat and spoke with authority, "Charles, after reading the selection you showed us, I can see why it's hard for you to accept Caroline abandoning Millicent."

Charles listened anxiously.

Jere continued, "So, Ingrid and I were talking while you were out. We believe our best approach is to come up with a list of possible suspects who might have abducted or murdered Caroline."

"Suspects? Just like you would do in one of your cases?" Martha asked wide-eyed.

Jere smiled, "Just like in one of our cases."

"So our most obvious suspects would be the Hessians," Ingrid said. She picked up a green marker, grabbed a piece of poster board, and wrote Hessians in large letters at the top.

"But we've told you all we know about…" said Charles in disappointment.

"Hold on now, Chuck," Jere said with a wink. "You're getting ahead of yourself again."

Charles' look of disappointment quickly changed to one of amusement. "Chuck…," he repeated with a chuckle.

Ingrid said, "Now what other suspects can you think of?" asked Ingrid magic marker poised.

"Well, I don't know," said Martha.

"Think now people," said Jere playing it to the hilt. He looked straight at Charles. "Didn't I hear someone speak of Loyalists roaming the woods looking to hook up with the British?"

"Oh," exclaimed Charles. "Now I understand what you have in mind. We have only been focusing on Hessians soldiers. In doing so we might have overlooked other possible suspects."

"There you go, Charles. You always have to look at the big picture," Ingrid said adapting Jere's demeanor.

"Yes at that time there were quite a few loyalists about," Charles said nodding.

Ingrid picked up a red marker, grabbed a piece of poster board, and wrote Loyalists in large letters across the top.

"Oh this is exciting," said Martha. "Don't you think this is exciting, Ingrid?"

Jere cleared his throat again, put on his serious face, and said in a stern voice, "Now, I hate to be the one to suggest this," he said, "but there is one possibility we cannot overlook."

Charles and Martha's eyes were glued on him. "What, Jere?" asked Charles.

"We can't overlook the possibility that someone in this house may have been responsible...a slave, a tenant, an indentured servant, or...," Jere paused for effect and then continued in a sinister tone, "or a relative."

Charles and Martha gasped. The room fell silent.

"Oh, no," said Charles. "Jere I can't believe that anyone at Oldfields Point had anything to do..."

Ingrid interrupted, "You got to realize, Charles, when there's a murder we always look at the family first."

"And most murders are committed by family members or someone the victim knows well," added Jere.

"Oh dear, Charles," said Martha. "Why it never occurred to us..."

"Well, let's not get ahead of ourselves again," said Ingrid as she picked up another marker, grabbed a piece of poster board, and wrote in big letters Someone at Oldfields Point across the top.

"Okay," said Jere. "Any other possible suspects you can think of?"

Charles and Martha still looked shocked at the possibility that someone at Oldfields Point might be responsible for Caroline's disappearance.

"No?" asked Ingrid looking from Charles to Martha. Getting no response, she continued, "All right seems to me we've got a plan."

"And we've got our work cut out for us," added Jere.

"Well, I don't understand," said Martha. "What do we do next?"

"What we do next is look for evidence, and we'll look right here," Jere said gesturing toward the bookshelves. "We'll start with the Hessians since they seem to be our number one suspects. Charles, we got real good insight into Millicent and Caroline's relationship from the selection you showed us on their childhood."

"Yes," agreed Ingrid, "but it's also necessary to learn just as much about your suspects as possible."

"Right," said Jere, "so can we find information here on Hessians…not so much on Hessians in general, but specifically about their occupation of Oldfields Point?"

Charles rose from his chair, shuffled to the bookcases, and began pulling volumes from the shelf. "Oh yes, yes indeed. Considering their impact on Oldfields Point, the Ford family has amassed a wealth of information on Hessians over the years. I'll pull what I consider to be the most relevant for our purpose."

Charles returned to the table with armfuls of books, journals, copies of old newspaper clippings, pictures, and maps. He dropped them on the table and smiled at Ingrid and Jere.

Jere exhaled loudly, "This should do for starters. Now here's what we'll do. We'll examine a book, a journal, a map or whatever. Remember we're not studying for a quiz on Hessians. We're looking for information that will tell us what happened at Oldfields Point under the Hessian occupation, and more specifically what happened to Caroline."

"And when I'm doing this sort of thing," said Ingrid, "I just jot down anything I think is pertinent."

"Later, we'll pool our findings, evaluate the significance, and then put it on the chart there," Jere said and nodded toward the poster with Hessians written in green across the top. "Now we need paper and pencils."

This time it was Martha who was up like a shot and returned with paper and pencils

Grinning from ear to ear Charles announced with aplomb, "Let the research begin."

"No, no, Charles," Jere corrected, "Let the *investigation* begin."

Charles and Martha smiled broadly at each other, and everyone reached for something to read.

They worked late into the evening taking only a short break to enjoy a rice and crab meat casserole that Martha 'just happened' to have in the freezer. The nor'easter soon arrived full force at Oldfields Point. The wind rattled the windows threatening to crash the shutters and invade their safe haven. Sheets of rain streamed down the windows and obscured the green and river beyond causing Martha and Charles to repeatedly express concern about the leaking cellar. Branches fell and knocked persistently against the house like an ancestor seeking to join the investigation taking place in the ancient library.

Finally Ingrid closed a book, dropped her pencil, and shook her hand. "I've had it for tonight," she said.

"I think we all have," said Jere noticing the dark circles under Martha's eyes. "And you two have to deal with a leaking basement tomorrow."

"Only if it stops raining," said Charles. "Sometimes the rain lingers for a day or so after the nor'easter moves out. But you are right. It's time to call it a night."

Ingrid and Jere slowly dragged themselves up the steps behind Charles. When they were half way up the stairs Charles paused, turned, and said, "I think I shall sleep for the first time in weeks. Just knowing that Martha and I are not alone in this pursuit lifts a tremendous burden. Thank you. Thank you so much."

Jere could not help but feel guilty knowing that the chances of ever discovering what really happened to Caroline were slim to none. Ingrid must have sensed his feelings for she passed him a pitiful look.

When they reached the top of the stairs, they paused and looked at the portrait of Caroline as if paying homage to one for whom they'd worked all day.

"Good night, Caroline," Ingrid said sleepily. "And don't disturb me until morning." Then she turned and walked to her room.

Jere stood and stared at the portrait for awhile. He wasn't sure, but he thought Caroline's mouth turned up ever so slightly in a wistful, haunting smile.

CHAPTER 18

Jere slowly made his way to his room. He noticed that Ingrid's door was closed, and he felt disappointed. He wanted to talk. He wished that they could go out on the balcony again where Ingrid would smoke her foul-smelling cigarette, and he would tell her how much he'd grown to like his cousin. He wanted to discuss how to help Charles and his devoted companion, Martha, and he wanted to rage on about dreadful Aunt Isodora. Jere wanted Ingrid's input. He needed to talk to his partner and friend.

Jere opened the door to his room and clicked on a small lamp beside his bed. Its gentle glow did nothing to dispel the dark mood he'd felt since delving into the mysterious disappearance of the mesmerizing Caroline. He strained to see out the window but the view was obscured by a dark sheet of rain. Jere sighed, undressed, and slipped between the soft cool sheets. As he turned off the light he wondered if Ingrid were as deeply affected by the bizarre turn of events as he.

* * *

Sleep was elusive, and Jere listened to the rain tap-tap on his window like some menacing spirit trying to win its way into his cozy chamber. The ancient house creaked and groaned as the wind found its way through cracks and crannies to far off rooms and dark hallways. Then Jere was suddenly startled by the sound of horses' hoofs. He dashed to the window and was surprised that the rain no longer obstructed the view. To his astonishment a company of Hessians in green uniforms galloping atop fiery white steeds appeared from the direction of the river. They were unlike any portrayal of Hessians Jere had ever seen. They were in full regalia and their mitre hats set upon ghastly vacant-eyed skulls. In their boney hands they brandished large ornate swords that dripped with blood. They waved the weapons menacingly at Jere and emitted blood curdling screams. Then to Jere's amazement a magnificent black coach drawn by four restless black horses pulled up directly under his window. The coachman was dressed in a long black cloak. His face was white, and he had a large scar on his cheek like Jere had seen in pictures of German swordsmen. He leapt from the coach, opened the carriage door, and with a sweeping gesture bowed and groaned, 'Come. You're one of us'. Then as abruptly as the apparition appeared, it was gone.

* * *

Jere suddenly awakened, bolted upright, and flung his feet to the floor. In spite of the cold air, he was perspiring heavily and breathing hard. He reached for his travel clock…four forty five. He knew it was hopeless to try to go back to sleep. He seldom had nightmares, but when he did they affected him deeply. 'You're one of us' the eerie voice had moaned. Were his spirit ancestors impinging on his psyche?

Jere didn't turn on the lights for fear of awakening Ingrid. He padded quickly across the room, found his luggage, and began rummaging through it. He dragged out a pair of rumpled jeans, a knit sweater, and socks. He dressed without making a sound. Then he dropped to his hands and knees and felt around the floor until he found his shoes. He groped about on the dresser, sent several coins jangling to the floor, and finally found his pocket flashlight. Then with shoes in hand Jere crept silently out of his room.

Jere didn't turn on his flashlight until he reached the stairs. Before starting down, he couldn't resist directing the beam on the portrait at the top of the stairs. Caroline smiled down at him as if to chastise him for his early-morning intrusion. Then averting the disapproving stares of his ancestors, Jere cautiously, quietly followed his flashlight beam down the steps to the dark hall below.

Jere finally reached the hall and turned toward the closed library door. He was startled to see an ethereal glow emanating from the cracks around the door. Was he still asleep? Was this a continuation of his nightmare? Of course not! This time he was certain he was awake. Nonetheless there was a light from inside the library. He could think of no plausible explanation for anyone to be there at this hour. Warily he crept toward the light. Instinctively his hand felt for the firearm that wasn't there. He stood motionlessly, placed his ear to the door, and heard a muffled cough...a cough he recognized immediately as Ingrid's cigarette cough. Jere opened the door.

"What the hell are you doing up?" asked Jere. "You scared the begeezus out of me,"

"I might very well ask you the same, Butthead," said Ingrid. "You just scared five years off my life. You get a sick kick out of spooking people or something?"

Jere took one look at Ingrid's pale face and knew she'd really been frightened. "Sorry, Ingrid," Jere said. "Didn't mean to scare you. But really, what are you doing down here?"

"Same as you, I suppose," said Ingrid. "Every time I dozed off, I woke up with this feeling that I'd read or heard something yesterday that I needed to check out."

"What was it?" Jere asked anxiously.

"Damned if I know," said Ingrid. "It keeps eluding me. I'm just cognizant enough of it that it bugs me and keeps me awake. What are you doing up?"

Jere looked exasperated and sat down across the table from Ingrid. "I had an awful nightmare. It came complete with ghostly Hessians and skeleton ancestors beckoning me to join them because 'I am one of them'. You know, I don't have bad dreams often, but when I do they really tear me up. I knew I wouldn't be able to get back to sleep, so I just got up." Jere grinned. "Glad to find some living, breathing company down here."

"Well, we've pulled a lot of all-nighters together," Ingrid said stretching her arms above her head, "but none quite like this. I just wish I had a cigarette."

The door squeaked, a footstep approached, and a soft, sweet voice said, "Why don't you have one of mine, dear?"

Jere and Ingrid almost jumped out of their skin. They turned and exclaimed, "Martha!"

Martha stepped gingerly into the room and held out a package of unfiltered cigarettes to Ingrid. "Why don't you take one of mine, Ingrid?" Martha repeated. "Of course you must not smoke inside."

Ingrid was shocked not only by Martha's sudden appearance but also by the fact that she smoked. She looked out the window. Although the wind had died appreciably, the rain continued. "Well, I, I…" Ingrid began.

"Oh, I didn't get wet when I had my morning smoke," said Martha. "There is a little stoop off the kitchen. I managed to stay completely dry under the roof. Come. I'll show you." And she started for the door.

Ingrid whispered to Jere, "Can you believe this? Martha's a closet smoker." And she hurried after her.

Jere smiled knowing that after her cigarette Ingrid would be lots easier to get along with. While he waited for Ingrid and Martha, Jere wondered what the hell to do next. He looked at the three poster boards with the headings Hessians, Loyalists, and Someone at Oldfields Point. Then he began to read through the notes he'd made the night before on the Hessian occupation of Oldfields Point. He noticed that the others had plenty of notes on the Hessians too. So logically they should discuss what they'd already found. In the meantime, perhaps Ingrid could resurrect those particulars that she couldn't remember.

"Who knows what we'll uncover," Jere wondered aloud.

Jere heard three voices in the hall and realized that Charles was a predawn riser today, also. Then Ingrid entered the library, hurried over to Jere, and whispered, "That Martha is a stitch. She's got her own smoking lounge complete with ashtrays, mouth wash, and breath mints. Wonder if Old Charles knows?"

"I don't know, but I won't tell," Jere said conspiratorially.

Their conversation was interrupted when Charles lurched into the room, "Good morning. Good Morning," he said in cheerful, robust voice.

"He must have slept much better than the rest of us," thought Jere.

"Martha is convinced that you were slighted where meals were concerned yesterday," said Charles rubbing his hands together, "and she's determined to make it up to you. Breakfast will be ready shortly. How did you sleep?"

Jere and Ingrid looked at each other.

"Oh, I see. Too much late night stimulation," said Charles. "I know exactly how you feel. Many are the nights that Martha and I stay up into the wee hours cataloging materials. We become so involved that when we finally call it a night, sleep does not come easily."

Jere thought how sad that Charles and Martha found cataloging library materials so stimulating that it kept them awake.

Ingrid said, "I hope Martha's not going to a lot of trouble. I thought yesterday's meals were delicious." She stood up. "In fact," she added, "I think I'll see if I can help out." And she started toward the door.

"Well, I agree with Martha. I think we will work better after a good breakfast...and, of course, after you and Martha have your morning cigarette," Charles winked at Jere and grinned.

CHAPTER 19

After breakfast Charles and Martha excused themselves to check on the cellar and confer once again with the plumber. Ingrid took advantage of their absence to grab an after-breakfast smoke, and Jere pinched another cup of coffee and went back into the study.

Jere chose one of the chairs in front of the fireplace, wrapped his fingers around his coffee mug, and stared into the flames. The logs popped and sputtered, and embers floated upward on the draft created by the enormous chimney.

Jere looked over at the library table. Documents were strewn everywhere. Books and maps lay open to places they'd thought were significant. The computer was turned on, and the screen saver continuously displayed a Hessian sword swirling and hacking its way through cyberspace. From time to time it paused and assumed an offensive position that seemed to be challenging Jere.

"What the hell are we doing?" Jere said aloud.

"Talking to yourself?" It was Ingrid, all smiles. Jere recognized that she was rearing to go.

"I'm beginning to question what we're doing again," Jere said.

"What do you mean?" Ingrid asked, her smile turning to a look of concern.

"For one thing, I think the chances of uncovering anything new in the Caroline story are slim to none," said Jere.

"So? You told Charles as much," said Ingrid.

Jere stood in front of the fireplace. "I want you to realize that I really like Charles."

"Yes? Go on," prompted Ingrid.

"I respect him too much to patronize him. So I'm asking myself, am I'm really trying to help him?" said Jere.

"Patronize him?" Ingrid sounded shocked. "Why on earth would you do that?"

"I wouldn't consciously," said Jere. "But I might if I had an underlying motive."

"Well this is getting stranger and stranger. Get to the point. Last night you were gung-ho to dig into those documents and books and come up with some new information for good old Cousin Charles. What threw water on you fire?"

"I told you I'm beginning to question my motive?" said Jere.

"What motive?" Ingrid was becoming impatient.

"Am I doing this to help Charles, or am I doing this because of Isodora?" said Jere.

"Isodora? What's she got to do with this?" exclaimed Ingrid.

"Yes, Isodora," Jere repeated. "She made me so damned mad going off on Charles the other day, and then she turned on us."

Ingrid looked skeptical.

"Yes, that's what she did Ingrid," said Jere. "She turned on us too. She's got no right to talk to Charles like that, and she damned well has no right to mow us down. You know how I hate that kind of attitude."

Ingrid looked away and stared into the fire. After a few seconds she said, "So, what do you want to do? Tell Charles, 'Hey Chuck we're not up to helping you any longer because I don't want to patronize you…and by the way, Aunt Isodora is right'. Don't you see what would happen?"

"What?" Jere asked ashamedly.

"Isodora wins. The old bat gets what she wants. We slink off, leaving Charles and Martha to rattle around in this two hundred fifty year old house full of dark shadows and somber portraits," said Ingrid.

"Well, I do feel sorry for them, but is pity a good reason to practice all this subterfuge?" Jere said waving a hand toward the library table.

Ingrid moved to stand close beside Jere. "Listen, Jer, I'm not even sure that Charles expects us to uncover anything he didn't already know," she said in a low voice.

Jere heard footsteps in the distance and looked toward the door. "Then why enlist our help?" he asked.

"Where's your sensitivity, Jer?" Ingrid asked. "How many times have they said how *happy* they are that finally someone is interested enough to listen to them and their problem? How many times?"

"Well…" Jere began.

Ingrid interrupted, "And how many times have they told us how **happy** they are we came to visit? They're lonely, Jere. Lonely. They want someone to acknowledge them, acknowledge their ideas, and acknowledge their work."

"I suppose you're right," Jere conceded.

"I know I am," said Ingrid. "And you know what else? I don't think it would matter one whit if we didn't solve their mystery in the next two weeks. They'd just be happy that we were interested enough to work their *case.*"

The voices moved closer and the library door opened.

"Now that is all taken care of," said Charles. "The rain should abate today and completely move out tonight. So the plumbers will begin work tomorrow. So shall we resume?" And he tottered toward the library table and sat down.

Everyone else followed suite. Jere cleared his throat and said, "Let's take a few minutes and review the notes we took last night and then we can pool our resources. I'm sure we came up with a lot of the same information, and that's all right. We'll discard the excess when we pool."

They spent the next hour reviewing and organizing their notes. Charles made several printouts from information he'd saved on the computer. Ingrid scribbled notes on practically every item she'd collected. Jere took a chronological approach in arranging the material he'd collected, and Martha nervously marked through at least half of what she'd written down. One by one they sat back and patiently waited for everyone to finish.

Finally Jere said, "Okay, let's see what we came up with. Martha would you like to write this down on the poster board under Hessians?"

Martha nodded and picked up a magic marker. For the next few hours, they read through each stack of information, wrote the facts on the poster board, and threw out any duplicates.

When they completed this process, Ingrid said, "Okay Charles, take a look. You want to add anything?"

Charles stared hard at the board mulling over what they'd just done. "I don't know," he said, "there's so much to know about Hessians. That certainly doesn't cover it all."

"Hey, remember, Charles," said Jere, "we're not gathering material on Hessian soldiers in general. We're looking at only those Hessians who were here at Oldfields Point when Caroline went missing."

Charles still seemed unsure.

"Okay let's go over what we have out loud. Here we have British General William Howe taking 264 transports into the Chesapeake Bay and arriving at Turkey Point on August 25, 1777. Okay?" said Ingrid pointing to the first item on the board.

"Yes," Charles looked pensive and slowly nodded in agreement.

"Okay," said Ingrid, "now on that same day there were about 16,500 seasick, exhausted men who disembarked down on Oldsfields Point beach."

"Yes," Martha said contemptuously, "and that's where the Tories came in. With the British soldiers so sick and exhausted, they relied on the local Tories and deserters from the American dragoons to help care for them and re-equip them." She pointed out information she had uncovered.

"Re-equip them with livestock from Oldfields Point," Charles added.

"Now let's not get ahead of ourselves," cautioned Jere.

In an effort to get back on point Ingrid said, "We also learned that because the militia was disorganized and the main army was so far away, Howe could give his army time to rest and reorganize."

"So," said Jere, "that means that they 'rested' here at Oldfields Point."

"Oh, to think of what might have gone on here," said Martha. "That poor family. That poor, poor family."

"Okay, let's stay on track," Jere said again indicating the next item on the board. "Now here we see that Howe divided his army into two divisions. One to be led by Hessian Gen. Wilhelm Knyphausen and the other by Major Gen. Charles Cornwallis, and we learn that Oldfields Point Manor House was commandeered and occupied by the Hessians. Right so far?"

Everyone nodded in agreement.

"We don't know a lot about the details of the occupation," said Ingrid.

"Perhaps that's just as well," Charles said sadly.

"I have a question, Charles," said Jere. "Do you know exactly what day Caroline went missing?"

"Yes, that's real important," said Ingrid. "How did we miss that?"

"Oh, yes, I have it right here," said Charles rummaging through a stack of documents. "You see I have a list of John and Millicent's children and their birthdays somewhere. Millicent gave birth to her second child then. Ah, here it is. The child was born on August 28. Caroline left the night before, which would have been August 27. Caroline disappeared on August 27, 1777."

"Two days after the occupation began," said Jere.

"Okay, let's move ahead here," said Ingrid. "The army started moving out on September 3. That would be nine days later."

"Yes, nine days with those heathens!" said Martha vehemently.

Ingrid ignored the outburst. "Charles, that's when they wiped out the family stores, huh?"

"Yes," said Charles, "and then set fire to the house."

"Charles, give us that list of stolen property again," said Jere.

Charles quickly rattled off the entire list.

Jere considered. "Could there have been other things taken? I mean items that family would not have recorded."

"Oh, most certainly," said Charles, "they took items from the house if that's what you mean."

"But they wouldn't have taken the crest," added Martha. "Caroline took that."

"Unless they took Caroline, too," said Ingrid.

"Yes," said Jere. "Charles, did Hessians ever capture civilians?"

"Why yes, as a matter of fact, that is why Millicent had the male slaves and freed blacks hide in the woods. Blacks were often taken to serve as laborers and even as weapon carrying soldiers. So kidnapping did occur during the war. Do you think Caroline was kidnapped and forcibly taken from Oldfields Point?"

"That's one possibility," said Jere. "But let's move ahead here. Where did the army go after leaving Oldfields Point?"

Martha pointed to the poster, "Here we show that only eight days later they are engaged in battle with General George Washington's army at Brandywine Creek."

"Wait a minute," exclaimed Ingrid. "Wait just a minute…" Ingrid leapt from her seat, raced to the book selves, and began pulling manuscripts off the shelves. "It just came to me. I found something yesterday that was interesting but I thought irrelevant. Now I'm not so sure."

Ingrid found the document she'd been searching for and brought it back to the table. After flipping through a few pages she stopped and rapped a page with her finger. "It's an account of a young black boy being taken from Oldfields Point by the Hessians. He escaped a few weeks later and came home," exclaimed Ingrid. "Maybe he wasn't the only one kidnapped."

"Yes, I'm familiar with that incident," said Charles and he reached across the table to receive the article from Ingrid. He examined the document for a few minutes and continued. "Yes, yes, I do remember."

"Well tell us about it, Charles," said Jere. "We might be on to something."

"I doubt it, Jere," said Charles. "You see German units often recruited and sometimes captured blacks, slaves and free, as part of their *feldmusik.*"

"What?" Jere and Ingrid exclaimed.

Martha simply nodded her head. "Yes I recall that story, too."

Charles continued, "*Feldmusik.* You see Hessians considered it a status symbol to have a black drummer lead your unit. The custom goes all the way back to the Ottoman Empire. The tradition was catching on in America just about the time General Howe landed at Oldfields Point. Also as we have already discussed, black men also served as soldiers and laborers for the armies."

"Was this young boy the only black person seized at Oldfields Point?" asked Ingrid.

"Yes," said Charles. "Remember, Millicent sent the older black males into the woods and swamps. This boy was so young I suppose it was felt he would be safe."

"But he wasn't," Ingrid said simply.

"No, he wasn't. The boy was mesmerized by the decorative drums and the ornamental uniforms the Hessians showed him. And when they taught him how to use the drum, he was captivated. When the Hessians marched out of Oldfields Point on September 3, 1777, the child was leading the procession."

"According to the account, his poor mother was beside herself with grief. She threw herself on the ground screaming, crying, and begging them not to take her baby. I suppose the proud little boy was quite confused," said Martha.

"Tell us about his return," urged Jere.

"Of course the child's feeling of adventure soon passed, and he became terribly homesick. He was, however, not allowed to leave. He was with the Hessian troops all the way to Brandywine Creek. It was there in the confusion of battle, that he was able to slip away and return to Oldfields Point," Charles said.

"That's an exciting story," said Jere, "but having heard it I'm not sure it can help us."

"Wait," said Ingrid. "There's more to the story than that…right Charles?"

"I suppose," said Charles, "but I feel it's been discounted."

"Don't make assumptions, Chuck," said Jere. "Finish the story."

Charles smiled at being called Chuck again. "Well it seems that when the boy finally arrived back at Oldfields Point, he told of having seen American women being man-handled by Hessians as they traveled en route to Brandywine Creek. He also stated that one such woman bore a striking resemblance to our Caroline."

Jere was excited, "Was this checked out?"

"Oh most certainly," said Charles. "When the searchers found no clue to Caroline's disappearance at Oldfield's Point, the older men who lived on the estate tracked the path the British army took to Brandywine and questioned extensively those people living along the route...especially the women."

"No one saw her?" asked Ingrid.

"No one, and Caroline was well known," said Charles. "Therefore, it was concluded with certainty that it was not Caroline whom the boy saw. In fact the boy himself repeatedly spoke only in terms of a strong resemblance."

"I say we still don't discount the possibility that she was taken off the estate by Hessians," said Ingrid. "Write that down, Martha."

On another poster board, Martha wrote the heading Possible Suspects in bold, large letters. Ingrid and Jere smiled. Martha was really getting into the case. Charles on the other hand looked troubled.

"What's the problem, Charles?" asked Jere.

"I am concerned that we might stray off the correct path. You see, I strongly feel that Caroline never left Oldfield Point. Something awful happened to her, and it happened right here," Charles said with certainty.

"But we agreed to examine all the possibilities," said Jere.

"Of course," Charles said with resignation, "You're right. Examine all the possibilities."

Martha stood, lifted her shoulders up and down, and smiled. "Well, I'm stiff," she said, "and now I must examine the possibility of lunch."

"And I'll help you," said Ingrid thinking that this would provide her an opportunity for a cigarette break.

CHAPTER 20

Lunch followed the same routine as the day before. Martha made a huge tray of delicious sandwiches and a large pot of tea. Sandwich choices included crab salad, egg salad, and Maryland barbecue. They ate hungrily, sipped herbal tea, and watched the subsiding rain tap gently on the windowpanes. Shortly their attention returned to the 'case of missing Caroline'.

"Where do you think we should go from here?" asked Charles who was anxious to continue.

"How about moving right on to our next possible suspect," said Jere nodding at the poster board that had Loyalists written across the top.

"Logical progression," said Ingrid. "Let's use the same process…find what we can on the Loyalists in the area at that time then come together to discuss it."

Everyone agreed, and the next few hours were spent gathering information on Loyalists. Since they were now familiar with the location of materials in the library they worked more quickly.

"You know," said Charles, "one could spend years researching the Loyalists or Tories and not glean all the information. Their's is a heartrending story. They were torn between the crown and their neighbors who were fighting for independence. Their decision was not made lightly."

"Yes," said Jere, "but let me remind you again, we are looking at only those Tories who impinged on Oldfields Point, especially around the time that Gen. Howe landed his army."

"Say Charles," said Ingrid, "was there like a list of the names of Loyalists around here?"

"Most certainly. I have it right here," said Charles reaching for a printout showing a list of names.

"Good," said Jere. "Now I suggest we just include all these names as Suspects."

"All of them?" asked Charles.

"All who would have been physically able to kidnap Caroline," said Jere.

Charles studied the list, marked through several names, and handed the list to Martha. Martha copied the names onto the poster labeled Suspects.

When she finished adding the names to the poster, Martha rubbed her hands together and said gleefully, "The list of possible suspects is growing."

Ingrid and Jere just smiled.

Charles said, "I realized as I studied that list that so many of the men were wealthy merchants. Trade was severely interrupted during the war, and merchants in America and in England wanted the war to end quickly. They worried how a victory for either side would affect trade. When things really got difficult, some of those families just fled to England."

"Charles, you amaze me," said Ingrid. "You speak of these people who lived over two hundred years ago as if they were alive now."

Charles smiled, "When you have spent as much time with them as I, you gather a lot of coincidental information."

"Give us another example of coincidental information," said Ingrid biting into a crab salad sandwich.

"Well, I don't want to sidetrack, but not all the Tories were wealthy merchants. For example, any Loyalist who brought in a recruit would receive five guineas. Offering oneself as a volunteer was worth ten guineas. For this paltry sum, men of lesser means than the merchants often joined the Tories. The British were able to provide monetary compensation which the Americans didn't have."

"Charles, what about the Tory who was obsessed with Caroline? Was he a merchant, volunteer, recruit, or what?" asked Jere.

"Yes," said Ingrid, "and what was his name?"

"Oh, he was the son of a wealthy merchant," said Charles flipping through the pages of a journal. Soon he added, "And his name was Chapman, Thomas Chapman."

"What do you know about him?" asked Jere.

"Oh that was a most unfortunate affair," Martha whispered.

"Yes, it caused a great deal of upheaval in the family, as you can well imagine," said Charles. "It was treated as quite a scandal. Consequently there's not a lot of recorded information about it...you know like in journals, diaries, etc. Most of what I know is more or less unverifiable family lore. Are you still interested?"

"Of course," said Jere.

"From what I understand, Thomas Chapman met Caroline at a party here at Oldfields Point. Now this was before it was known which side families would take in the war. He declared undying love for Caroline and apparently for a short time his feelings were reciprocated."

"What do you mean for a short time?" asked Ingrid.

Charles leaned forward, looked uncomfortable, and said diffidently, "You see...Caroline never seemed to remain interested in a young man for very long, and Thomas Chapman was no different. Soon Caroline had another interest, and that left Chapman distraught."

"So that was the end of the affair?" asked Jere.

"Oh, no," said Martha. "That was half of it."

Charles continued, "Martha is correct. When the Chapmans and other families declared their loyalty to the Crown, fear and hatred spread like a stain seeping into the hearts and minds of Patriot families. It caused a schism between Caroline's family and the Chapmans. Thomas Chapman, however, would not be deterred. He continued to pursue Caroline in spite of her rejections and her father and brothers' more definitive actions of which I told you earlier. He even proposed marriage via a letter, which happens to be the only real proof of the situation that I have."

"Do you have the letter?" asked Ingrid.

"Oh, yes," said Charles, "but I must search it out."

"Fine," said Jere, "we might need it. So did Caroline's father and brothers finally run the scum bag off?"

Martha laughed at the word 'scum bag'. Charles continued, "No, actually that was unnecessary. You see, the entire Chapman family fled to England."

"You don't say," Jere said with heightened interest. "I don't suppose you know when do you?"

"Oh, yes," said Charles digging out a printout listing the names of American families that fled to England during the war. "Here it is. The Chapman family sailed for England September 5, 1777."

Jere looked at the poster headed Hessians. Then he exclaimed, "That's two days after the Hessians moved out of Oldfields Point!"

Ingrid said, "Martha added Mr. Thomas Chapman to the Suspects list."

Martha excitedly wrote the name on the list and said, "More and more suspects! Charles, this is developing into a real investigation."

"Now that we're on the topic of Loyalists," said Ingrid, "we can't overlook the Loyalists you told us about who cared for the British and provided them with food and supplies when they landed here at Oldfields Point."

Martha picked up her marker, smiled broadly, and happily wrote 'Loyalist Helpers'. She grinned at her joke and said, "There's some more suspects!"

Unexpectedly the wind and rain stopped, thrusting the room into a disturbing silence. The fire burned low, and the four investigators felt suddenly flattened. The last two days of intensive scrutiny of old documents, the family party, the crazy dreams, and visits from Isodora the 'dragon lady' had taken its toll. Charles rubbed his eyes wearily, and Martha studied him with concern.

Martha stood, stretched, and said, "I say we call it a day. Just look at all we have accomplished," she gestured to the poster boards that were rapidly being filled. "I suggest that we stop where we are and I shall prepare us a delicious Eastern Shore dinner."

"And I'll help you," said Ingrid laying her pencil on the table and standing.

"Me, too," said Jere.

"No, no, you must keep Charles company," Martha said. "And Charles it is time for your medication. Jere, would you come with me and bring Charles his pills? Now Charles, you relax and think of anything other than Caroline."

Charles watched adoringly as she left the room. Jere and Ingrid followed her.

Jere returned quickly with Charles' medication and a glass of water. As he handed it to him, Charles said, "She really does take care of me, you know."

"I can see that," said Jere. "She's quite a gal."

Charles smiled and took the glass. "Yes, quite a *gal.*"

* * *

Martha and Ingrid entered the big kitchen. Ingrid admired the modern conveniences located at one end of the room. It looked like a picture from a gourmet kitchen magazine. At the same time, she was in awe of the other part of the room where the ancient fireplace and oyster oven stood undisturbed for over two hundred years.

"Martha, did you design the modernized part of the kitchen yourself?" asked Ingrid.

"Oh, heavens, no," said Martha. "When Charles realized how much I enjoy cooking, he hired a designer and contractor. Of course, he made it perfectly clear that the other end of the room was to be left as is."

Ingrid crossed to the other end of the room and examined more closely the gigantic fireplace. She sat on one of the benches and looked admiringly at the masonry. "What a remarkable piece of masonry," she said. "It's not only beautiful, but stable."

"And functional," added Martha who was busy banging pots and pans in preparation for cooking dinner. "I could prepare a meal on it tonight if I had to. Things were built to last back then."

Ingrid nodded, stood, and walked back to join Martha. She watched as Martha took fresh vegetables from the refrigerator and placed them in a stainless steel tub. Then Martha walked to the pantry and returned carrying a full bushel basket of apples.

Ingrid rushed to help her. "Here let me help you with that."

Martha shrugged her off and said, "This is nothing. It's not really that heavy. A strong girl like you should know that." And she lifted the basket onto the counter.

Martha began to fill the steel tub with water. Her expression was composed, serene, and her lips revealed a faint smile. Ingrid wondered at this pleasant, happy woman who lived in such a secluded place.

Ingrid said, "Martha, don't you ever get lonely out here?"

Martha looked surprised and stopped what she was doing. "Why no, Ingrid," she said. "There's so much to do with the house and our research…and of course, there's Charles. No, I'm most certainly not lonely." She resumed placing the vegetables in the tub.

Ingrid smiled wickedly and whispered, "You're in love with Charles aren't you?"

Martha stopped what she was doing, turned, and with a shocked expression on her face, said, "Why Ingrid!"

"Aha!" said Ingrid. "I knew it."

"Oh!" Martha said exasperated. Then she smiled a naughty little smile and said, "Ingrid, you're awful."

"I think it's great," said Ingrid. "I know Jere would feel so relieved to know that Charles had you to love and care for him."

Martha looked as if she were going to cry. "Would he really?" asked Martha. "You think he would approve?"

"Approve?" repeated Ingrid. "Hey Martha, wake up. This is the 21st century. No gentry versus working class here. Not only would Jere approve, he'd be delighted. I know Jere well enough to know how he'd feel."

Martha said, "Oh, thank you, thank you for telling me that. You see the rest of the family…"

"The rest of the family meaning Aunt Isodora? Well, I suspect Aunt Isodora has her own agenda. Just try to ignore her," said Ingrid.

"Well, it sometimes hard to ignore Isodora," said Martha shaking her head and returning to the sink.

"How does Charles feel about you? Is he in love with you?" asked Ingrid.

Martha smiled with her eyes. "That's two questions you know. How does he feel about me? He cares for me very deeply. He's told me that. Is he in love with me? Well, I don't know. How do you define love? Right now I'll settle for 'cares for me very deeply'."

"You're some piece of work, Martha. I really do like you and old Cousin Charles," said Ingrid and she gave Martha a hug. Martha seemed embarrassed by Ingrid impulsive display of affection.

Ingrid looked around the vast kitchen with the dark corners and pantries off its sides. She felt uneasy when she thought of Martha slamming about in what amounted to a dungeon.

"Martha, don't you ever get spooked roaming around in this enormous house with so many closed rooms, dark hallways, and shadowy stairways?" asked Ingrid suppressing a shudder.

"Occasionally I do," admitted Martha. "Sometimes I even imagine I hear little noises."

"Really? What kind of noises?" asked Ingrid.

"Oh, just noises...like rustling about. It's probably just field mice. The house is in the middle of a forest you know, and it has all kinds of cracks and crevices for mice to slip through," said Martha. "On dark and windy nights, one's imagination plays strange tricks."

Ingrid did not consider Martha a fanciful person and found her comment about noises at night disturbing. "Has Charles ever heard these noises?"

"Oh, no," said Martha. "Charles sleeps upstairs, and I sleep downstairs. Usually the noises come from the kitchen area."

"Whooo!" said Ingrid faking a shudder and moving to the sink. "We'd better change the subject. I'm getting the creeps. Now give me my marching orders. I'm not an experienced cook like you, and I'll need lots of instructions."

Martha seemed relieved to change the subject and said, "Really? Don't you cook at home?"

"Not unless I have to," said Ingrid. "With Sean away at school and my other half on the west coast, it seems kinda pointless...at least as long as there's a pizza parlor down the road."

Martha clicked her tongue and shook her head. "My, my, then we must prepare an especially nutritious meal tonight. You may begin by scrubbing these vegetable for our salad." She placed the vegetables in the sink.

Ingrid looked at the pan of fresh vegetable, shrugged her shoulders, and began to scrub. "Rub a dub, dub," she chimed.

CHAPTER 21

After dinner, it was decided that they'd call it a night. Charles looked particularly tired, and his climb up the steps took much longer than usual. Martha stood at the bottom of the stairs and watched anxiously as Ingrid and Jere stepped guardedly behind him. When they reached the top of the stairs Charles turned, looked down at Martha, and smiled affectionately. Martha smiled back, turned, and disappeared down the long dark hall.

Charles said, "I'm sure you realize that I am quite tired this evening, but I must assure you that this is a positive thing. So many evenings I have retired in frustration. Now I am finally pursuing a puzzle that has mystified me for years, and although I am weary I feel a profound sense of satisfaction. Thank you both. Goodnight."

Jere and Ingrid watched sadly as Charles ambled towards his room. Ingrid whispered to Jere, "Couple of things to tell you."

They walked back down the hall and Jere motioned for Ingrid to come into his room.

"I had an interesting talk with Martha while she was giving me cooking lessons. I was right about her feelings for Charles. Love, love, love," Ingrid said with a grin.

Jere looked impatient. "Now that's got nothing to do with us, Ingrid. How did it even come up?"

"I asked her," Ingrid replied simply.

"Oh, geez," was all Jere could think of to say.

"But there's more," said Ingrid milking it for all it was worth.

"Go on," Jere said in a tired voice.

"Martha expressed concern that you may not approve," said Ingrid.

"What? Why on earth would she think that?" asked Jere.

"Aunt Isodora," Ingrid said simply.

"I see," said Jere. "I gathered as much from the way Isodora spoke to her. She probably thinks that Martha may compromise her control over Charles. The old biddy! Did you assure her that I'd approve…for whatever my approval is worth."

"Of course," said Ingrid. "She was so grateful that I thought she was going to cry."

"That's pathetic, Ingrid," said Jere.

"And there's something else," said Ingrid.

"Lay it on me," said Jere. "It seems like we're getting pulled deeper and deeper into this family drama."

"This may not be anything," said Ingrid, "but I thought you should know. Martha spoke of hearing noises downstairs…mostly in the kitchen."

"What kind of noises?" Jere was suddenly interested.

"She said it was mostly rustling noises which she attributed to field mice. But I don't think she really believes that," said Ingrid.

"Well Martha doesn't strike me as the kind of person who's easily rattled," said Jere. "I don't think she would mention it if she weren't concerned."

"That's what I thought," said Ingrid. "Anyway, this place is beginning to give me the creeps."

"I know what you mean," said Jere. "At least the rain has moved out. Maybe a little sunlight will put a better face on things tomorrow."

* * *

As usual Jere woke up before Ingrid. He walked quietly to the window and looked out upon the green. "What a difference a day makes!" he thought.

The sun shined brilliantly. A shaft of sunlight penetrated the old wavy glass in the window and created a kaleidoscope of color on the opposite wall. The trees were outlined against a startling blue sky, and pinpoints of light pierced their lacy leaves. A mist hung like smoke above the river and a fish leapt eagerly from the water in search of an early breakfast.

Suddenly the serene ambiance was interrupted by boisterous voices, clanking tools, and the deafening sound of an engine. Jere stepped onto the balcony and walked to the end of the porch. He peered around the house and there he watched as three scruffy men clad in grungy bib overalls crawled out of a battered truck. Charlie's Plumbing and Sewage Works was painted on its side. Jere watched the men disappear inside what he assumed was an entrance to the cellar. Shortly they returned and attached a long hose to a pump in the back of the truck. Soon water was very slowly being pumped out of the basement into a ravine that fed into the river.

Jere rushed inside and put on the same clothes he'd worn the night before. He hurried from his room, down the stairs, and into the kitchen. Martha turned as he entered, put her hands over her ears, and frowned.

"Sorry for the disturbance," she said. "I am glad, however, that the plumbers were true to their word and came first thing this morning."

"Looks like a lot of activity," said Jere looking toward a door that was the source of the commotion. "Mind if I take a peep?"

"Certainly not. Be my guest," said Martha.

Jere walked to the door and looked down steep wooden steps that descended into a dark cavernous void. He started down cautiously and as he rounded a bend in the stairs, a light appeared. He breathed a sigh of relief, and as he did his nostrils filled with the damp smell of stagnant water. He spotted the workmen standing on steps on the other side of the basement and waved a greeting. They waved back. Jere looked down at the muddy water. All kinds of debris floated aimlessly about...medicine bottles, wine bottles, old shoes, baskets, pottery, jars.

Jere climbed back up the steps and went outside. He found the outside steps, went down, and joined the workmen below.

"Morning. You've got quite a job here," said Jere.

The men nodded but said nothing. The man who appeared to be in charge was a tall, awkward, skinny man of about fifty. He wore a filthy baseball cap and one strap on his bib overalls hung loose revealing a gray sweatshirt with sweat ring under his arms. His ears were pasted to his head like a boxer's and his beard was at least two days old.

Jere said, "I was just looking at the debris floating around down here. I'd really like to take a look at that stuff when the water is pumped out."

The men exchanged curious glances. Then Mr. Tall and Lanky said, "Makes no never mind to me. Gonna be a while before all the water's out though. Might take best part of the day."

"Then there'll be mud," added a pudgy red-face young man who wore the same garb as his boss.

"Mud?" repeated Jere.

"That's right," said the boss. "This cellar is always wet, and when it floods like this you got several inches of boot sucking mud."

"I'll take my chances," said Jere recalling how he'd climbed into an abandoned well at Jamestowne to retrieve an English musket that had been buried in mud for almost four hundred years. "Try not to discard anything until I have a chance to examine it?"

Boss looked at Jere like he'd swallowed a frog. "Sure," he said. "We'll leave all that trash just where it is." The other two workers snickered.

Jere smiled, turned, and climbed toward the daylight at the top of the steps. There in the doorway stood Charles.

"Good morning, Jere," he said cheerily. "I'm sorry that you were disturbed so early. The workmen like to get an early morning start since this can be a lengthy job."

"So they told me," said Jere. "Say Charles have you seen all that debris that the water uncovered. Some of that stuff looks like really old artifacts. I just told those guys I'd like to take a look at it when they pump the water out."

"Of course," said Charles.

"Where did all that water come from anyway?" asked Jere.

"Let's walk over here," said Charles, "and I'll show you. It's easier to explain if you see what I'm referring to."

Charles led Jere up a slight incline. There situated under an enormous shade tree was a small lovely one room stone building. It, too, had been immaculately maintained.

"It's called a spring house," said Charles as he opened the wooden door and motioned for Jere to enter. As they stepped inside they were swept with a waft of cool air.

"I've heard of spring houses, but never had a chance to examine one...especially one in A-1 condition," said Jere. "It's really cool in here. Just think how good this would have felt back then on a hot summer day," said Jere.

"That's the point," said Charles. "A spring house was used in the days before refrigeration."

The little house had dirt floors, and a stream of water ran freely through the center of it. Jere put his hand in the water and discovered it was very cool. He touched the stone walls and found they too were cool. Shelves were built on the cool stone walls, and Jere noticed a rusty dipper laying on one of the shelves. He thought how refreshing a cool dip of water from the stream would taste. A large wooden trough lay several inches below the water and ran lengthwise in the stream. Slots were cut in the sides of the trough so water could run through it as well as over it.

"Explain this, Charles," said Jere pointing to the trough.

"Bottles, jars, and crocks containing food were placed in the water inside the trough to keep them cool. The trough kept the containers from floating away or turning over. They stored butter, eggs, and milk anything that would require refrigeration today. This was their refrigerator."

"How ingenious," said Jere. "These people were survivors."

"Yes, they were, Jere," Charles said proudly, "and just think, you are one of them."

Jere smiled. "Tell me about the shelves"

"Shelves were used to store vegetables or prepared foods such as custards or pies," said Charles. "But all this talk about food must surely be making you feel hungry. Shall we go in?"

As they started back to the house, Charles looked concerned. "What's up Chuck?" asked Jere knowing that calling Charles 'Chuck' would boost his spirits.

"Oh, it's the cellar," said Charles. "You see, ideally spring houses were built over an existing, natural spring. In the case of this spring house, there was no natural spring, so a stream was created by diverting water from a nearby creek. For many years that worked fine. However, about five years ago, somewhere between the creek and the spring house the watercourse produced another diversion and directed a flow to the cellar, thus the flooding. And what is so troublesome is that it keeps getting worse."

"Surely there are experts that can take care of this kind of problem," said Jere.

"Yes, there are," said Charles. "But it is a costly restoration which is why I've put it off this long. After this, however, I'll delay no longer."

"It won't disturb the spring house will it?" asked Jere.

"Not at all. They will be working outside. They'll just dig up the yard until they find the problem and fix it," Charles said.

Charles and Jere entered the dining room to find Martha and Ingrid already seated. Their plates were almost empty.

"We apologize for not waiting," said Martha. "We're so anxious to get back to the investigation that we started without you."

Ingrid grinned at Jere and said, "You never know what you'll find on the very next page."

CHAPTER 22

The slow steady drone of the pump served as background noise for the four investigators who were lost in their notes, books, and other documents. First they discussed the information they'd already recorded on the poster boards. Then they turned their attention to the poster with Someone at Oldfields Point written across the top. There was nothing written below the heading.

Jere reached across the table and tapped the poster with his pen. "This is the last place to go," he said. The others nodded.

"This is the category with which I have the greatest difficulty," said Charles, a pained look on his face. "I just can't believe anyone in the Ford family would deliberately have caused Caroline to disappear."

Jere tapped his pen on the table a few times then dropped it. "You know, we may have placed too much emphasis on family when we wrote that heading. There were other people in Oldfields Point at that time. For example uh, uh...the male tenants. Some were too old to fight...and they searched for Caroline when it was discovered she was missing."

"Possibly...," said Charles doubtfully.

"How about disgruntled slaves?" suggested Ingrid.

"None that I've read of," said Charles.

"The woman! How about the woman who was attending the birth? You know the one who carried the hunting knife. Anyone who'd carry that kind of weapon certainly would be capable of killing..." Ingrid stopped abruptly when she saw a doubtful expression cross Charles' face.

Martha saw it too and quickly said, "Oh no, not Anna. Everything we've ever read or heard of Anna indicates that she loved those sisters like they were her very own."

Charles agreed. "Captain John trusted Anna with Millicent's life, and I feel sure Anna felt the same devotion to Caroline."

"So nix on the family, nix on the disgruntled slaves, and nix on Anna. Do we just leave this board blank?" asked Jere.

"Wait," said Ingrid, "don't forget the carpenter."

"That's right," said Jere. "What about the carpenter?"

"Charles, when you mentioned him earlier, you said the carpenter was strange. What did you mean by strange?" asked Ingrid.

"I suppose I meant strange in the sense that he was mysterious. You see unlike most indentured servants he was obviously well educated and well trained in the protocol of a gentleman. Captain John even allowed him to teach some of the children to read and write. Caroline used to help him. In the evening she'd go to his cottage and by candlelight they would teach the children," Charles paused thoughtfully. "Caroline's family thought she stayed **too** late in the evening."

Martha picked up the story, "Caroline always seemed to reject her family's opinion of her suitors. She also seemed to have an attraction for the atypical...and by the way, the carpenter had a club foot."

"A club foot? What happened to the carpenter? What was his name?" asked Jere.

"James. James was his name, and I've never seen a last name, which is also strange. As for what happened to him, no one knows. He disappeared as mysteriously as Caroline...," said Charles.

"And about the same time," added Martha.

"And you didn't think that was suspicious?" asked Ingrid.

"At first," said Charles. "But then we read that the *friendship* between the two had ended some time before. If you will recall I told you that Caroline did not remain interested in one young man very long."

Martha leaned forward and whispered, "You see I think it was the chase that excited Caroline."

"You mean once she had him hooked, she lost interest?" asked Ingrid. Martha nodded distastefully.

Charles attempted to draw attention from Caroline's foibles. "It seems that with maturity her attention turned to more serious minded lads. She wrote with admiration of several brave young Patriots she'd met who took up arms to fight for the American independence."

"How romantic that must have seemed to her," said Martha.

Jere leaned forward in his chair. "Just listen to yourselves. We're not through here yet. Martha, write down James, the carpenter and...Charles do you have names for the 'brave young Patriots'?"

Charles said, "Of course, in a folder of letters Caroline wrote to Millicent when she was visiting a cousin on another estate." He stumbled across the room, pulled a leather folder from the shelf, and brought it back to the table. He carefully removed a crinkled faded paper with handwriting so light as to be hardly discernable. The page was carefully protected in a sheet cover.

"You know these young men were not in the house at the time of Caroline's disappearance," said Charles protectively.

"Not that we know of," interjected Ingrid.

Jere continued, "Didn't you say that Patriots **and** Loyalists scouted the woods at the time General Howe landed?"

"Yes," said Charles hesitantly.

"Well, how do you know one of these guys here wasn't one of the patriot scouts?" said Jere.

They went through Caroline's letters and found reference to four young Patriots she'd admired. Martha quickly copied the names onto the poster underneath James the carpenter.

Martha finished, placed the marker on the table, sat back as if to say 'what now?' All eyes turned expectantly to Jere. The silence was deafening. They had not even noticed that the noise from the pump had stopped.

"So where do we go from here?" asked Charles.

Jere cleared his throat. "Well, Charles, do you have any strong feelings about any of the suspects we've..."

Suddenly a deep anxious voice echoed in the hall. "Mr. Ford, Mr. Ford. You better come down here. Please hurry up, sir!"

Charles pushed himself up from the chair and stumbled toward the door. "Oh no! Now what? Please, Jere, would you come with me?"

Jere and Ingrid dashed out the library door, through the kitchen, and to the door that led into the cellar. They paused briefly to allow their eyes to adjust to the darkness before racing down the dimly lit stairs.

Jere called back to Charles, "Don't come down here, Charles. Too dangerous." Charles and Martha stood frozen at the top of the stairs and peered down into the blackness.

As the detectives rounded the bend of the stairwell, startled voices could be heard below. "Hell," said one shrill, high-pitched voice. "Just look at dis here…"

Ingrid and Jere stopped abruptly when they reached the bottom step. The workmen were standing in mud so deep as to cover the tops of their boots. They were bent over examining something protruding from the mud. The man with the shrill voice turned, looked at them, and said, "Ain't dis here a hand?"

Jere and Ingrid gasped and stared in disbelief. Then they were shaken from their incredulity when shrill voice repeated, "Well ain't it? Ain't it a hand?"

Jere and Ingrid gathered their wits. "Now listen carefully," Jere said calmly yet firmly, "Listen carefully. You need to come out of there. I want you to retrace your footsteps as best you can. Try not to step anywhere you've not stepped before." Jere coached the men as they slowly retreated, "Go slowly, look down, and come back the same way you went in. Slowly now…slowly." The men began to look frightened but they followed Jere's directions precisely.

Ingrid and Jere suddenly realized that two anxious voices were calling from the top of the steps as Martha and Charles repeatedly asked, 'what's going on', 'is someone hurt', 'shall we call 911'. Ingrid said, "I'd better tell them what's going on, Jere. If I don't they'll try to come down here." And she darted up the steps. Soon Jere heard gasps and exclamations. Then the door closed and he listened as footsteps crossed the kitchen and headed back toward the library.

When Ingrid returned she stooped on the bottom step and watched as Jere slowly made his way toward the object reaching out of the mud. On the stairs on the other side of the cellar, the workmen watched spellbound. When Jere reached the object, he began to carefully wipe the mud aside. Slowly, slowly it became apparent that indeed a hand was reaching up as if beseeching someone to unearth its.

"It's a hand, all right," Jere called.

"Tolt ya' so," shrill voice declared triumphantly.

Jere called over his shoulder, "Ingrid, call Julia. And fellows," he said to the workmen, "you need to clear out of the cellar, but don't run off anywhere."

CHAPTER 23

Julia, Ingrid, and Jere worked late into the evening. The digging skills that Ingrid and Jere used so many times in archeological digs made the job move faster and rendered the evidence more reliable. They were also joined by two forensic anthropologists who had been lecturing at the Salisbury University about the human skeletal system and how it changes with age. The anthropologists immediately raced to the scene when Julia contacted them about the find and asked for their help. One man was considerably older and appeared to be serving as mentor to his younger cohort.

The workmen had become real sidewalk supervisors and had not budged from the yard. Occasionally a head appeared around the bend in the stairwell, and then quickly returned to the yard to report the progress.

Martha did her usual excellent job of feeding the entire crowd. The gathering now included a television news crew that had picked up the rumor from a university source that an ancient skeleton had been found in the cellar of a two hundred and forty year old mansion in Cecil County. Charles was wringing his hands with excitement since Julia assured him that the remains were most certainly from an earlier period.

More and more bones were unearthed, and slowly their excavation revealed a large grave filled with a mass of twisted, jumbled bones.

Finally Julia declared, "I think I found the prize." She held a mud-caked, oval shaped object. After she rinsed away most of the mud, she held a skull close to the light so all could see. "And I think we got a woman."

"Certainly looks that way," said the younger forensic anthropologist.

"I'd agree judging from the shape of the upper margins of the orbits," the older anthropologist withdrew a pen that was clipped to his shirt pocket and pointed to the eye cavity. Then he continued, "Also, look at this smooth, high forehead and the muscle attachment marks. These are most definitely consistent with a female."

The workman who was on surveillance at the moment stumbled and almost fell back into the mud as he rushed up the steps to pass the news to the crowd in the yard.

They had no sooner completed their examination of the skull when the younger digger cried, "Hey, I think I've found another one here. Another skull! And this one…" The cellar became morbidly silent and the young digger rinsed mud from the newly found skull. Then the digger announced, " This time, I think we got ourselves a man."

Jere and Ingrid gawked at each other. "What in the world have we got?" Ingrid asked incredulously. "What went on here?"

Julia and Jere continued to work together closely. "Julia," said Jere breathlessly, "Do your think this could possibly be…"

"Possibly? Yes," said Julia. "But I think we'll be able to make that determination definitively. These teeth and bones could provide us with some reliable DNA…"

"We've got to tell Charles," said Jere.

Ingrid agreed that Charles should know right away. Jere nodded, and soon three muddy diggers trudged up the steps to the kitchen.

Charles was sitting in a rocking chair beside the fireplace. He had not left this post since the discovery of the hand. He was startled by the muddy figures that tromped into Martha's clean kitchen. Julia went to his chair and dropped down beside him. "Charles, the skull in the cellar is ancient. And besides that, it's the skull of a woman." She did not mention the man.

"And the crest medallion?" Charles asked hopefully.

Julia said, "No Charles. No crest."

Charles looked disappointed. "Then without the crest, how will we know with certainty if it is Caroline?"

"There are ways, Charles. Definitive ways," Julia assured him.

"As far as the crest goes," said Jere, "that could have been stolen by the assailant." Ingrid nodded in agreement.

Martha was just entering the kitchen after serving the backyard onlookers yet another round of refreshment. She dropped the empty tray to the floor and rushed toward Charles.

"Charles, what is it? Are you all right?" Martha asked concern etched in her voice.

"Martha, you do realize what this means don't you?" A look of confusion spread across Martha's face.

Charles looked at Martha, "The skeleton in the basement is probably that of dear Caroline." He began to weep.

Jere and Ingrid exchanged sympathetic glances. "We don't know that for sure, Charles," Julia said softly, "but surely you must have known that after over two hundred years, a skeleton would be the only remains we could hope to find."

Charles reached up and touched his stepsister's cheek. "I know, Julia," he said. "It's just that I have looked at her lovely portrait for so many years that it's hard to think of her in any other way. But if it is she, we shall at least have some closure. We'll have proof that Caroline did not abandon Millicent. Have I not said she was here?"

Jere said, "Charles, there's something else you should know. There's another skeleton down there."

Charles looked stunned. Then slowly he gained his composure, and his face took on a dark look. "Do you suppose you have discovered the remains of Caroline's assassin?" he said.

"Not very likely Chuck," said Ingrid. "Most likely he was a victim, too."

"I see," Charles said slowly trying to assimilate all that was being thrown at him so quickly. "Then we must continue our investigation. We mustn't leave any loose ends."

Ingrid, Jere, and Julia moved toward the cellar stairs. "Right now we have a more urgent investigation going on here," said Ingrid. "But don't worry, Chuck, we're in it for the long haul." And she gave him an exaggerated wink.

Charles smiled. "That Ingrid! Martha, she can bring levity to the most serious situation."

They worked through the night taking turns to grab short cat naps. When the first shaft of sunlight peeped through the cellar door, five exhausted muddy, excavators stood and stretched their smarting muscles. They looked down into the grave that had held the jumbled bones of two victims of so long ago.

Julia said, "Well we've done all we can do for the time being. I want to get someone down here for pictures. Then I'll move these remains to the lab for closer examination. You two are welcome to come along if you'd like."

"I'd sure like to see how this plays out," said Jere.

"Me too," said Ingrid. "But right now, all I want is a shower, food, and to catch a short one. By the way, did we eat last night?"

Julia laughed, "As a matter of fact, I don't think we did."

"Martha's fallen asleep on the job," Jere charged.

"Oh, no Martha has not fallen asleep on the job," a sing-song voice from the top of the stairs called out.

Julia, Jere, and Ingrid smiled, pulled themselves up wearily, and trudged to the bottom of the stairs.

The Salisbury University team left at daybreak and checked into a motel. They agreed to meet Julia at her lab after they cleaned up, ate breakfast, and caught a few hours of sleep. Only the television news people and a few curiosity seekers still remained in the yard. Martha served coffee and pastries to the small crowd. She did not, however, notice one figure that stood apart from the others in a stand of small slim trees on the other side of the spring house. The sunlight of dawn would soon pierce the heavy ground fog and the watcher would become visible. So gradually the figure slunk back into the dark shadows and soon appeared to be merely the silhouette of another tree trunk.

CHAPTER 24

After a field-hand sized breakfast, a hot shower, and sleep Ingrid and Jere announced that they were going to meet Julia at the Medical Examiner's lab. Charles and Martha said they would eagerly await information about any findings Julia had made.

As Ingrid and Jere drove down the driveway, they met an old, very large, four door, black Cadillac moving slowly, cautiously up the drive toward the house. The aged driver sat with her eyes glued fixedly on the road her tiny hands firmly gripping the enormous steering wheel that she peeked over. So intent was she on her task that Jere was forced to drive onto the side of the driveway, stop, and let her pass. As the car passed Ingrid studied the other silver-haired elderly ladies in the vehicle. Their mouths moved non stop and no one seemed to notice that they just ran another car off the road. Ingrid recognized the occupants of the car as ladies she'd met at the party although she couldn't remember their names...except for Mrs. White and Mrs. Gray.

"Looks like the neighbors are comin' to call," Ingrid mused.

"You can't have this much activity without finding out what's going on," said Jere as he pulled the SUV back onto the drive and started in the direction of the main road. Just as his vehicle was completely on the drive, they heard a racing engine, and suddenly a silver Lincoln bounced around the curve careening from one side of the drive to the other. Jere saw an enormous gleaming grill smile at them like a Cheshire cat and head straight for him. Jere swore and jerked the wheel hard to the left, drove his van off the road, bounced across several ruts, and came to rest against a small pine tree. For a moment they feared they'd turn over, but fortunately the tree yielded, bent to the ground, and stopped the van.

Ingrid immediately turned and strained for a looked at the crazy driver. This one she recognized too. She was not one of the gentle women with whom Ingrid had spent an enjoyable evening. This driver was one of the arrogant, drunken interlopers who attached herself to Isodora's entourage and crashed Charles' party. And as she drove away toward the house, she looked over her shoulder and smirked at Ingrid and Jere.

"What the hell...,"exclaimed Jere. "Who was that crazy woman?"

Ingrid collapsed against the seat. "She's one of Isodora's inebriated idiots," said Ingrid panting hard.

"You all right?" Jere asked with concern.

"Oh sure," said Ingrid. "But do you think that Martha and Charles will be?"

"Good question. We better go back," Jere said. "There's no telling what that kook might say or do. Judging from the way she's driving, she's probably already loaded."

It took Jere a while to get the van back on the drive and headed toward the house. He saw the news crew walking toward the back of the house.

"Bet they tried to interview the ladies," said Jere.

"Bet they didn't get anything out of them either," said Ingrid.

The crew looked back, saw Ingrid and Jere get out the van, and decided not to bother. Several times they'd struck out trying to interview them. Jere and Ingrid went inside and directly to the parlor. The visitors were seated, including the mad driver. Jere and Ingrid exchanged appropriate greetings with the ladies. All were friendly and reiterated what an enjoyable evening they'd had at Oldfields Point...except Isodora's friend who sat in stony silence. She sat somewhat apart from the other guests and her eyes were glassy and unfocused. Her head bobbled as her eyes darted about the room aimlessly always avoiding Jere and Ingrid.

"Just look at her," whispered Ingrid. "It's not even noon and she's drunk as a coot."

"Shh," cautioned Jere as he smiled, nodded, and acknowledged the gentle ladies who sat sedately smiling at Charles. They seemed at a loss as to how they should begin their conversation.

Finally Mrs.Gray cleared her throat and said to Charles, "My dear, what on earth is going on? When I saw the plumber's truck I thought nothing of it. But then a crowd gathered and a television truck appeared. I was most alarmed for you, Charles. So naturally I called Mrs. White."

"Naturally," smiled Charles. "Thank you ladies for being so concerned. It's comforting to know that one's neighbors are watching out for us isn't it, Martha?"

Martha smiled, "Most assuredly."

Charles continued, "You mustn't be alarmed. While the plumbers were working on our drainage problem they discovered, of all things, two skeletons."

Gasps of horror rippled through the room. Questions, exclamations, suppositions were tossed about as all the ladies began to talk at once…except Isodora's buddy.

Then Mrs. White leaned forward prepared to speak, and the room fell silent. And it was she who breached the subject of the identity of the skeletons in the cellar. "Charles dear, I do not mean to be presumptuous, but have the remains found in the cellar been identified yet?"

All eyes turned back to Charles. "Quite possibly, Mrs. White," Charles said. "It appears that we might have found the remains of Caroline, sister of Millicent Ford."

"Oh!" swooned Mrs. White and she fell back against her chair for support.

Then an eerie silence fell over the room as if in reverence to the woman found in the cellar. For generations Caroline's mysterious disappearance had kindled the imagination of many on the Eastern Shore. Storytellers would sit before a cozy ebbing fire surrounded by wide-eyed children clad in night clothes and tell the saga of how the beautiful Caroline vanished one misty night over two hundred years ago. Then the children would refuse to go to bed until they each took a turn guessing what happened to Caroline.

It was Mrs. Gray who spoke dubiously. "Charles, are you certain you've found Caroline? How can you be sure?"

"That's right," said another gentle lady. "She's been dead for over two hundred years."

Charles smiled and continued, "Julia feels confident that scientific tests will make the identification conclusive."

Gasps went up and suddenly the room was alive with murmurs and speculation. Then there was excitement and words of congratulations to Charles for they all knew how long he'd worked to unravel the mystery of Caroline's disappearance.

Then from the back of the room still sitting slightly apart from the other ladies, Isodora's crony spoke in a loud and slurred voice. "Is that all you found?"

"What?" Charles asked appearing to be somewhat confused.

"Is a bunch of bones all you found?" the voice repeated.

"Yes, madam," said Charles, "that and the remains of a young woman who has left a mark on this family for years. Yes, that's **all** we found."

"Huh," she scoffed, stood up, and staggered out.

* * *

The sign on the door read Medical Examiner, Cecil County.

Jere immediately recognized that the best security system was being used to safeguard the lab. They knocked on the door and Julia shouted, "Just a minute." Soon they heard a click, and the door opened. The detectives knew that security was imperative since every safeguard must be taken to prevent contamination or any other compromise of potential evidence. There were two long metal tables under lights in the middle of the room. Green sheets covered the remains. Jere was impressed that even though the corpses were only skeletons, Julia showed them the utmost respect. There was a closed white cabinet with a red cross on it indicating that the contents were for Staff Emergency Use. On a section of the wall instruments of different sizes and types hung from wall hooks, and shelves were lined with jars and bottles that held liquids and small body parts. Two sinks…one labeled for Specimen Use, the other Staff Use…stood on opposite sides of the room.. There was another long table at the end of the room. It was tagged Evidence Table. On display were objects they'd brought from the cellar.

"Welcome to my kingdom…the kingdom of the dead." Julia said affecting a menacing face.

Although Jere and Ingrid had seen many Medical Examiners' Labs, they were really impressed with Julia's layout and told her so.

"So," said Jere. "Tell us what you got."

Julia walked to the metal table where the smaller skeleton lay. She reached down and slowly drew back the green sheet. The bones were white, delicate, and brittle. The skeleton was so small and fragile that it could easily have passed for that of a child. The bones had been discovered in disarray, but Julia had assembled them perfectly. A few small bones were missing especially noticeable was the absence of the right fourth metacarpal bone. Ingrid and Jere had seen skeletal remains many times before. However the bones lying before them now had a special significance. Jere felt an inexplicable reverence that caused him to swallow hard against the lump that rose in his throat. From the corner of her eye, Julia saw his pained expression and moved quickly to begin explaining her findings.

"We have here a very young woman although she is nevertheless fully mature. We also know our victim is female by the shape of her occipital lobe, high smooth forehead, and muscle attachment markings." Julia pointed to areas of the skull and began using a more practiced tone. She cleared her throat and continued, "There is no evidence of recent bone growth, and her collar bone is mature so she's at least nineteen or twenty. Her pelvic area is also mature. I would place her height at approximately five feet three inches."

Julia paused allowing time for Jere and Ingrid to ask questions. They simply stood without speaking and stared down at the bones on the table.

Julia continued, "Now this is the painful part. The evidence indicates multiple defensive wounds…and when I say multiple, I mean multiple. And you must remember that not all defensive wounds can be seen on a skeleton. Most of the wounds we see here were made by a heavy edged weapon, probably a sword. I'll talk about that a little more later on. The right upper arm or humerus had numerous nicks and cuts. And as you can see, the right metacarpal is missing altogether indicating that she might have held her right arm and hand upward in a defensive position." Julia raised her hand and arms affecting a defensive pose.

"In addition to the defensive wounds, there are other potentially deadly wounds," Julia continued pointing to the skull. "There are signs of brutal trauma to the head. There're several fractures to the skull, and there was a sword thrust through the right eye socket which most certainly entered the brain. The fractures on the right leg could have been the result of being stomped, and these two ribs are broken." Julia pointed to two right ribs.

Julia paused, and they stood silently trying to comprehend the brutality of such an attack. No one moved. No one spoke...only the click, click, click of the exhaust fan blades as it labored to rid the laboratory of the stench of death and dust and fleshy tissue.

After what seemed to be a respectable period of silence, Julia spoke softly, "She died a dreadful, violent death, Jere. This was most certainly over-kill possibly perpetuated by the fear of being discovered. I feel most certain that she was killed in the cellar since moving two bodies would have greatly increased the possibility of being observed."

Jere exhaled loudly, "What are the chances that this is really Caroline's body?"

Julia spoke cautiously, "Oh, given the knowledge of the circumstances surrounding Caroline's disappearance, I'd say we can take it to the bank. However, fortunately we have more accurate means of determining skeletal identification today."

"We're familiar with some of the techniques," said Ingrid, "but what can be done to this specific skeleton?" asked Ingrid.

Julia said, "Call it family curiosity, but the first thing I'd like to order is a computer generation of the skull done by a sculptor anthropologist friend of mine in Baltimore. By using the skull and a computer, she'll do a facial restoration of our victim. Then we can compare it to portraits of Caroline. Lord knows we have enough of those hanging in Oldfields Point."

"We're familiar with computer generated facial restoration. It's been used in Jamestowne. Talk about putting a face on a victim," said Jere, "that'll surely do it."

"How about DNA?" asked Ingrid.

"Most certainly," said Julia. "There are lots of Caroline's descendants around here, and they'll probably vie for the chance to be chosen as a DNA donor."

"You're fortunate there are so many descendants still here. Back in Jamestowne they found a skeleton believed to be the remains of Captain Bartholomew Gosnold, a founder of the Jamestowne colony. He'd worked with Captain John Smith in 1605 to set up the colony and died in 1607 of some kind of illness. Archeologists made effort to verify that the skeleton was Gosnold including DNA. They tried to find the grave of Gosnold's sister back in England for DNA purposes, but couldn't. So the skeleton remains unidentified, although Gosnold is still the leading candidate."

Julia reached down and pulled the green sheet over the skeleton. "Of course, after I place these orders, we must decide on the disposition of the remains. Unlike so many cases of very old remains, there are plenty of family members available who will want input. I for one would like Charles to make those kinds of decisions, but we'll see…"

Julia moved on to the other metal table. She pulled the green sheet down and began, "Now here we have an entirely different case. The remains are that of a male somewhere between twenty five and thirty. Here our victim was taken by surprise and died almost immediately. I believe this because there are no defensive wounds. Also, here on the right side of the skull is a bullet entrance wound. There is no exit wound, and a lead bullet and shot fragments were found in the skull. Death must have been instantaneous."

"That means that he had no chance to defend Caroline…uh, the woman," said Jere.

"That's right," Julia confirmed. "Also there's something else that is of particular significance." She pulled the sheet down below the feet of the skeleton. Ingrid and Jere were struck by the difference between the left and right feet. They were not symmetrical. The left foot looked smooth and natural, but the right side showed a shorter leg and a foot was twisted and showed boney growth. Julia pointed to the deformity.

Julia said, "And this victim had a club foot."

Ingrid and Jere ghasted. "The carpenter," Jere said.

"James," whispered Ingrid.

Julia covered the skeleton and motioned to the table in the back of the laboratory. "Let's take a look back here." And they moved to the evidence tables. "We aren't concerned with fingerprints and that kind of thing in this case, but the finds are important historical artifacts."

They looked at the items some still caked with dried mud. A young woman and a young man were busy cleaning the objects on the table. "Ben, Sara, meet Detectives Fairchild and Ford from Richmond, VA. The workers smiled up at the detectives and then returned immediately to their work.

"Ben is working on a metal buckle. Sarah is working on a small sword. I'm real anxious for Charles to take a look at these two artifacts. If anyone can tell us about them Charles can," Julia explained. Then she pointed to small items on another table. "This is the lead bullet and shot fragments found in our male victim's skull."

"Whew," Ingrid gasped. "Not bad for a morning's work, Julia."

"Thank you," said Julia smiling. "But this kind of case doesn't have the same kind of constraints as a murder that occurred yesterday. Jere, you look troubled. What is it?"

"I was just thinking about Charles," said Jere. "He's dedicated his adult life to finding Caroline. Is he going to feel relief or regret?"

Julia and Ingrid nodded perceptively.

CHAPTER 25

Ingrid and Jere drove back to Oldfields Point in silence. When they arrived they found Charles and Martha in the kitchen talking with the plumbers about the leaky basement.

"Mr. Ford, if'n we don't get this fixed right now, next rain you're gonna have a mess that'll make this one look like a picnic," the crew chief was saying.

"I understand," said Charles, "and I agree. How do you propose to proceed?"

"Well," said the chief scratching his head and looking thoughtful, "first off, we got to find that leak. My best guess is that it's coming off the stream they diverted to cool the spring house."

"I certainly bow to your opinion, but I don't understand why it has taken so long for it to begin to leak into our cellar," Charles said.

"That's easy," a younger member of the team said, "erosion. Trickling streams of water like that create slow changes in the earth. Called erosion."

Crew chief looked proudly at the young man and said, "This here's my boy, Henry. He's studying down there at the Salisbury University."

"I'm so pleased to meet you, Henry, and I respect your opinion," said Charles. Then turning to the chief he said, "I leave this in your capable hands. Do what you must just take care not to damage any old structures."

The work crew left through the back door, and it was then that Charles realized Ingrid and Jere were standing at the kitchen door.

"Jere, Ingrid!" Charles exclaimed. "We have been anxiously awaiting your return. Come in, let's go into the study and you can bring us up to date on your findings." And Charles ambled toward the door.

"Oh, by all means," Martha clucked, "and I shall light the kettle."

"Doesn't that woman do anything without serving tea? She serves tea, and then I have to pee," Ingrid muttered to Jere. Jere rolled his eyes in disgust.

Soon they were all settled with the customary cup of tea in hand. "Please, tell us," urged Charles.

Jere began, "Charles, we found additional evidence that indicates that the female might indeed be Caroline."

Charles set his cup on the table his hand trembling so badly tea sloshed into the saucer. "Jere, I need no additional evidence. I knew immediately that she was Caroline. I realize that Julia will try to confirm identification. That is her job, but I still knew. I knew it was Caroline," he said in a trembling voice. "Just think of all the years she's been down there just waiting for someone to find her…to rescue her. And then the water." He looked up at them with revulsion on his face. "She was covered with muddy, odorous water. That poor girl. That poor, beautiful girl! How despicable! How irreverent!"

Jere and Ingrid knew that Charles's anger was tantamount to grief. They'd seen it too many times before. So they listened to him rant without interruption, and soon the tears came, and then the stillness.

"I'm so sorry," Charles said softly. Martha sat by his side and gently held his hand. "Julia was right. Intellectually I knew we'd find only a skeleton at best, but emotionally I dreamed of, of…more."

Ingrid said, "That's all right, Charles. After all the years you've put into finding Caroline, you deserve to grieve any way you damned well please."

"And most of the time you were searching without the help or support of anyone else" Jere added. Then he looked at Martha. "Martha if it hadn't been for you, Charles couldn't have done it."

"Oh, I couldn't abandon my Charles," she said and gently patted his hand again.

Charles smiled at Martha and held her gaze for just a moment. Then he turned to Jere and Ingrid and said, "Now please, tell me everything you've learned."

Jere and Ingrid spent the next hour recounting Julia's findings to Charles and Martha. They saw nothing to be gained from hiding the brutally of the crime. After all they had spent years searching for Caroline. Surely that had earned them an honest account of what happened. They did, however, spare them the most gruesome details of the assault on Caroline. They also told them that the crime most certainly took place in the cellar since moving two bodies would have been observed. They reminded them that reports indicate that the Hessians discovered the wine in the cellar. It was therefore presumed that Caroline was snatched as she walked by the cellar door. Lastly they reported the most powerful clue to the identification of the two victims.

"Charles, as you know, the second victim was a male," said Jere leaning forward in his chair. "And the man had a club foot."

Martha's hands flew up to cover her mouth. Charles fell back against his cushions. "The carpenter," Martha said. "She was running away with the carpenter?"

Charles regained his composure. "Oh no, my dear. She need not have been running away with the carpenter. He might have been there to accompany her and protect her as she went to fetch her mother."

Ingrid spoke up, "I agree with Charles. I think James tried to defend Caroline and was killed in the process. Besides, if Caroline and James wanted to run away together, they'd had many chances to do that when the place wasn't swarming with Hessians."

"Or," said Jere, "that could have been a perfect time. In the confusion of the occupation, they may have hoped to slip away unnoticed."

"No," argued Ingrid, "would you…"

But Ingrid's argument was cut short when they heard the front door slam. Immediately, Jere thought of Isodora or a member of her clique. Apparently he wasn't the only one who had thought of this for all eyes turned anxiously in that direction. Then Julia rushed in clutching two brown paper bags.

She went immediately to Charles. "How are you feeling today, Charles?" she asked looking at him with her most analytic expression.

"Julia, dear," Charles said, "of course I'm over excited, but I am also relieved. We've found her haven't we?"

"Looks that way," Julia said as she pulled a chair in close and set the bags on the floor. "Now I could use a little help from you if you're up to it."

Charles eyes lit up. "Most certainly! I have felt so helpless just sitting here waiting for others to bring me news. I welcome any opportunity to contribute."

"Great," said Julia reaching for one of the paper bags. "Now Charles, these are items from the dig in your cellar. I think…in fact, I know that they are related to the murder of Caroline. I need your help in identifying the items. Still up to it?"

"Yes," Charles' response was little more than a whisper.

Julia reached in the bag and slowly removed a crude metal belt buckle. "What can you tell me about this?" she asked handing the item to Charles.

Charles received the object with trembling hands and began to examine it by turning it over and over. "This," he said definitively, "is a metal belt buckle definitely from the 1700 period. It is crudely hammered, probably homemade…perhaps even here at Oldfields Point."

"Charles, I don't like asking you to do this, but you're our local expert on eighteenth century artifacts," Julia said as she reached into the bag and slowly began to remove the second object. "I think this was one of the weapons used to kill Caroline, and I'd like to know as much about it as possible. Are you still sure you want to do this?"

Charles and Martha looked at each other in horror. "A weapon used to kill Caroline?" Martha asked in a whisper. Julia nodded.

Charles sat upright and said definitively, "Most certainly. I cannot expect you, Jere, and Ingrid to endure the entire burden of this investigation. May I see what is in the bag please?"

Slowly, slowly, Julia removed the object. Charles eyes opened in amazement and he reached for the artifact.

"*Der saebel*," Charles murmured. "…a saber." He held the saber in his trembling hands and examined it admiringly. It is not of the fine workmanship as the Hessian sword hanging above the mantle, rather it was standard equipment issued to the Hessian Soldier." Briefly he seemed lost in wonderment. He let his hands curve around the grip and pointed the weapon upright. His fingers caressed the cold metal blade, and he slid his finger gingerly along the cutting edge. Then as if suddenly remembering that this was the weapon used to cut the life from Caroline, he recoiled and handed it back to Julia.

"Yes," he repeated. "This is indeed a Hessian Sword."

Julia put the sword back in the bag. "Sorry to put you through that Charles."

"Where were the items found?" Charles asked.

"That's an interesting question," Ingrid said. "We found the sword and the buckle in the grave with Caroline."

"What?" Martha exclaimed.

"How strange," Charles said. "Why on earth would the assassin do that? It's a perfectly good weapon, you know."

Julia said, "Who knows why he did that. I've seen situations where the murderer threw the weapon into the victim's grave. Perhaps it's grief, regret of some kind, or simply wanting to rid himself of any reminder of his deed. It may be symbolic of disassociating himself from the crime. At any rate, it is not uncommon."

Charles pondered all he'd been told. Then he looked at the table strewn with volumes of research they had used in the search for Caroline. He nodded at the table. "All the work we did, Jere, Ingrid. It appears that it was unnecessary. Nature and the passage of time brought Caroline back to us. I'm sorry if we wasted your time"

Ingrid, Jere, and Julia protested loudly. Then Julia said, "Charles, the research you all did was certainly not for nothing. For instance, you revealed that the carpenter had a club foot making it possible to identify the second skeleton."

"And you were the only one who could identify the buckle and sword..." said Jere.

"And the sword in turn identifies the perpetrator," Ingrid added. "No Charles, don't you dare think your research was worthless."

"And there's something else," Jere said. "This investigation gave me a chance to get a real look at my ancestors. Not many people have that opportunity."

"Thank you," Charles said in his usual humble manner. "I do believe you." A smile spread across his tired face.

Finally Jere said, "Charles, Julia shared some plans with us that you may find exciting. Julia, tell him about the computer generation."

"Oh yes," said Julia, "Charles I have a friend who can take the skull of a deceased and using her computer skills, she can generate a picture of the victim. I called her this morning after Jere and Ingrid left the lab, and she agreed to do this for us with the skull we found in the cellar. In fact, she said she'd put a rush on it."

Charles looked amazed, "She can do that?"

"Yes," said Julia. "Then we can compare her work to Caroline's picture." And Julia nodded in the direction of the portrait.

"How wonderful!" Charles exclaimed. "Martha what do you think?"

"Oh yes, Charles this is simply mind-boggling," Martha replied. "What on earth will happen next?"

As if in answer to Martha's rhetorical question, a frantic voice bellowed up the hall. "Mr. Ford! Mr. Ford, better come quick, sir. We got another one!"

Jere, Ingrid, and Julia looked at each other. Had they missed a corpse in the cellar? Confused, they raced for the door…Charles and Martha close behind.

CHAPTER 26

Jere, Ingrid, and Julia raced down the hallway and into the kitchen. There they were shocked to see the beckoning crew chief, not at the entrance to the cellar, but at the door leading into the backyard. Impatiently he motioned them to follow him outside. Jere caught the screen door and smacked it open. Ignoring the steps he leapt directly into the yard and followed the chief who raced up the hill toward two other men waving frantically for him to hurry. Jere realized they were running toward the stone spring house at the back of the yard. He could hear Ingrid and Julia's heavy breath behind him.

As he approached the workers outside the spring house he heard one declare, "I ain't never coming back to this place to work again. Even if I ain't got food on the table, I won't come."

"Shut up, you fool," another worker warned, "don't never say never. That's just asking for trouble."

The crew chief had dropped to one knee panting loudly his hand supporting his head. He tried to speak but couldn't. He pointed wordlessly at the door to the spring house, looked at Jere, and shook his head.

Jere approached the open door and motioned the other two men to stay back. Behind him he heard Julia and Ingrid's footsteps on the crushed shell path. Jere pushed the door open slowly and stepped down into the spring house. Cool air floated upward and brushed his sweating brow. His eyes had not yet adjusted to the dim room, and he reeled slightly as the murky odor of earth and mold and wet stone assaulted his nostrils.

His vision cleared just in time to avoid stumbling on a bundle that lay on the damp earthen floor. Then reality set in. He realized the bundle was a person…an arm, a leg, a mass of brightly colored fabric…and a grotesque face. The face was waxen, set, and lacking any animation. It resembled the face of a pale, painted doll. It was heavily powdered, wore orange rouge, bright red lips, one long vulgar earring, and heavily shadowed eyes that were empty and dry.

Jere stooped down and looked at the woman on the floor. Then he stood and whispered, "Isodora."

Julia and Ingrid had entered the spring house just in time to hear Jere. They stood silently looking down at Isodora who stared back at them lifelessly.

"Jere, Ingrid, you'll have to get out of here, and call the sheriff," Julia said.

"Right," said Jere, and he and Ingrid backed out of the cool spring house into the warm, muggy air outside.

Inside, Julia reached into her pocket, pulled a pair of rubber gloves from her pocket, and snapped them on. Then she knelt beside Isodora's body. The only sound was the sweet trickle of water moving gently through the wooden trough as it had for so many years.

* * *

Jere and Ingrid reached Charles and Martha as they trudged up the hill. Jere told them briefly what they'd found. Then Jere held Charles' arm as they walked back to the house and to the parlor.

Jere notified the Cecil County sheriff, and then they sat silently for a long time grappling with this latest calamity. The sound of a vehicle engine broke the silence, and Ingrid dashed to the window.

"It's the fuzz," she said instinctively attempting to lighten the seriousness of the situation. No one laughed.

Charles spoke, "I don't understand what possible reason Isodora could have to be in the spring house?"

"And at night," Martha added. "She must have gone at night."

"And where is her car?" Charles added. "She most certainly could not have walked the distance."

Jere said, "These are the kinds of questions that Julia and the sheriff will attempt to answer. As soon as Julia finishes examining the body in her capacity as medical examiner, the sheriff will go in and look for evidence. Then we'll have a better idea of what happened."

"The *body,*"said Martha. "How impersonal...even though I had issues with Isodora, that sounds so impersonal."

Much later Jere looked out of the window and saw Julia emerge from the spring house. Then the sheriff and two other men went in to begin their investigation.

"Jere," Charles suggested, "why don't you assist the sheriff in his investigation? It would certainly move things along."

Jere said hesitatingly, "First of all, we don't have authority in Cecil County, Maryland," Jere said. Then he and Ingrid exchanged a knowing glance before he continued, "Also, the sheriff will probably want to question us, too."

"Question *you?*" asked Martha with some alarm.

Charles looked startled. "Surely he cannot think that you had anything to do with Isodora's death!"

Ingrid explained, "Knowing Isodora, I'm sure he'll have enough suspects without adding us to his list. But it's his job to question anyone who might have information about her death."

"And, after all," added Jere, "The workmen, Ingrid, Julia, and I saw the body. We'll all be questioned. That's just procedure."

"Oh," said Charles, but the expression on his face indicated that Jere's explanation had not completely allayed his concerns.

"Well, in that case," Martha said definitively, "I shall light the kettle."

Ingrid looked at Jere and rolled her eyes. Jere shot her a look of disapproval and walked to the window to view the activity outside. He watched as the sheriff exited the spring house and began talking to Julia. Julia pointed toward the house, and the two of them began to walk down the hill. A second man followed close behind.

"Here come Julia and the sheriff," Jere said.

He had no sooner made the announcement than they heard footsteps in the hall. Julia entered the parlor first. Her face was flushed and she immediately looked at Charles with concern.

"Are you all right, Charles?" asked Julia. Charles seemed unable to speak. He just nodded. Julia continued, "Sheriff, this is my stepbrother, Charles Ford. Charles, Sheriff Regan."

Charles nodded again and extended a slightly trembling hand. "Good to meet you, sir," the sheriff said as he shook Charles' hand. "Sorry about this. We'll try to take care of business and move on out as soon as possible." Charles nodded and smiled appreciatively.

Julia turned to Jere and Ingrid. "And, Sheriff," she continued with introductions, "this is Charles' distant cousin Jere Ford and his partner, Ingrid Fairchild." The sheriff raised an eyebrow when Julia used the term *partner*. Julia explained quickly, "Jere and Ingrid are homicide detectives on the Richmond, Virginia police force. They work together...partners."

The sheriff relaxed and smiled, "You don't say...so, big city cops eh? Well, how about that."

At that moment, Martha entered. She carried a clattering tray that held teapot, cups, and a plate of cookies. "Tea anyone?" she sang out. Ingrid shook her head and turned away. Jere shot her a warning glance. Without bothering to ask, Martha moved stealthily about shoving cups of tea in each one's hand.

The sheriff continued undeterred by Martha's activity. "I'll bet you never discovered three bodies in two days over in Richmond."

Ingrid said, "Not three bodies where two are over two hundred years old that's for sure."

"Yeah, Julia mentioned that you did a lot of digging. You just go around looking for...for...for what?" the sheriff asked.

"It's just a hobby," said Jere. "We volunteer to dig at archeological sites anywhere they need help. We've dug at dinosaur pits, old Indian village sites, over at Jamestowne, and Colonial Williamsburg. When we finish up a really horrific homicide case, like the one we just completed in Richmond, it's a relief to get outside and do something physical."

The sheriff nodded. "I can understand that," he said. "And you certainly never expected to find all this excitement over here did you?"

"That's for sure," said Ingrid.

"Julia tells me there's no doubt that those bones down in the cellar are over two hundred years old, and I know Julia knows her business. But just how in the world did you happen to find them?"

Taking turns they explained how the rain from the nor'easter flooded the cellar; how the workman were called to drain the cellar and find the leak; how instead the workmen found a hand protruding from the mud; and how excavation yielded not one but two skeletons.

Since the skeletons did not seem to represent a crime he could address, the sheriff had few questions and moved on to the discovery of Isodora's body. At first he questioned that the workmen again found the body, but he quickly accepted the explanation that they were to examine the spring house as a source for the diversion of water to the cellar.

"When was the last time you saw Isodora Ford?" the sheriff asked. They all began to answer at once. But it was quickly concluded that the evening of the party was the last time any of them had seem her…alive.

"Mr. Ford, was this a big gathering?" he asked.

"Oh, most certainly," Martha interceded. "This was a celebration in honor of Jere."

Charles continued, "We invited quite a few members of the family and neighbors in order that Jere might become acquainted with them."

"Did anything unusual happen that evening involving Isodora Ford?" he asked.

Again they all began to answer at once. Ultimately, they deferred to Jere and he explained Isodora's scene and how she left abruptly almost running down poor Alice.

"Hummm…," said the sheriff. "With a crowd such as you describe, there could be lots of people to question."

The man who had accompanied Julia and the sheriff into the room spoke for the first time, "And there's no shortage of people who'd like to see Isodora Ford dead." The sheriff glared at him.

"I suppose a lot of folks witnessed this scene," the sheriff said.

"Definitely," said Martha. "One could not help but notice such a spectacle."

The sheriff muttered to himself. "Now let me get this straight," said the sheriff. "This party took place on the same evening the nor'easter blew in. Right?" They all concurred.

"Actually the nor'easter blew in later that same night," Ingrid said more exactly.

The sheriff nodded and turned to Julia, "This gonna help you with time Julia?"

"Well, somewhat," she said. "There are a couple of other conditions I have to factor in."

"You gonna make this hard for me aren't you?" the sheriff said with a wry smile. Jere could tell they were accustomed to working closely together, and he was surprised to feel a brief pang of jealousy.

Julia smiled. "Not intentionally. Just so you know, Isodora wasn't killed in the spring house."

"Julia, how do you know?" Charles said a cautious look of relief on his face. "You're not just saying that to make me feel…"

"I wouldn't do that, Charles," she said moving to the couch to sit beside him. "I can tell by the appearance of the body, that it has been moved. In fact, Isodora had been dead for some time before she was moved."

"How do you know that?" he asked warily.

Julia paused for a few seconds collecting her thoughts as to the best way to explain to Charles. Finally she said, "It's called lividity. After death the cardiac pump stops and gravity causes the blood to pool in the lower parts of the body. This blood collection produces a bluish discoloration on the skin in that lower part of the body. This discoloration begins to appear about thirty minutes after cardiac arrest and will continue for a couple of hours. If the body is not moved for eight to twelve hours after death this discoloration or lividity will not change position. This lividity not only helps determine time of death, but also indicates if the body has been moved. So, Charles, Isodora died laying on her right side, so the blood collected on the right side. Some time passed and her body was moved, but the collected blood remained on that right side. Isodora was laying on her back in the spring house, but lividity appears on her right side. This tells me that Isodora died laying on her right side then was moved to the spring house and was laid on her back."

"So we know that Isodora was moved to the spring house from eight to twelve hours after she was murdered," Ingrid said.

"And that would have been just as the storm subsided or just after it ended," Jere said.

Charles wasn't sure he understood, but he nodded confidently trusting Julia's expertise. Julia turned to the sheriff and said, "The other factor I have to consider is the temperature. As I'm sure you noticed the spring house is very cool. Environmental temperature changes affect body temperature thus affecting a precise determination of time of death."

Jere looked thoughtful. "This may be why the body was moved to the spring house," he said.

"That and the fact that it wouldn't be found right away," said Ingrid.

"Right," said Jere. "Whoever did this didn't count on the workers having to go into the spring house."

"I am still baffled," said Charles. "How did Isodora get to the spring house?"

"When we answer that one," said the sheriff, "we'll know who the murderer is."

"Murderer?" whispered Martha. "How dreadful!"

"Well, folks," said the sheriff, "thanks for your cooperation. By the way, I need a list of the party guests."

"Oh, right away," said Martha scurrying away.

The sheriff turned to Ingrid and Jere, "Nice to have met you folks. Always enjoy meeting big city cops. By the way, you're not planning to leave anytime soon are you?"

Jere gave him a knowing grin. "No, sheriff. We'll be here as long as it takes."

"Good," the sheriff said and he turned to Charles. "Now sir, don't you worry about this one bit. We'll catch the b…" He stopped himself. "We'll catch the bum."

CHAPTER 27

Julia returned to her lab to begin Isodora's autopsy, and the sheriff went to notify her next of kin. Ingrid, Jere, Martha, and Charles sat silently in the study each lost in their own thoughts. They glanced at the work table covered with piles of books, maps, and their suspects' chart. For days they had concentrated their efforts on finding Caroline. Now abruptly she'd been found...mystery solved. Case closed. Jere had met other descendents of Capt John Ford. He'd been honored by Charles' neighbors and friends. Their purpose on the Eastern Shore appeared complete. Suddenly Jere felt at loose ends. He began to think of returning to Richmond. Then he remembered the sheriff's subtle admonition and realized that leaving now was out of the question.

It was Charles who broke the silence. "What will happen next?" he asked unaccustomed to investigative procedures.

Ingrid explained, "Julia will autopsy Isodora to find out exactly how and possibly when she died. The sheriff will deal with why she was killed and who did it."

"Just how will he go about *dealing* with why and who killed her?" asked Charles.

"Question, questions, questions," said Jere. "He's gonna have to question anyone and everyone he thinks can provide him with information."

Ingrid added, "That includes her family and friends and her enemies."

"Family and friends shouldn't take very long," Martha said, "but enemies…that's going to take quite some time."

"Will they question those who attended the party?" asked Charles.

"Most certainly," said Jere. "and me and Ingrid and you and Martha. Even Julia."

"Oh dear, Jere, this has become quite a predicament," said Charles.

"Yes, how thoughtless of Isodora to die at Oldfields Point," said Martha.

"Don't forget, Julia said she didn't die here," Ingrid reminded her.

Jere walked to the window and peered out. There was still one police car, several curious onlookers, and the television news crew who justified their on-site time by asking neighbor after neighbor how they felt about such a thing happening in their quiet community.

Jere turned away in disgust. "I can't take just sitting around here waiting for something to happen. Ingrid, why don't we go down to Julia's lab?"

"I don't think so Jere," she said. "You know we went into the spring house. We can't take a chance of being accused of contaminating evidence at the lab."

Jere slapped his fist into his hand. "You're right, of course," he said. "I'm just not used to being on the sidelines."

Ingrid sensed her partner's restlessness. "Well I know one thing I can do," she said. "I can put away some of these books and material that we used in our missing Caroline investigation."

Taking Ingrid's lead, Martha said, "And, Charles, we should document every detail of the discovery of Caroline's remains. We mustn't leave unanswered questions."

"You're right of course," said Charles. "The best time to document is when it is fresh in our minds."

Soon Charles began to dictate as Martha wrote down details of the flood, excavation, and discovery of Caroline's skeleton.

Hours passed. Finally Jere couldn't take it any longer. He said, "I think I'll just go outside and see what I can find out from the sheriff's men."

Jere climbed the hill toward the spring house. He passed the crowd of onlookers and news people with so much resolve that no one dared to question him. Jere thought that the officers had probably been warned not to answer any questions, so he planned to quiz them obliquely. He soon realized there was no reason to be so cautious, as their answers were quite forthcoming. Unfortunately, he concluded they didn't know as much as he. So he spent the afternoon listening to the officers relate perilous accounts of nor'easters and hurricanes that had pounded Eastern Shore Maryland.

Finally Jere heard the sound of a familiar car engine. He looked hopefully at the driveway and breathed a sigh of relief as Julia pulled into the parking area, cut her motor, and made a dash for the house with reporters in hot pursuit.

When Jere entered the study, he found Julia sitting next to Charles. She looked up and smiled as he entered the room. They exchanged greetings.

"Well, I've finished the autopsy," she said.

"Can you share it with us?" Charles asked nervously.

"Certainly," Julia said, "not that there's any real shockers."

Julia settled back, retrieved a small note pad from her purse, and flipped to a designated page. "Okay…as I already told you, Isodora was not killed in the spring house. She was killed somewhere else where the body lay on the right side for some time. Then she was moved to the spring house."

"Could you determine just how long she lay on that right side before being moved?" asked Ingrid.

"Probably around eight to twelve hours," Julia said shaking her head. "However, as I said earlier the temperature in the spring house makes determining time more difficult."

"What about cause?" asked Jere.

"Isodora died as a result of a broken neck," said Julia. Everyone looked shocked. "My Lord!" exclaimed Martha.

Julia continued, "There were bruises on the neck indicating that someone intended to choke her. But her bones were so brittle that they snapped like a chicken's."

"But how did she get into my spring house?" Charles asked fretfully.

"That I can't say, Charles," said Julia. "However, it wouldn't take a very strong person to move her. She was four feet eleven inches and only weighed ninety two pounds."

"Even so," Ingrid said, "she must have been brought in by vehicle."

"Tire prints!" squealed Martha. "I'll bet they'll be able to identify the murderer's tire prints." Martha had slipped back into the role of detective.

Jere shook his head regretfully, "I wouldn't count on it Martha," he said. "That parking area is full of tracks. Just think about the cellar workmen, then the crowd of rubber-neckers who showed up when the skeletons were found."

"Also, think about the nor'easter. Had the body been moved before the storm ended, there would be no tracks left," Julia added.

"Fingerprints?" Martha tried feebly.

"We'll see," Julia smiled not wanting to squelch Martha's enthusiasm. "The crime scene investigators will let us know about that. But inside the spring house...I doubt it. The door handle? Maybe."

"So what have we got here? Isodora creates a scene at Jere's party and leaves in a huff. Then sometime later...we're not sure when...someone tries to choke her and breaks her neck in the process. Then he, she, or they moved the body to the spring house where the temperature confuses time of death and where the body is not likely to be found for a long, long time," Ingrid summed up the case to that point.

"That's about all we have," said Julia.

"I think this calls for a cigarette!" And Ingrid walked toward the hall.

"And I think I'll join you," Martha said.

Jere noticed that Julia did not admonish Martha or Ingrid for their nasty little habit.

Charles sat silently, pensively for a while. Then he looked at Julia sadly and said, "What about arrangements Julia?"

Jere looked confused. "Arrangements?"

Julia explained, "Arrangements for Isodora's funeral." Then she turned back to Charles. "I don't know, Charles. I suppose Jefferson T. or Alice will let us know. Do you really feel up to going to a funeral, Charles?"

Charles sighed, "No, I don't Julia. I was just thinking that in spite of my ill feelings for Isodora, someone should be there. Do you think anyone will go?" He looked at Julia with such innocence.

Before Julia could answer Jere said doggedly, "Don't you worry, Charles, someone will go. I'll be there."

* * *

It was one of those ambivalent September mornings. There was a chill in the air and heavy drops of dew dripped from trees causing early colored leaves to fall and stick to Jere's windshield. A great orange ball of a sun rose and pierced the heavy mist promising at least one more short-sleeve day.

Jere and Ingrid had left Oldfields Point early to search for the cemetery where Isodora's graveside service would be held. They planned to arrive before the mourners and scout out a surveillance position. Their plans proved futile as they searched in vain driving from one cemetery to another. Somehow they'd thought Isodora would be buried in the well-maintained memorial park beside Dan Ford, but apparently that spot was already taken by Dan's first wife. So Isodora was to be laid to rest beside her father. They bumped onto a path filled with ruts and debris. They dodged old soda cans, wrappers from fast food cafes, and white garbage bags filled with unknown contents.

"Are you sure there's a graveyard back here?" asked Ingrid gripping the dashboard.

"No, I'm not. I'm just following the gas station attendant's directions," Jere said swerving to miss a broken beer bottle.

Jere began to think they were on the wrong path and started looking for some place to turn around. Then suddenly they emerged into a clearing. Old tombstones lay toppled on the ground and faded plastic flowers in broken vases lay pitiably at the head of the unkempt graves. Grass and weeds grew knee high and so much trash was strewn about that it resembled a garbage heap. In the very back of the cemetery a large tent was erected. Its enormous size laid emphasis on the small number of mourners gathered there. Six rows of folding metal chairs were set up, but only two rows had occupants.

"Charles was right," said Ingrid. "There's hardly anyone here."

"Looks like this is just a gathering of her party pals," said Jere recognizing faces of those who accompanied Isodora to Charles's celebration. "Far as I'm concerned, I can see all I need to see from here. What do you think?"

"Me too," said Ingrid.

Jere and Ingrid opened their door and stepped out of the car. They froze when an earsplitting unnatural wail suddenly pierced the thick damp air. At first Jere thought it was the cry of some pitiful animal in distress. Then it came again and they realized that the heart-wrenching wails came from Jefferson T…sobs and mourning cries that emanated from the very core of his being.

They started when they heard the crackle of footsteps on the dead grass behind them. They turned as a voice said, "He's been going on like that for fifteen minutes. They can't get on with the service 'cause of him." It was Sheriff Regan. He continued, "So guess you're here for the same reason as me."

"I suppose," said Jere. "We just wanted to see if Isodora had friends other than those who came with her to Oldfields Point. Looks like she didn't. That's the same bunch as attended the party."

They watched as a man in a wrinkled gray suit slipped a silver flask from his inside coat pocket and sipped from it. He made no attempt to hide the deed.

"Yeah, and they all been drinking and it ain't even eleven o'clock yet," said the sheriff.

Another wail pierced the air, but the preacher determinedly began to speak. He had apparently decided he could no longer wait for Jefferson T. to get control of himself.

Ingrid said, "Look at Alice. She's still holding that dead-pan expression…no emotion at all."

"Hummm," said the sheriff. "I noticed that. Can't really blame her though. Probably relieved not to have to deal with Isodora any more wouldn't you say?"

The service was brief and the mourners staggered to their feet. Two men moved in to assist Jefferson T., but when he almost collapsed it was the minister who rushed forward and actually prevented the fall.

The sheriff moved toward his car. "I'm gonna lead this group out of here real slow like. Don't want any one burning rubber and speeding out of here just to show off," he said. Then he paused and said, "You two gonna be around this afternoon?"

"Yes," Ingrid said.

"Good," he said. "Then if it's okay, I'd like to come over to ask a few questions."

"Sure," Jere said. "See you then."

Ingrid and Jere watched as the sheriff pulled in front of the cars and slowly, slowly led them out of the cemetery toward the highway. As the cars crept pass, they could see Jefferson T. and Alice sitting alone in the back seat of the big black limousine. Although not a sound could be heard they saw Jefferson T. thrashing about, hands gesticulating, and tears streaming down his face. Alice, on the other hand, looked straight ahead showing no emotion at all.

"Alice in Wonderland," Ingrid said shaking her head.

"What?" asked Jere.

"Oh, nothing," said Ingrid. "You'd have to have read the book.

CHAPTER 28

When the sheriff arrived at Oldfields Point he found Jere, Ingrid, Julia, Charles, and Martha waiting in the parlor. He nodded a greeting, took off his hat, and stared appreciatively about the room.

Charles welcomed him and pointed to a chair. "Would you like to have some privacy when you speak with Jere and Ingrid?" he asked.

"Not necessary," said Sheriff Regan. Then he turned to Jere. "Talked with the Homicide Department over in Richmond."

Jere smiled. "I felt sure you would."

"Yes, sir," said the sheriff. "They spoke very highly of you and Detective Fairchild."

"Glad to hear that," said Ingrid smiling.

"Yeah, they told me about this comp time you get when you finish out a real rough case. Yeah, sounds like a good deal to me," the sheriff said pensively. "We don't have anything like that over here...not that we have many real hard cases either. But still it'd be nice to have that perk just in case."

Ingrid and Jere nodded in agreement.

The sheriff continued, "They also confirmed this hobby of yours...digging around in geological and historic sites and all. Now I don't see as how that could be very relaxing, but then everybody's got their own notion. Certainly came in handy here didn't it."

The sheriff sensed that his audience was getting restless so he moved on to the business at hand. "So maybe you can tell me just how you came to be here at Oldfields Point at the very time a couple of two hundred fifty year old skeletons was found."

Jere wanted to say sarcastically…'just luck I suppose'…but thought better of it. Jere explained how working archeological digs stimulated his interest in genealogy, and researching his family line eventually led him to Charles.

"And just how'd you find Mr. Ford?" asked the sheriff.

"On the internet," said Jere.

The sheriff looked thoughtful. "On the internet? Humm. Well, I'll be darned. Just by accident?"

"No," said Jere, and he explained some of the on-line procedures which ultimately helped him find Charles.

The sheriff looked at Charles for confirmation. Charles said, "That is correct sheriff. I was so pleased to meet Jere that I invited him here for a visit. The rest is history."

"History? And, of course, you had no idea two skeletons would just happen to show up in your cellar while these two diggers are visiting you here?" the sheriff asked.

Martha cried out, "Of course not, sheriff. We have been searching for Caroline for years. Ask anyone who knows us. Had we known she was down there, we would have immediately buried her properly."

"Thank you, Ms.Stevens, for explaining that to me. Now maybe you can answer a couple more questions," the sheriff said.

"Most certainly," Martha said stiffly.

"Just what was your relationship with Isodora Ford like?" he asked.

Martha looked stunned. "Relationship? Why we had no relationship."

"Guess what I mean is did you get along with her?" the sheriff asked more bluntly.

Martha stiffened. "Sheriff, I can assure you that I have never done nor said anything to offend Isodora Ford. Her attitude toward me, however, was less that congenial. In fact she was actually hostile."

"And why's that do you think?" asked the sheriff.

Martha looked flustered. Her face turned red and she looked frantically from one person to another.

Julia spoke. "I can answer that sheriff," she said. "Isodora was jealous of Martha. Isodora wanted to control Charles, so she was jealous of anyone who had a closer relationship with him than she."

The sheriff raised an eyebrow, grinned, and said, "Including you, Julia?"

"Yes, *Sheriff Regan*, including me," Julia said tauntingly. Again Jere felt that twinge of jealousy.

The sheriff turned to Charles. This time his demeanor was more respectful. "Mr. Ford do you agree with Julia's explanation that Isodora was jealous of Ms. Stevens because Isodora wanted to control you?"

"Yes, I'm afraid that was her motive," said Charles.

"If you don't mind my asking, sir," said the sheriff, "why did she want this control?"

Charles looked perplexed. "I don't really know, Sheriff. She's such…"

Martha had regained her composure and blurted, "She wanted Oldfields Point and everything in it. That is what she's always wanted even when she married Dan, Charles' uncle. She thought that marriage would bring her one step closer to being *mistress of Oldfields Point.*" Martha said with great sarcasm.

The sheriff looked cagily and asked, "And where would that leave you, Ms. Stevens?"

Martha was again taken aback. Jere and Ingrid exchanged knowing glances. Charles began to shake, and Julia leapt from her chair.

"Now hold on there, Sheriff Regan," Julia sputtered. "Of all the people in Cecil County to have motives to kill Isodora, Martha Stevens is your least likely candidate. Why don't you talk to some of her low-life friends?"

"I'm just about to do that, Julia," the sheriff grinned. Then he turned to Martha again. This time he was more contrite. "I didn't mean to rile you, Ms. Stevens, but I have to ask these kinds of questions. If something came up later that indicated I should have asked hard questions and I hadn't…well, then we'd both be up the creek without a paddle."

"I understand, sheriff," Martha said compliantly.

"Now I have one more question," he said. "Remember you told me about Isodora's friend who paid a visit to Oldfields Point after the

186

discovery of the two skeletons." Martha nodded. "I don't suppose you know the name and address of that particular visitor do you?"

Martha stood and walked to the desk, "Of course. I'll write it down for you right now."

The sheriff stood and said, "In that case, I'll just move on and talk to some of Isodora's *friends* that Julia spoke of." And he gave her a wink.

Martha handed him a piece of paper on which was written the name, Carrie Goldsmith, and her address. The sheriff moved toward the door. Then he stopped and turned to Jere and Ingrid. "Since this isn't one of those rough cases, don't suppose you'd want to tag along would you?"

Ingrid and Jere stood up. "We thought you'd never ask," said Ingrid.

* * *

At one time the house had been beautiful. It was a large, two story brick Georgian place, but now the wood trim was in desperate need of a fresh coat of paint and there were several loose bricks. The house was situated above a trickling creek that flowed over rocks and stones. Giant old trees shaded the banks and a broken rope swing hung from one of its sturdy limbs. A path leading from the house to the creek was almost obscured by weeds. Flower beds lay untended except for an occasional persistent perennial struggling to survive the neglect. What little grass that existed was brown and sparse adding to the place's sad appearance.

The sheriff parked in front of the house. As he, Ingrid, and Jere stepped out of the car, a curtain in a downstairs window drop concealing the watcher. They walked up on the porch and rang the bell. They waited for quite some time listening to rustling noises inside. Just as the sheriff was reaching to ring again, the door sprang open.

They gawked at the woman who opened the door. Ingrid immediately recognized her as one of Isodora's party pals and one of the mourners at Isodora's service. She wore a brightly colored, wrinkled, and stained caftan with metallic gold house slippers. Golden chains hung around her neck and golden bracelets climbed almost to her elbows. Her makeup was brash and her smile revealed lipstick stains on her front teeth. She beamed at Jere and Sheriff Regan flirtatiously, but when her eyes fell on Ingrid she glared contemptuously.

She quickly recovered her composure and said, "Why sheriff, how nice to see you. Won't you come in?" she cooed, threw open the door, and stepped aside to allow them to enter. Then she eyed Jere. "And just who is your friend, sheriff?"

The sheriff and Jere exchanged perceptive looks and the three officers walked in. "Mrs. Goldsmith, this is Jere Ford here on a visit. He's a relative of Charles Ford."

"Is that right?" Carrie said batting her eyelashes in surprise. "I believe I saw you at Charles' party, but I had no idea you were family."

"That's right," Ingrid said. "The party was given to introduce Jere."

The woman shot her a look of condescension. Then the sheriff said, "This here is Ingrid Fairchild. She's Jere's partner."

"Partner?" repeated the woman. "You mean you're...ah...are involved?"

Jere said, "We're homicide detectives on the Richmond City Police Force."

A look of alarm briefly crossed her face, but she quickly recouped and said flightily, "Well let's not stand here in the hallway. Come into the study." As she brushed pass Jere he smelled liquor.

They walked into a room with heavy furniture, heavy upholstery, and heavy draperies. The room was dark and smelled of cigarette smoke, stale alcohol, and drug store perfume. A bar extended across the far end of the room and bottles of liquor and several used glasses were setting out.

She moved to the bar. "Can I offer you something?"

They answered 'no thanks' in unison. "Suit yourselves," she said as she poured herself a drink.

The sheriff said, "Mrs.Goldsmith, I understand you paid Mr. Charles Ford a visit right after those bones were found in his cellar. Do you mind my asking why you did that...beings you're not a close friend or relative."

Mrs. Goldsmith sat on the sofa and spread out her brightly colored, badly wrinkled caftan much as a debutante would display her gown. She paused, sipped her drink, and lifted her head haughtily. "I went as a favor to a friend," she said with finality.

"And I suppose this friend was Isodora Ford," it was a statement not a question, and the sheriff watched intently for her reaction.

"And so what if it were," Mrs. Goldsmith said challengingly.

"Mrs. Isodora Ford couldn't make the trip herself?" Ingrid asked flatly.

Mrs. Goldsmith's head jerked so abruptly in the direction of Ingrid that she spilled her drink on her skirt. Her eyes burned with hatred and when she spoke spittle spewed from her mouth. Her voice was deep and menacing as she snarled, "Who asked you, you troublemaker? What business is it of yours anyway?"

Ingrid realized she'd made a mistake by speaking at all. Jere and the sheriff stirred nervously ready to restrain Mrs. Goldsmith if her anger escalated to violence. Finally the sheriff spoke calmly, "Mrs. Goldsmith, I'm afraid I'll have to ask you that same question. Why didn't Mrs. Isodora Ford go over to Oldfields Point herself to see what was going on?"

The transformation was amazing. Mrs. Goldsmith's face softened. As she turned to face Sheriff Regan a smile slowly crept across her lips, and she batted her eyelashes enticingly. Her voice was suddenly soft and amiable, "Well, you see Isodora...ah Mrs. Ford...had not felt very welcome at Charles' party. In fact, she was not allowed to even speak with Charles. After such inhospitable treatment on the part of the host and hostess, I was asked to inquire on her behalf," she paused, smiled, and then added, "You see, Isodora cared very deeply for Charles and was concerned that outsiders may take advantage of him." She shot Ingrid another abhorrent look.

Jere was anxious to question Mrs. Goldsmith but was fearful of another angry outburst. Finally he garnered the nerve and spoke contritely, "Mrs. Goldsmith, would you mind if *I* ask you a question?"

Mrs. Goldsmith smiled sweetly and murmured, "Why of course not, dear. What is it?"

Jere couldn't believe it when he heard his voice actually cracked. "Ah...Mrs. Goldsmith, when you visited Charles you seemed to think that something besides bones might have been found in the cellar. Am I correct in that assumption?"

She brushed her hair from her face and lifted her chin before replying pleasantly, "Oh yes, your assumption is most definitely correct."

Jere felt encouraged so he thought he'd try again. "And just why did you think there would be something else found with the skeletons…if you don't mind my asking."

"Oh no, my dear boy, I don't mind at all. **You** may ask me anything," she cooed. Then she continued, "Everybody knows that Charles has been searching for Caroline's remains for years and years. And common sense would tell you that nobody is going to waste that much time hunting for just a bunch of bones. Ha!"

"So you're saying that it was believed that Charles was looking for something else. Something valuable?" asked Jere.

Mrs. Goldsmith said, "Yes, I believe that's what I'm saying." Then she scolded, "Don't be so naïve." And she rose and lurched to the bar to replenish her glass.

The three officers looked at each other incredulously. Then the sheriff hunched his shoulders and spread his hands in a helpless gesture and the three of them stood and walked out. Mrs. Goldsmith stood with her back to them filling a glass and mumbling incoherently.

When they piled into the car, the sheriff said, "We couldn't get anything else out of her in that condition," he said as he started the engine.

"Well, at least we found out one interesting fact about our Mrs. Goldsmith," said Ingrid.

"What's that?" the sheriff said driving the car away from the curb.

"We found out she likes her police officers lean, meek…and male," she laughed elbowing Jere.

CHAPTER 29

That evening Martha served another gourmet dinner of crab puffs, fresh asparagus-artichoke casserole, fresh green salad, and of course Martha's special Maryland biscuits. As they dined Ingrid and Jere filled them in on the interview with Mrs. Goldsmith. Charles was amazed that Isodora had actually believed his search for Caroline was a mere treasure hunt, and Martha was appalled at her rudeness toward Ingrid.

Martha cleared the table replacing dinner plates with dessert plates. Then she brought out a scrumptious-looking linzer cake crowned with a generous topping of fresh raspberries. Just as she was cutting generous slices the front door opened, and they heard rapid footsteps tapping along the hall.

"Hey, where is everybody?" It was Julia, and Jere was surprised that he felt so thrilled.

"In here dear," called Martha, "in the dining room."

Julia rushed into the room. She was still wearing her uniform. Her eyes were bright, animated, and her face flushed. Damp coils of hair fell in disarray onto her forehead and neck. She went immediately to Charles and kissed him on the cheek.

"Ummm," she said, "linzer cake. I'm just in time. I haven't eaten since eleven thirty this morning."

Martha said, "Oh my, dear, then let me fix you a plate. We had crab…"

"No thanks, Martha," said Julia. "Just a piece of my favorite dessert will do."

"Well, if you insist," Martha said reluctantly cutting Julia an unusually large portion.

Julia walked around the table to a chair beside Jere. As she slid her leg under the table, her knee brushed slowly against his. He knew the move had been on purpose.

A sensuous feeling rushed through him.

"So tell me about your interview with Isodora's drinking buddy," Julia said attacking the cake ravenously.

Ingrid and Jere repeated the entire interview again as Julia held out her plate for a second helping.

"So how do you think that helps you…besides discovering that she'd rather be questioned by men." Julia asked with a twinkle in her eye.

Everyone laughed. "For one thing," Jere said in an effort to move the focus away from him and to something relevant to the case, "it appears that Isodora didn't want to pay another visit to Oldfields Point while we were here."

"Makes sense. If you were here, she couldn't harass Charles without interruption," added Julia.

"Also, her story helps with time of death," said Jere. "We now know that Isodora was alive right before the time Mrs. Goldsmith came to call."

"Hmm," said Julia, "I'll have to think about that one. What's the next step?"

Ingrid said, "Sheriff Regan is going to talk with Jefferson T. and Alice sometime tomorrow. He's invited us to come along again."

"Good luck! Probably no point in going over there until late afternoon," Julia said. Then she hastily looked at her watch, crammed a large piece of cake in her mouth, and said, "Gotta go. Thanks for the cake, Martha. I'm meeting Bernie for dinner."

Jere looked surprised. "Bernie? I thought Bernie went back to North Carolina after the party."

Julia was already heading toward the dining room door. "Nope. The weather was so bad that he stayed over with a friend."

Jere called after her, "You know the Sheriff is gonna want to talk with him too."

But Julia was out the door. Ingrid and Jere exchanged troubled looks.

* * *

Apparently the sheriff agreed with Julia concerning the best time to question Jefferson T. and Alice. He called to say he'd pick up Jere and Ingrid about two pm. Sheriff Regan seemed to enjoy the Richmond Detectives' company, and he asked endless questions about their investigative techniques and procedures. They in turn were interested in rural law enforcement. Jere's thoughts kept returning to Julia and the comment she'd made about Bernie still being in Cecil County. He wasn't sure that Sheriff Regan knew that Bernie had not returned to North Carolina. If he didn't, Jere dreaded the idea of being the one to tell him. He also knew that if he failed to mention Bernie's whereabouts that Ingrid would, and then she'd give him hell to pay.

Finally Jere asked, "Who else are you planning to question?"

"I still need to talk to other members of Isodora's party. But I hope to have other leads when I get through interviewing Jefferson T. and Alice Wainwright," the sheriff answered.

"How about Bernie Caswell, Julia's brother?" Jere blurted.

The sheriff looked quizzical. "No plans to question Bernie. He'd returned to North Carolina when all this came down."

Ingrid couldn't look at Jere. She knew how difficult it was for him to reveal Bernie's whereabouts.

The sheriff glanced at Jere and continued, "You know something I don't?"

Jere tried to look detached. "No. Last night Julia just happened to mention that she was having dinner with Bernie. I thought he'd gone to North Carolina too."

"Damn!" swore the sheriff and he struck the steering wheel with the heel of his hand. "Well, I gotta question him you know. It would have been much simpler if they hadn't hid the fact that Bernie was still in town."

Ingrid said, "Oh, I don't think anyone was trying to hide anything. The question just never came up."

Sheriff Regan looked skeptical. "You probably don't know the history of Bernie and Charles Ford. They were stepbrothers, but the bond couldn't be stronger than if they were twins."

"Yes, Julia told me that," said Jere.

"Bernie was always a fragile boy. He was a ready target for every bully on the playground. Charles was his big brother. You see Charles was always a big healthy child and later a husky, strong man. Makes what's happened to him later even more tragic. Anyway, Charles always defended Bernie as a child and later as a man. Bernie worships the ground Charles walks on and I'm sure he didn't like what he saw Isodora doing to him."

"Motive," Ingrid said simply.

"Yep, that's what we call it in Cecil County too…motive," the sheriff said. "Please tell me Bernie wasn't staying with Julia."

Jere said, "No. Julia said he was staying with a friend."

"A friend? Well, I can believe that much anyway. I know all about *Bernie's friend,*" the sheriff said.

They ate lunch in a diner not too far from Isodora's home. Most of the time they ate in silence each lost in their own thoughts about motives and means. Finally the sheriff looked at his watch and announced that it was almost three o'clock. They threw some bills on the table and walked out to the car.

"I find three o'clock is a pretty good time to catch a drunk. He's more or less recovered from yesterday's spree and not completely into today's."

The sheriff turned onto a shell driveway and pulled up in front of Isodora's home.

"Jefferson T. and Alice live here with Isodora?" Ingrid asked.

"Knowing Isodora, she wouldn't have had it any other way," said Sheriff Regan.

"No wonder Alice walks around like a zombie," Ingird said as she swung out of the car and started toward house.

It was another one of those beautiful old homes that cried out to be taken care of. It was a three story, eighteenth century home constructed of brick probably used as ballast in English trading vessels. Some bricks were missing and mortar was in need of replacement in several places. Peeling paint and rotting wood could be spotted everywhere. Shrubs reached above the window castings, and weeds pushed their way pass shells in the walkway. There were two large dead trees dangerously close to the home probably victims of hurricanes or nor'easters. Their limbs stretched precariously over the house awaiting just the right wind to send them plummeting onto the roof.

There was no doorbell only a large brass knocker in need of being polished. The sheriff reached for the knocker and gave it several hard thuds. The sound could be heard reverberating inside. There was total silence. He tried a number of times. Still no response.

"I don't like this," said the sheriff trying again. "We've already had one murder in this crazy family. I gotta know what's up in here."

Jere and Ingrid nodded remembering how many times they'd knocked on the door of a victim's family member and got no response. They also remembered times when they finally gained entrance only to discover a ghastly scene.

The sheriff knocked persistently again…this time much longer and harder. Just as he was reaching for his phone, they heard the sound of slow shuffling footsteps. Then they heard the sound of metal on metal as safety locks were being slowly slipped from their casing. They watched as the door slowly opened and red blurry eyes squinted out at the visitors.

"Whatta you want?" Alice said not yielding an inch.

Sheriff Regan said, "We are here to talk with you and Jefferson T. about the murder of Isodora Ford."

She recoiled and stumbled backward. After a few second, she regained composure and said, "You can't talk with Jefferson T., and you can't talk with me. We're in mourning." And she tried to close the door.

The sheriff was too quick for Alice and inserted his foot in the doorway just in time to stop the door from slamming shut. "Mrs.Wainwright, I am *going* to talk to you and your husband. It's just a matter of *where* I talk to you. Now we can come on in there and get this over with or you can take a ride down to my office. Take your pick."

Alice had the frightened look of a baby rabbit caught in a snare. She blinked from one officer to the other then she stepped back and slowly opened the door. When they entered the dark hallway, they were struck by the smell of mold and dust. The scene was almost surreal. The place was ill kept, and dust was thick on everything. The hall was wide and surrounded with intricately carved woodwork and an impressive grand spiral staircase. Adorning the wall along the steps were oil portraits of Isodora at various ages and in different attire. In one portrait she wore a tennis skirt, in another a formal ball gown. Another one featured her in a riding habit and yet another in a fur coat over a velvet cocktail dress. Jere studied the metamorphosis of Isodora Ford from attractive alluring young lady to the hard, callous old woman she eventually became. Large heavy doors closed off rooms that opened into the corridor, and large pieces of oversized furniture were haphazardly set. Ingrid noticed that except for the portraits of Isodora, the place was completely void of unique or expensive accouterments.

Alice looked straight ahead. Her eyes totally averted the officers. She just stood there like a robot waiting to be activated. The officers looked from one to another. Ingrid hunched her shoulders in a 'what do we do now' motion.

Finally the sheriff said, "Can we go somewhere and sit Mrs. Wainwright?"

Alice turned slightly and looked about as if she did not recognize the house…didn't know which door to chose. Then unexpectedly a bellow burst from the top of the steps and thundered down the stairway ricocheting off the walls and through the house.

Startled the officers shrank back and jerked around fixing their eyes on the stairway and the source of the rant. They stood transfixed as they watched Jefferson T. virtually crawl down the steps, gripping the banisters with both hands, and wailing hysterically. His harangue was incomprehensible, and tears poured profusely down his cheeks. He was dressed in dingy satin pajamas and was barefoot.

The officers caught an occasional word, "…torture me…mama…can't even mourn…why…cold, she's cold."

"We're not going to get anything here," the sheriff said to Ingrid and Jere. "Have to come again later."

"You think it'll be different tomorrow?" Jere asked dubiously.

"Probably not," Sheriff Regan said. "I'll get a doctor in here...or a straight jacket."

"Or maybe both," said Jere.

"What about her?" asked Ingrid shouting to be heard above the din. They looked at Alice who had not moved since admitting them into the hall.

"I gotta talk to their doctor first. Don't want to be accused of harassing a grief stricken family," the sheriff said. Then he turned to Alice and spoke loudly, "Mrs. Wainwright, we'll be back tomorrow. Meantime, I'm gonna get your doctor over here."

Alice gave no indication she'd heard a word. She continued to stare straight ahead seemingly oblivious to the furor taking place on the steps only a few feet from her. The officers backed out of the hall and closed the door. As they walked down the steps they could still hear the wails of Jefferson T.

The officers settled into their car and rode in silence for a few miles. Finally the sheriff said, "You see, investigating a crime in a small community is different from the cases you work in Richmond. Here everybody knows everybody else. People take sides. You have to be careful not to move too fast or you'll blow the whole case."

They rode in silence and finally Jere said, "Could that have been an act back there?" he said.

"No," said Ingrid and Sheriff Regan simultaneously.

"I just gotta get their doctor out here. I need some medical input before I go dragging those two in," the sheriff said turning out of the driveway and onto the highway.

"Well, I'll tell you one thing," said Ingrid. "If that was an act, Jefferson T. deserves an academy award."

Jere and the sheriff nodded in agreement.

CHAPTER 30

Jefferson T.'s doctor verified what the officers already knew. Jefferson T. and Alice were in no way able to answer questions.

"It'll just mess up your case," the doctor said. "Neither one of them even knows the time of day. I gave them both sedatives and Jefferson T. quieted down. Now maybe Alice can get some rest. Try again tomorrow."

So Sheriff Regan decided to try again tomorrow. In the meantime, he tracked down Bernie and set up a time and place to question him. Bernie chose Oldfields Point. When the sheriff arrived at Oldfields Point and entered the parlor, he immediately knew he'd made a mistake by not having Bernie come to the office. The usual group had assembled: Jere, Ingrid, Martha, Julia, and Charles. This time, however, Charles did not offer to leave the room during questioning. The sheriff knew that Jere and Ingrid would not interfere, but Charles and Julia were capable of coming to the most ferocious defense of Bernie. He knew he'd have to tread lightly.

Everyone exchanged greetings and the sheriff noticed that Bernie sat close to Charles on the sofa. The sheriff began, "Thanks Bernie for coming over to talk to me. I suppose Julia's told you this is routine."

"Yes," squeaked Bernie and he cleared his throat. Then he looked at Charles and Charles gave him a reassuring smile.

The sheriff continued, "I thought you planned on heading back toward North Carolina after the party. What made you change your mind?"

Bernie said nervously, "Well…you ah, ah see the storm. I didn't, well…wasn't sure how fast it was going to move in. And I, I don't like to drive on the Bay Bridge/Tunnel in the rain. That is in a big rain. Like a nor'easter."

Julia spoke up, "That's right Sheriff Regan. Bernie has never liked to cross that bridge/tunnel even under good weather conditions."

The sheriff smiled at Julia and said, "Makes perfect sense to me." Bernie exhaled and seemed to relax a little.

Then Martha said, "You know Bernie you could have stayed here. You know there's plenty of room." All eyes turned on Martha and immediately she knew she'd said the wrong thing.

Then the sheriff said, "Yes Bernie, now why didn't you stay here at your brother's house. After all you grew up here. You know there are plenty of rooms."

Although the sheriff had been especially gentle in his questioning of Bernie, bead of perspiration formed on Bernie's forehead and ran into his eyes. Bernie took out a handkerchief and mopped his brow with a shaking hand. Martha looked horrified that she'd raised the question. Julia watched him with empathy, and Charles was becoming more and more agitated.

Finally Bernie said, "Ah actually I didn't decide to postpone the drive until I got on the road and realized that the storm was getting worse. So I decided to take this opportunity to visit a, a, ah friend…a friend of mine."

"Makes perfect sense to me," said the sheriff.

Bernie seemed to relax even more. Jere and Ingrid knew he'd not ask the hard questions yet.

"I'm changing the subject here, Bernie. Tell me how you feel about your brother Charles. Or should I say stepbrother," the sheriff said.

Bernie smiled for the first time.

"Brother is more accurate. I know we're not blood kin, but Charles is my best friend, my brother, and my surrogate father," Bernie looked at Charles and smiled. Charles nodded his head and smiled back.

"You'd do anything for your brother wouldn't you, Bernie?" asked the sheriff.

"I sure would," said Bernie. "He's looked after me all my life. I'd do anything for him." And he reached over and patted Charles' arm.

"Makes perfect sense to me," said the sheriff.

Everyone was silent for a few moments. Martha thought the interview was over and that refreshments were in order. She slipped to the front of her chair and prepared to stand, "Can I..."

The sheriff interrupted, "Bernie, you know I'm doing all of these interviews because there has been a death. It was a murder. The murder of Isodora Ford. So now I have to question everyone who had contact with Isodora Ford...especially on the night of the party. You and many others, of course, were at that party."

"I understand," Bernie said.

"Now, were you aware of rumors that Isodora was harassing your brother, Charles?" asked the sheriff.

"I had heard that she ridiculed him for his research on the disappearance of Caroline," he said. "I also heard that she made fun of him...taunted him."

"How'd you feel about that?" asked the sheriff.

Suddenly Bernie looked angry and distressed. "I didn't like hearing that," he said. "I didn't like that at all. Charles is my brother. He took care of me...still does. It makes me angry to hear that someone is being unkind to him."

Julia started to say something but the sheriff lifted a hand in a silencing motion and continued, "Makes perfect sense to me."

The sheriff sat quietly lost in thought. He tapped a pen on the spiral notebook he held in his lap. Occasionally noises made by the cellar workmen broke the silence. Bernie began to squirm.

"Did you witness the scene at the party? You know the scene when Isodora left in a huff causing such a fuss. Did you witness that?"

"Yes," said Bernie. "At first I didn't realize what was going on. Then...well, I couldn't help but...ah...witness it."

"What did you think about that?" the sheriff asked.

Bernie again became angry. "I thought it was a rude and thoughtless thing to do. Charles had looked forward to that party. We all had. She deliberately set out to wreck it. I thought she was cruel to Charles!"

"Makes perfect sense to me," said the sheriff. "How did you feel when she acted like that?"

"Why, I felt angry at her, of course," said Bernie.

"That too makes perfect sense to me," the sheriff said simply.

Jere and Ingrid knew the question that the sheriff was leading up to, and when Jere saw the concerned look in Charles' eyes he realized that Charles knew too.

"I want you to think about my next question real carefully, Bernie," the sheriff said watching him intently. "Were you angry enough with Isodora to choke her for how she'd treated Charles?"

Gasps went up, and Charles reacted to the sheriff's question more deftly than Jere and Ingrid had ever seen him. With glaring eyes he reared up in his chair and grasped Bernie by the shoulder and drew him protectively toward him.

"Leave the boy alone, Sheriff Regan," Charles sputtered. "Please leave him alone. You know the bond that exists between my brother and me. Do you really think he would come back here, murder Isodora, and secrete her body in *my* spring house? Don't you think he'd consider the trauma and anxiety such a thing would inflict on me? Don't you think he'd know that would cast suspicion on me? No sir, he would not do that. This kind boy would never torment me like that. He cares for me as much as I for him."

The sheriff was somewhat taken aback by Charles outburst. He sat without speaking. The room grew still and the air seemed suddenly thin and hard to breathe. Finally, Sheriff Regan tapped his pen on the notebook again and said, "Makes perfect sense to me, Mr. Ford." And he slipped his pen in his shirt pocket and stood up.

Jere, Ingrid, and Julia stood also. "Guess that's all I have to ask you right now, Bernie. Just so you'll know, I've been questioning a lot of people. Just has to be done, Bernie, part of the investigation."

Bernie said in a shaky voice, "Sheriff, I didn't answer your last question. Just so *you'll* know, I did not kill Aunt Isodora."

The sheriff looked pleased. "I'm glad you said that Bernie. Real glad." And he punched him playfully on the arm and walked out.

CHAPTER 31

It was one of those clear crisp fall evenings that is savored with the knowledge that porch sitting will soon be replaced by winter evenings in front of a glowing fire. A mantle of twinkling, silver stars was pasted against a cloudless blue velvet sky, and the melodious call of a night bird occasionally broke the silence.

It was one a.m. and Ingrid and Jere sat on the porch outside their rooms relieved to finally have some privacy and a chance to unwind. The search for Caroline, the discovery of the skeletons, the dig, and Isodora's murder had made for a nerve-racking vacation. Jere was restless and Ingrid was becoming a chain smoker. Ingrid crushed out another cigarette and reached for the pack.

"Stop it," demanded Jere as he paced back and forth. "You're gonna kill yourself."

"Well, you're wound up tighter than a drum," she retorted. "You think that's good for you. And don't snap at me."

Jere said. "I just want to get out of here."

"Whoa…that doesn't sound like you. I've never seen you walk off a case before. Where's the determination? The old curiosity?" Ingrid chided.

"Quite frankly," he said, "I'm trying to stifle it. Too many people I've come to care about could be hurt."

"So you're caving?" Ingrid said.

Jere said nothing. Ingrid continued, "What's this all about Jere?"

"I told you...generally," he said.

Ingrid studied her partner. "And more specifically? Is there someone in particular you're concerned about?"

Jere looked at Ingrid beseechingly. "We learned a long time ago that you don't investigate a case you have a personal interest in. Now I know why...even though this is not our case."

"And who's this specific person you don't want to be hurt?" Ingrid asked again doggedly.

Jere relented, "Ingrid, I don't want Julia to be hurt. I'm concerned about her, and the sheriff hasn't even questioned her."

Ingrid was silent then she said slowly, "Oh, I see. You're thinking that Julia could be suspect the same as Bernie."

"Right," Jere said miserably.

"Whew!" said Ingrid. She tapped another cigarette out of the package impervious to Jere's intense scowl. Finally she said, "How do you know that the sheriff hasn't already questioned her? Just because we weren't *invited* to the interview doesn't mean he didn't sit little Julia down and give her the third degree just like he did the others."

Jere thought for a few seconds. Then he said, "Yes, he could have done that. You're probably right. Just because he took us along on a couple of interviews doesn't mean that we're privy to his entire investigation."

"There you go," said Ingrid.

"You want to do the suspects and motives thing?" Jere asked his enthusiasm returning.

"Yeah. Does that mean you're not going to take off for Richmond tonight?" Ingrid asked. Jere smiled.

"Who do you want to start with?" Jere asked conceding the lead.

Ingrid thought for a moment, smiled, and watched Jere closely as she said, "Martha. I'd like to start with Martha."

"Martha?" Jere was dumbfounded. "With all the suspects to start off with why on earth would you choose Martha?"

Ingrid shrugged. "She's here...and I suppose I'm thinking we should start close to where the body was found."

Jere relented and began the analysis, "Okay...Martha had motive." Ingrid nodded in agreement. "Martha resented Isodora's interference in their research into Caroline's disappearance."

Ingrid nodded in agreement and said, "And that research was the glue that held Martha and Charles together."

Jere continued, "Martha also resented the way Isodora treated Charles. She wanted to protect him."

Ingrid said, "And there's also a pecuniary motive. If Isodora gained control over Charles and Oldfields Point, which everyone seems to think she wanted to do, what would happen to Martha?"

"She'd be out of here before the sun went down," Jere said. "Okay, that's enough motives for Martha. Let's do means."

"I've been thinking about that and..." Ingrid began.

"Seems like Martha's really been on your mind. Thought you liked her," said Jere.

"I do like Martha, but *I'm* not going to let personal feelings interfere with my judgment," Ingrid said. Then she continued undeterred, "Do you remember my telling you that Martha heard strange noises at night? And do you remember my telling you that Mrs. White and Mrs. Gray were concerned because Isodora snooped around Oldfields Point?"

"Yes and yes," said Jere.

"Just suppose those noises Martha heard were Isodora on one of her snooping expedition. And just suppose she caught her in the act, a fight ensued, and Martha breaks Isodora's neck."

"That's a lot of supposing, but how about getting the body to the spring house," Jere asked.

"Jere, one evening I was in the kitchen with Martha, and I saw her lift a bushel basket filled with apples. With little effort she simply hauled up that load, lugged it all the way to the other end of the kitchen, and heaved it onto the counter. And that's a big kitchen. Now Isodora weighed less than one hundred pounds, so I think Martha could easily move her to the spring house."

"And Martha certainly knows the property," said Jere. "She'd know all the vacant out buildings. And the spring house is convenient to the kitchen."

"There you go," said Ingrid. "Motive and means."

"Well, that's got lots of holes in it, but it does present possibilities. "Who's next? Charles?" Jere said in jest.

"Okay," Ingrid said quickly. Jere looked startled.

"Sure...no one had more reason to want old Izzy to catch the bus than Charles," Ingrid said nonchalantly.

"Motive...okay, but just think for a minute," Jere said. "Do you really think Charles has the strength or coordination to choke Isodora...much less move her?

"I was thinking along the lines of accomplice," said Ingrid. "Just keep in mind my little scenario of Martha taking out Izzy. Suppose Charles found out about it after the murder took place. Maybe Martha became frightened post act or maybe he walked in on her. Anyway, Charles might help her hide the body."

"You're joking, of course," said Jere. "Charles move a body? Why he can hardly move his own."

"I didn't say move. I said hide," said Ingrid. "Remember, Charles had just taken you to the spring house. It was fresh on his mind. So Martha says, 'where can we hide the body until Jere leaves', and Charles says, 'in the springhouse...I was just up there'."

"So we're saying that Charles had motive to want to see Isodora dead, and so when she was killed, he gladly helped stash the body."

"Bingo!" said Ingrid.

Jere looked troubled. "I don't want to talk about Martha and Charles anymore. They're two of the people I was telling you about. I've really grown fond of them. Let's talk about Bernie."

"Yeah, now his alibi for the night of the murder was thin," said Ingrid who was really into the game.

"I'm not so concerned about that," said Jere. "I'm sure the sheriff checked his alibi right away. But say the alibi does have holes in it...when I watched his interview today there was no doubt in my mind that he idolizes Charles and would do anything for him."

"Including murder?" asked Ingrid.

"Including murder," said Jere. "Bernie could easily have gone to Isodora's house to confront her. For all practical purposes, she was alone.

Jefferson T. was blitzed, and Alice…well Alice was in outer space somewhere. At any rate chances are they were in effect unconscious. He could have killed her, moved her to the spring house, and gone to his friend's house for the night."

"And since he grew up there, he also knew his way around Oldfields Point. And he certainly knew about the spring house." Ingrid added. Ingrid hesitated and Jere recognized the troubled expression on her face.

"So what's bothering you?" asked Jere.

Ingrid spoke reluctantly, "You know we could apply an accomplice theory here too."

Jere froze. "What do you mean? Who?"

"Julia. Julia could have helped Bernie move the body. Don't forget, she grew up at Oldfields Point too," she spoke rapidly not allowing Jere to interrupt. "Bernie could have accidentally (or not) killed Isodora, got scared, called his big sister, and the two of them moved her to the spring house. Accomplice!"

Jere looked somber. He walked to the porch rail and leaned out looking down on the green lawn that stretched to the river now hidden in mist. The place would soon be a wilderness of autumn colors…red, gold, and purple. A wind was rising and it made a low wild sound. This home of his ancestors was a sweet mysterious place, and he had grown to love it and the family he'd found here. Now he was probing their lives and mores and he felt embarrassed, remorseful.

Jere turned suddenly and said, "I can't talk about my family anymore, Ingrid. I'm beginning to feel guilty like I'm betraying them by merely entertaining these thoughts. Let's talk about someone who doesn't mean diddly squat to me."

Ingrid understood Jere's feelings, and said, "Okay then, let's talk about Jefferson T. and Alice in Wonderland."

"Good choice," said Jere. "There's certainly no end to opportunity. They lived with Isodora, socialized with her, and apparently never questioned her. And you saw how they tagged along after her at the party."

"And motive," said Ingrid. "She was such a bitch that I could have almost killed her myself. I don't think I've seen a more domineering, hateful woman in all my life."

"I'm sure it was hell for both of them, but especially for Alice. I can't believe that she's always been like she is today," said Jere.

"What about moving the body to the spring house? Why would they choose the spring house?" Ingrid wondered aloud.

"Maybe to cast suspicion on Charles or Martha…or even us," said Jere. "And again Jefferson T. and Alice may not know the house well, but the spring house is in plain view for anyone to see."

"Right now they are my pick," said Ingrid reaching for her pack of cigarettes.

"You know, there's one other person I'd look at carefully if I were running this show," said Jere. "I'd want to take a long hard look at Isodora's party pal. What was her name now? Carrie…Carrie Goldsmith. There's something real strange about that friendship."

"What do you mean?" asked Ingrid blowing smoke rings.

Jere waved smoke away from his face, looked disgusted, and said, "Why is she the chosen friend? She came to the party with Isodora and stuck to her like glue the whole time. Then after Caroline was found she showed up here behaving rudely and asking questions that were none of her business. Then there she was at the funeral. I know this sounds like the kind of things a friend would do, but she just seems to have such a presence."

"You know what struck me as strange about Ms. Goldsmith?" asked Ingrid. Then without waiting for Jere to answer she said, "It struck me as strange that Isodora would have a friend so much younger than she. I'm surprised Isodora didn't see her as competition. I know Carrie's no spring chicken, but Isodora was as old as dirt. And couldn't Carrie Goldsmith find friends her own age?"

"Well, there's no understanding the dynamics of relationships, but she must have been chummy with Isodora. After all Isodora sent her over here to find out if our digging had uncovered buried treasure," Jere said and shook his head in disbelief.

They sat silently for a long time each lost in their thoughts. They breathed deeply and felt the cool damp air on their skin. As they looked up at the sparkling sky a shooting star streamed across the heavens and disappeared somewhere beyond the horizon. They listened to the wind's song and the katydids and thought how sad it was that such tranquility was being tested by the brutal murders of two women…Isodora Ford and Caroline.

Suddenly Ingrid bolted upright. "That's not what she said."

"What are you talking about?" asked Jere.

"That's not what Carrie Goldsmith said. She didn't say Isodora sent her to Oldfields Point to find out about treasure. She said 'I went as a favor to a friend'."

"Right," said Jere. "And then when the sheriff pressed her she said Isodora wasn't well and didn't feel welcome at Charles' house. But she *never* said Isodora told her she wasn't well or Isodora told her she didn't feel welcome."

"Partner, I think we should suggest to Sheriff Regan that he pay another visit to Mrs. Carrie Goldsmith and find out if she actually spoke with Isodora or even saw her," Ingrid said.

"I agree," said Jere excitedly. "Now I just hope I can sleep."

"Me too," said Ingrid. "The problem with our late night discussions is I get so keyed up I can't get to sleep."

The room next to Ingrid's also opened onto the porch, and its door was slightly ajar. A shadowy figure sat hunched in a rocking chair ear tuned to the conversation outside. Ingrid and Jere stood, said good night, and walked to their rooms. The figure shrunk back into the shadows and sat very still until two doors clicked shut. Then slowly the face of the figure turned toward the moonlight, and Martha stepped out of the shadows and crept slowly toward the hall.

CHAPTER 32

"Sure am glad you caught the discrepancy between what Ms. Goldsmith actually said and what we thought she'd said," the sheriff said. "If she didn't directly speak with Isodora, then where was Isodora? If she was already dead at that time, this is going to put a whole new light on the situation."

"Well, you have to admit that interview with Mrs. Goldsmith came with a lot of distractions," Jere said.

"Maybe she meant for it to," said Ingrid. "Her dress, her manner, the booze might have been intended to throw us off our game."

Sheriff Regan turned off the main road into the Goldsmith driveway. "Well if she intentionally tried to mislead us she almost got away with it, and I don't like being made a fool of."

The sheriff pulled the car in front of the house, switched off the engine, and stared at the neglected house for a few seconds. "She should take some of that money she spends on liquor and fix up this proud old place. This kind of neglect is outrageous, unpardonable."

Then the sheriff said. "I don't want to give her a chance to weasel out of answering our questions. Short, sweet, to the point, and we're out of there. I don't intend to play games with her anymore."

The sheriff got out of the car, slammed the door, and stomped to the front porch. Jere and Ingrid raced to catch up with him. He rang the door bell. Then impatiently rang it a second time. Further demonstrating his impatience, he knocked long and hard until the door sprang open and the angry, painted face of Carrie Goldsmith popped out.

"What the hell..," she began. Then she recognized Sheriff Regan and her tone immediately changed from rage to sweet and apologetic. "Oh, sheriff, I had no idea it was you. Please come in." And she stepped aside holding the door open. The sheriff walked with authority into the hall.

When Carrie spotted Jere she grinned widely and said softly, "Oh, a return visit how flattering." Then she spotted Ingrid and a sour sneer crept across her face. "So you brought the agitator too, huh?" she fairly spat the words out.

When they were all inside Carrie Goldsmith said, "Well, shall we sit in the parlor? A drink? I admit that it's a little earlier," she said turning toward the parlor, "but I will if you will."

"Mrs. Goldsmith, we aren't here to socialize. We're here to ask you two questions, and I want a straight answer to both of them," the sheriff said emphatically.

"Why sheriff," Carries Goldsmith said affecting an innocent look, "haven't I always been straight with you?"

The sheriff ignored the remark and continued, "My first question involves your visit to Oldfields Point after Caroline's remains were found. I believe you said you went as a favor for friend. My question is did Isodora Ford ask you face to face to go to Oldfields Point?"

Carrie was silent. Jere could almost hear the wheels turning.

The sheriff continued, "Now you be real careful, Mrs. Goldsmith. I want to know if you actually *saw* Isodora and if she *personally* asked you to make the visit."

Slowly Carrie Goldsmith said, "I did...I did not see Isodora face to face, and she did not ask me personally to go to Oldfields Point." She breathed deeply and looked frightened.

"All right," said the sheriff, "you told us that Isodora didn't make that visit because she wasn't well and didn't feel welcome at Oldfields Point. Now, once again I ask you, did you actually speak *personally* with Isodora? Did she tell you in person that she wasn't well?"

Carrie Goldsmith stood silently, her face pale and drawn. "Isodora did...did not tell me in person that she wasn't well."

"Okay then," said the sheriff. "I want a straight answer here Mrs. Goldsmith, and I want it quick. We've wasted enough time. Who told you to go to Oldfields Point when Caroline's remains were discovered?"

Carrie's answer was inaudible and her hand covered her mouth as if to prevent the words from escaping.

"Speak up, Mrs. Goldsmith," said the sheriff. "I can't hear you."

She dropped her hand and fairly shouted, "Jefferson T. Jefferson T. told me Isodora wanted me to go to Oldfields Point and find out if they'd found anything other than bones in the cellar."

"Did Jefferson T. tell you Isodora was sick?" asked Jere not wanting to leave a stone unturned.

Carrie Goldsmith looked at Jere as if he had betrayed her. She began to cry softly. Then she whispered, "Yes, Jefferson T. told me Isodora was ill."

The sheriff turned, stomped out the door, and called back to Jere and Ingrid, "Let's go. We've wasted enough time." Jere and Ingrid reached the car just before the sheriff tore up the driveway to the main road.

Meantime inside the house, Carrie reached the door just as it slammed shut. She threw herself against it sobbing. Mascara streaked down her painted cheeks, "Don't leave me. Please don't leave me, Jefferson T. Who'll take care of me? Who...?"

Her agonizing sobs bounced off the walls of the long hall and resonated through the house. Then she slowly turned and stared terrified into its foreboding emptiness.

* * *

Sheriff Regan sped up the driveway. He failed to stop before pulling onto the main road and almost ran into an old rusty truck its bed filled with fire wood. The old driver was not intimidated by the patrol car and shook an angry fist at the sheriff. Ingrid and Jere were jolted about as the car bounced from one enormous pot hole to another.

"Damned pot holes big enough to raise catfish in," the sheriff complained. "That's Jefferson T's job you know...he's suppose to take care of county roads. Jefferson T...should have known from the beginning that he's our man. A bigger piece…" The sheriff's rant was interrupted when he almost passed Jefferson T.'s place. Brakes squealed and Ingrid was slammed against Jere as the sheriff cut sharply and wheeled onto the driveway. He braked in front of the house and the car had hardly stopped before all three officers were out of the car and rushing toward the porch. The sheriff lifted the tarnished knocker and pounded loud and long. No response. He pounded again even more persistently.

Then he called, "Jefferson T. open up. This is Sheriff Regan. I've got some questions for you Jefferson T." There was more knocking. Finally Ingrid said, "Shh. I think I hear something."

From inside the house they heard a slow dragging sound. At first it was so faint as to be almost inaudible. It came nearer and nearer. Slowly the door opened slightly and two panicky eyes blinked out into the sunlight.

"Mrs. Wainwright this is Sheriff Regan. Sick or not we're here to see Jefferson T. and this time I won't take no for an answer. Now I can talk to the two of you here or this time for sure we'll take a ride to my office. So what'll it be?"

Alice slowly opened the door admitting the three officers. Immediately the odor of dust and mold assaulted their nostrils. The hall seemed even darker and the portraits of Isodora more severe and intimidating than before. This time there was silence…deafening silence. The stillness was so overpowering that they heard their own hearts beat.

"Where is he, Mrs. Wainwright?" the sheriff asked. For some reason he found himself almost whispering.

Alice did not speak nor did she look at any of them. She simply pointed a trembling finger toward the stairway.

Sheriff Regan took the steps two at a time with Jere and Ingrid close behind. As they ascended the stairs they sped past Isodora's gallery. In some portraits she seemed to laugh as they rushed by…from others, she appeared to scowl at their intrusion. Meanwhile, Alice shuffled slowly behind them. The officers reached the long upstairs hallway covered by a thread bare rug of undistinguishable colors. The gloomy atmosphere that had overwhelmed them downstairs suddenly vanished as they faced a dazzling, dancing pattern of color on the dinghy wall. They were surprised to find this effect was caused by the morning sun pouring through a magnificent Tiffany stained-glass window.

The first three doors opened into cluttered bedrooms filled with massive furniture, shabby rugs, and faded draperies. Next they opened doors to two lumber rooms latched shut with eye hooks and crammed with an assortment of out-dated and outrageous stuff…a harp with no strings, boxes of dusty moldy books, discarded household items, broken furniture, portraits in busted frames, a rusty short wave radio, and other useless items. Another room appeared at one time to have been used as a chapel. An enormous Bible was cradled on a make-shift pulpit, and a shattered candelabrum lay on the floor missing one arm. There were several crudely constructed kneeling benches with stuffing escaping through moth eaten holes in their velvet covers. Particles of dust floated in shafts of light that shined through two narrow, elongated windows.

Finally they came to five steps that led up to a short hall that had only one door. As they reached the top step, animal-like groans and whimpers could be heard behind the closed door at the end of the dimly-lit hall. Sheriff Regan unsnapped his holster, lifted out his gun, and pointed it upward. Jere and Ingrid instinctively reached for their firearms then remembered they were not armed. They stepped softly, cautiously toward the door. Sheriff Regan reached down and turned the doorknob. The macabre sounds grew louder as he slowly opened the door. Then they stepped into a scene that was so bizarre as to be surreal.

The room was alive with the flickering light from countless candles dispersed endlessly around the room…on tables, on chests, in candelabras, on the floor. The officers were struck with the overwhelming odor of dust and candle wax and cheap perfume. Here too they found mammoth pieces of furniture but no piece was as large as the bed. The king-sized bed was covered with a feathery purple satin spread on which countless matching downy pillows were scattered. A dusty purple canopy hung precariously above the bed, and on the bed the officers viewed a scene that later they vowed they'd never forget.

Jefferson T. lay atop the satin cover clutching a massive pillow to his chest. The pillow cover was wet with tears and he wallowed and squirmed about hugging the pillow to his body and yammering unintelligibly. They were able to grasp only a few words. "Mommy, I'm sorry…so sorry, Mommy…don't know why…had to do over…I wish I could go back…sorry, Mommy."

"Jefferson T.," the sheriff tried to out-scream him. He moved closer. "Jefferson T. this is Sheriff Regan. I mean to talk with you, Jefferson T."

The sheriff's attempts were to no avail. He moved cautiously to the bed, reached down, and touched the bed giving it a little bounce. Suddenly Jefferson T. sprang upright with fury blazing in his eyes and spittle oozing from the corners of his mouth. "Don't you touch my Mommy's bed! Don't you ever touch her bed. This is Mommy's bed and I'm the only one she lets touch it…**ever**!"

He slapped at Sheriff Regan's hand. Then he looked beyond the sheriff to Jere and Ingrid. Then Jefferson T. was on his knees screaming and pulling his hair. "Oh the desecration!!! The violation, the unholiness of it!!! You can't come in her room!!! You are defiling her sacred place. Her place. Oh Mommy, Mommy what to do!!!"

"Somebody call the doctor. Tell him to get some help out here right now," said the sheriff not daring to take his eyes off the mad man who was now bouncing up and down on his knees.

Ingrid slowly edged toward the door. Jefferson T.'s eye caught her movement. Suddenly he stopped moving and gawked maniacally at her. Ingrid simply stared Jefferson T. down. Then when she reached the door she bumped into Alice who was just entering the room. Jefferson T.'s eyes registered recognition and hate. He let out a piercing, ear-splitting scream, dived off the bed, and lunged for Alice. Ingrid tried to stop him but Jefferson's anger fueled his strength and he pushed her to the floor. Without warning he was on top of Alice and had her by the throat shaking her mercilessly until they feared her neck would break. Then Jere and Sheriff Regan were on him prying his hands from Alice's neck. After what seemed an eternity, they subdued Jefferson T. and secured him face down on the floor.

Ingrid was up and rushed to help Alice. But when she put her arm on her shoulder Alice's face took on a vacant stare, and she squirmed from Ingrid's grasp. Then Alice stretched her shaking arms toward Jefferson T. as if imploring him to hold her. Then with tears swimming in her dazed eyes she babbled incoherently.

Jefferson T. looked up at Alice from his face-down position on the floor. Then he raged contemptuously, "Do you really think I'd touch you. You stupid slut! Mama always said you were a no good, low life, stupid bitch."

Alice continued to babble as tears streamed down her face. "Shut up!!!" screamed Jefferson T. "Get out of Mommy's room. There was no stupid treasure. There never was. Mommy kept telling you there was no treasure with Caroline. But no…you thought you knew more than Mommy. You had to keep badgering her over and over." Then Jefferson T.'s voice took on a mimicking tone, "*How do you know there's no treasure? How do you know there's no gold medallion?* She couldn't take your whining anymore. That's why she smacked you. And you killed her, Alice. You killed Mommy for no reason at all. No reason at all!"

Jefferson T. began to bang his head on the floor. The three officers looked at each other stunned. Alice continued to babble and stared into space.

Ingrid gently guided Alice toward the door. Alice moved like an automaton offering no resistance. As they reached the door Ingrid suddenly stopped, turned back to face the bed, and gawked at a portrait hanging above it. It was a portrait of a very young Isodora. She looked to be about sixteen. Her smile was soft and broad, and she was wearing a pale yellow sweater set. Around her neck was a gold necklace and attached to the necklace was a medallion. Ingrid stepped closer and studied the medallion. It bore a crest…the Ford family crest.

Jere noticed Ingrid's intense scrutiny of the portrait and moved to stand behind her. "What's up, Ingrid?" Jere asked.

Ingrid pointed to the portrait. "The medallion," was all she could say.

Jere stepped in for a closer look. "My God! It's the crest…the Ford family crest. She had it. She had it all along."

Ingrid whispered something. "What did you say?" asked Jere.

Ingrid repeated, "I just said 'Poor Alice in Wonderland'."

CHAPTER 33

Ingrid and Jere stayed with the sheriff until medical attendants arrived and Jefferson T. and Alice were carted off to the County Mental Health Center. Then they got out of the way and let the law enforcement teams move in to complete the job. They hurried back to Oldfields Point their bodies still pulsing from the adrenalin rush they always experienced when a case was cracked. Jere was anxious to share how the investigation worked out with Charles and Martha. After all, they too had an interest in bringing Isodora's murderer to justice.

When they arrived at Oldfields Point Martha and Charles were just sitting down to dinner. With flushed faces Ingrid and Jere rushed into the dining room beaming.

"Have we got a story for you!" announced Jere.

Martha and Charles suddenly became energized. "Do sit down and tell us what you have been up to all morning," Martha said.

Between mouthfuls of succulent roast beef and creamy mashed potatoes washed down with sweet ice tea Jere and Ingrid excitedly related what had occurred after they arrived at Isodora's place. Then they got to the part about the portrait of Isodora wearing the crest medallion.

Ingrid said, "Now, Charles, hold onto your skivvies. Have we got a shocker for you! In Isodora's room above bed there was a portrait of young Isodora wearing…are you ready for this…wearing the crest medallion."

"What?" Charles and Martha cried. They couldn't assimilate what was being said.

"I don't understand, Jere, Ingrid," said Charles. "What are you trying to tell us? What medallion? Surely not the Ford family crest medallion. How? How could that be?"

Jere leaned forward, arms on the table. He spoke slowly, distinctly. "Yes, Charles, she was wearing the Ford crest. I'm positive. As we speak Sheriff Regan is searching the house for it."

Charles was still bewildered. "But how on earth did she get it?"

Martha quickly came out of her daze. "Oh, do you think she found it on one of her prowls through Oldfields Point?"

Ingrid said, "No, Isodora didn't find it here at Oldfields Point. She's had it a long time. That portrait of her wearing the crest medallion was taken when she was a girl."

Charles spoke slowly, thoughtfully. "This could explain so many things," he said.

"Sure could," said Ingrid. "For one thing, it explains why she didn't want you to look for Caroline."

"Yeah…because you might just find her and discover the crest wasn't with her remains," said Jere.

"And that is exactly what happened," said Ingrid.

Charles' face took on a look of amazement, and he leapt into the discourse. "And then…and then if it were ever discovered that Isodora had the crest medallion her ancestors would have been implicated," Charles said. "Remember Isodora is of German ancestry. It had to have been passed down to her. How else would she have gotten it?"

"And all this time I thought she was just jealous of Charles," said Martha. Then her expression turned dark. "Oh, it was much more sinister than that. No wonder she berated Charles for researching the Hessian occupation of Oldfields Point. She was afraid he would discover one of her ancestors was a participant in the occupation."

Ingrid reached for another serving of roast beef, cut off a small piece, lifted it to bite, then stopped midway. "You know what? This may even have spawned Isodora's attraction to Richard and Dan Ford."

"How, Ingrid?" asked Jere. Then he went on to explain, "Ingrid always focuses on the romantic aspects of a case."

"How?" Ingrid repeated ignoring his last comment. Then she explained. "Well, Isodora already had the Ford family crest medallion, so why not legitimize its possession by marrying a Ford?"

"Well, it didn't do that...legitimize the possession. I think it was Isodora's own sick version of *who's the winner now?*" said Jere.

Ingrid and Jere continued to help themselves to large servings of roast beef and mashed potatoes. After some time passed Jere and Ingrid realized that Charles and Martha had suddenly grown quiet and sat with sheepish grins on their faces.

Finally Jere said, "Charles, is something wrong?"

"Yeah, don't tell us you've found another body," Ingrid added in a effort to inject humor into what had become a tense moment.

Then Charles and Martha smiled broadly at each other, and Charles nodded to Martha. Martha said, "We know." Then she giggled and grinned at Charles.

Jere and Ingrid looked puzzled. Then Jere said, "Know what, Martha? What do you know?"

"Let us in on the secret too," said Ingrid.

Charles actually sniggered, "We know that we were suspects," he said clumsily.

Now Jere was confused. "Charles, what are you talking about?"

Charles looked at Martha, "You must tell them Martha."

Martha spoke with embarrassment, "I was listening last night, and I heard you say that Charles and I were suspects." Then she and Charles nodded their heads and smiled broadly at each other again.

Jere and Ingrid were embarrassed. They realized that Martha must have been listening when they were playing the 'everybody has a motive' game on the porch the night before. Jere didn't know what to say. He couldn't let his new cousin and friend think that he seriously considered them suspects. He immediately began kicking himself. How ungrateful!!! How mean spirited he must appear to them. What could he say to convince them that they'd never seriously been a *suspect?*

Jere began, "Charles, Martha, please don't think that we ever seriously thought of you as capable of murder. You see when Ingrid and I hit a brick wall in a case, we do this thing of looking at everyone involved and try to think of motives that would…"

Martha interrupted abruptly, "Oh, Jere dear, please don't apologize. We've been so excited!"

Ingrid couldn't believe it. "Excited…to be a suspect?"

Charles said, "Oh yes. You see we never thought that anyone would think we possessed the passion necessary to commit a murder."

"Yes," said Martha. "Oh, I just loved the scene you created of Charles and me toting Isodora to the spring house. I can just see us now in the dead of night…rain in our faces. Oh, Charles can't you just see us?"

Jere and Ingrid gawked at each other. "Well, don't become too fascinated by that picture," Jere said. "Murder is no motion picture you know."

Martha said, "We know that Jere. We can most certainly separate fantasy from reality. You believe that don't you?"

Jere said, "Yes, but…"

Martha continued, "But being a suspect just put the icing on our cake so to speak. And what better victim for us than Isodora?"

Charles said, "Think of this from our point of view, Jere. Night after night we've sat here in this house dreaming, hoping that some day we could solve the mystery of what happened to Caroline. Then you two come for a visit and voila…mystery solved. And we were a part of that investigation."

"But you were never a suspect in the murder of Caroline," said Jere still confused.

Charles continued undeterred, "Then a murder victim is found in our spring house. A victim, I might add, who has really tried our patience sorely. You two enter the case and voila…suspects apprehended. But this time we had nothing to contribute to the case. We actually felt at a loss. Then we learned that we are suspects, and suddenly we were a part of the investigation again."

Jere and Ingrid were stunned. They didn't know what to say. Finally Ingrid said, "Well glad we made you feel better."

Suddenly the bizarre dinner conversation was interrupted by a signature beep of a car horn. The front door flew open, footsteps tapped along the hallway, and Julia bounced in. She went immediately to Charles and kissed him on the cheek. Then she looked at Jere and Ingrid's bewildered faces.

"What's up?" she said taking a seat beside Jere and repeating the old touch knee thing.

"You wouldn't believe it if we told you," Jere said. Then changing the subject abruptly, he said, "What's going on downtown?"

"Big News!" said Julia. "Jere, have you told Charles about the portrait of Isodora wearing the crest medallion?"

Jere was still so stunned at Charles and Martha's exuberance at being suspects that he simply nodded.

Julia continued, "Good. Well Sheriff Regan found it!" Then she shouted, "He found the crest medallion!" And she clapped her hands exuberantly.

"Then it's true," said Charles. "She's had it all along. She had the Ford family crest medallion."

"How cruel!" said Martha. "Just think, all these years of ridiculing and tormenting Charles just to shield her ancestor's misdeeds."

"Well, it's true," said Julia. "Retribution for sins of her ancestors descended on Old Aunt Isodora."

"How about Alice?" asked Ingrid. The sadness she felt for Alice Wainwright somehow made the moniker Alice in Wonderland sound insensitive, cruel.

"Poor Alice," said Julia. "Alice was convinced that there was something of value to be found with Caroline. Apparently she hoped that this *treasure* would provide Jefferson T. with independence from Isodora."

"How?" asked Jere. Julia simply shrugged.

Martha had fetched a plate and Julia was eagerly filling it with copious amounts of roast beef, potatoes, and vegetables. "Julia, dear," said Martha, "you must start eating better. You're as skinny as a rail."

"That's why I come over here," Julia said between mouth-stuffing bites.

Jere would not be put off. "What's going on downtown?" he repeated his earlier question.

Julia swallowed and said, "Well, as you know, both Jefferson T. and Alice are at the County Mental Health Center emergency unit for observation and tests...only I don't know how you could test either one of them now. Sheriff Regan says they found evidence that Isodora was killed at home and her body moved to Charles' spring house. Right now, it looks like Alice did it."

Ingrid sighed, "Poor Alice. She never had a chance in that family. Julia, exactly why do the old ladies around here call her Alice in Wonderland?"

Julia swallowed, "Because for Alice nothing was ever what it seemed. She thought she married wealth...nix. She thought Isodora would accept her if she'd be her toady...nix. She thought that someday Jefferson T. would love her...nix. She thought she could please Jefferson T. if she got rid of his brow-beating, ball crushing mother...nix. Alice couldn't separate fantasy from reality. Alice in Wonderland."

"Pretty much what I thought," said Ingrid.

After dinner Martha served large portions of fresh apple pie topped with homemade vanilla ice cream. They ate silently for a while, and Jere had the feeling that Julia had something else to say.

Finally, coffee was poured in the parlor, and Julia spoke up, "Charles, Sheriff Regan asked me to ask you what he should do about Jefferson T. and Alice?"

Charles looked startled. "What does he mean, Julia?"

Julia set her cup on the coffee table. "I don't think the County Mental Health Center can handle them very long. They're in a temporary unit. They can't go on trial in their conditions. You see, they are going to need the kind of help and treatment not available here."

Martha looked at Charles nervously. Charles sat silently for several seconds. Then he said, "So what does this have to do with me?"

"I suppose you're the closest thing to family that Jefferson T. has so in cases like this law enforcement turns to family," Julia explained.

Jere interceded, "Charles, I doubt that legally you can be held responsible for any of Jefferson T.'s financial responsibilities. Your relationship to him is through marriage only."

Julia agreed. "He's right, Charles. Don't let anyone pressure you into doing something you don't have to."

Charles' face took on a brooding expression. These people had tormented him for years with their ridicule, hostility, and subterfuge. He felt no family bond there at all...if fact he felt disgust at their greed, brashness, and hedonistic lifestyle. Yet they were human beings, and Charles felt compassion for the suffering...especially for Alice. He perceived her as a helpless animal that had been caught in a cruel snare.

Solemnly he shared these feelings with the others and then said, "I must first talk with my lawyer. My assets are not inexhaustible, but I should like to help. However, I shall help on one condition. I want all contributions I make to be anonymous. I want to sever all ties of a personal nature with Jefferson T. and Alice. This means, that I would require your confidentiality, too." There was unanimous agreement.

Jere said, "Charles, it was a privileged day when I came up here and met you. You are some man! I'm proud to share the same blood line." They all laughed.

"And I, too, am grateful that our paths crossed," Charles said. "Please look upon Oldfields Point as your ancestral home...a home that you will visit often."

Julia stretched her arms above her head and said, "Jere, would you like to take an after-dinner walk?"

"Sure," said Jere and he followed Julia out of the parlor and out of the house.

Julia reached over and took Jere's hand, and they walked toward the river. It was a cool, crisp autumn evening. Somewhere someone was burning leaves and the pungent smell filled the air resurrecting memories of leaf fights, Halloween, and fields strewn with orange pumpkins. The sound of katydids blended with the lapping river water and somewhere the lonesome low pitched sound of a night bird blended with the rustling leaves. Then a gigantic yellow harvest moon appeared on the horizon floating upward like a magnificent golden orb. Occasionally small gray translucent clouds raced in front of the moon producing a magical effect.

Julia and Jere sat on a log on the bank of the river. They listened to the wind's song and watched the mist wind its way through the moving branches of the trees. They surrendered to the sound and the feel and the smell of the riverbank. Then Jere put his arm around Julia's shoulder and drew her to him. Her lips were wet and eager, and her warmth and softness aroused feelings he'd held in check for too long. They sat together for a long time experiencing excitement much like a couple of adolescents.

Julia finally pushed him away. "Can it work?" she asked breathlessly.

"I think it can work," said Jere. "Can you come to Richmond?"

"Yes. Can you come to Oldfields Point?" Julia asked.

"Yes," Jere whispered and he drew her to him again.

Julia pushed him away again. "When?"she asked.

Jere looked thoughtful. "How about Christmas?" he said.

Julia threw her arms around him and kissed him hard and long. "Christmas! Yes, Christmas! Then we can take it from there."

"Yes," said Jere with bated breath. "Then we can take it from there."

* * *

The SUV sped southward toward the Chesapeake Bay Bridge/ Tunnel. Resting on the back seat was an assortment of cookies, pies, homemade candies, sandwiches, and deviled eggs. Martha had been determined that Jere and Ingrid should not go hungry on what she had described as 'their long journey across the Bay'.

Ingrid rattled on and on about Caroline, Isodora, Oldfields Point, Jere's 'family from another era', and anything else that came to her mind. Jere on the other hand drove in silence. A smile often creased his lips, and his eyes took on a far-away look.

Apparently Ingrid had asked Jere a question and gotten no response. She persisted, "Jere, Jere. Are you listening to me?"

Jere was shocked out of his dream-like state. "No, I'm not listening to you," he said crossly.

"Then what are you thinking about?" she said.

Jere smiled and said, "Christmas. I'm just thinking about Christmas."

EPILOGUE

Combining fiction and history is a challenging effort, one that requires the author to provide some clarification and differentiation between the two. To this end, I submit this brief explanation.

In fact, on July 23, 1777 British General William Howe accompanied by General Charles Cornwallis and Hessian General Wilhelm Knyphausen left New York City en route to Philadelphia, the capital of America and the meeting place of the Continental Congress. Their mission was to disrupt the Continental Congress in Philadelphia and capture its members. They devised a rather circuitous route for their voyage. They sailed down the east coast to the mouth of the Chesapeake Bay. Upon entering the Bay they sailed north to what is now known as Northern Eastern Shore, Maryland. On August 25, 1777 they sailed into the Elk River where they found the river provided a safe harbor in which to anchor and a wide cleared beach upon which to disembark. Here the British rested and recovered from their long sea voyage before commencing their march to Philadelphia.

It is not pertinent to my purpose to examine why General Howe chose such a roundabout course to Philadelphia except to place him at Oldfields Point, the estate of Captain John Ford. Captain John Ford was indeed away fighting with the Continental Army when General Howe landed at

Oldfields Point, and undeniably General Knyphausen occupied his home. Captain John wasn't there when his livestock was stolen, his winter stores taken, and his home plundered and partly burned. And indeed, as fate would have it, Captain John Ford commemorated the Patriots' ultimate victory over the British by displaying a Hessian sword above his fireplace.

Nonetheless, it is at this point that I depart from fact and draw upon imagination. In writing this story, I would not have the reader think I am trying to amend the courageous deeds of our brave Patriots or alter the facts that led up to such. In my opinion, their feats of bravery and eventual triumph are beyond comparison. However, the creation of the enigmatic Caroline and her mysterious disappearance are simply a product of this writer's imagination.

It is hoped that this embellishment of the Oldfields Point occupation will provide the reader with a pleasant diversion as well as providing some insight into this little known incident in American history.